The Adventurer's Guild

#1-Jaikus and Reneeke Join the Guild

The Adventurer's Guild
#1 Jaikus and Reneeke Join the Guild

Brian S. Pratt

The Adventurer's Guild
#1-Jaikus and Reneeke Join the Guild
Copyright 2009 by Brian S. Pratt

ISBN: 978-0-9843127-0-2

Books written by Brian S. Pratt can be obtained either through the author's official website:
www.briansprattbooks.com
or through select, online book retailers.

Books by Brian S. Pratt:

The Morcyth Saga

The Unsuspecting Mage
Fires of Prophecy
Warrior Priest of Dmon-Li
Trail of the Gods
The Star of Morcyth
Shades of the Past
The Mists of Sorrow*
*****(Conclusion of The Morcyth Saga)**

Travail of The Dark Mage
Sequel to The Morcyth Saga

1-Light in the Barren Lands
2-(forthcoming Spring 2009)

The Broken Key

#1- Shepherd's Quest
#2-Hunter of the Horde
#3-Quest's End

Qyaendri Adventures

Ring of the Or'tux

Dungeon Crawler Adventures

Underground

The Adventurer's Guild

#1-Jaikus and Reneeke Join the Guild

This is for my children:

**Joseph
Breanna
Abigayle**

A Little Bit of History…

Rumor has it that the great city of Reakla had its beginnings nearly a millennium ago. Back then, it didn't even have a name. In fact, the only thing that could be said for what would one day be the preeminent city of the realm, was that very few people knew of, or cared about, the place.

A solid league from the road now called the Adventurer's Way ran the main trade route linking the production centers of the east with the populations of the west. This collection of huts housed less than a score who barely scraped out a living. Situated as this gathering of the destitute, poor, and unwanted was, at the northern fringe of Keot's Swamp, a swamp whose reputation for being infested with creatures of great evil and ferocity, they saw very few strangers willing to join their ranks.

The world ignored them, didn't care about them, and those that did manage to find their way there more often than not continued on their way without so much as a how-do-you-do; which for the most part, the residents of this backwater cesspool in the middle of nowhere preferred. That was, until the day when the great warrior Reakla decided to retire.

His deeds were legendary. Why, even to this day, bards still regale their audiences with his exploits. One of his most famous adventures, the one people have requested for centuries, was how he slew the Frost Drake Theriocula and rescued the Lady Eay from the Sorcerer Vultun. A tale of great daring-do and romance that makes men thump the table in applause, and women weep at the tragic ending. And this was but one of a dozen such tales that still survive from his day.

In the winter of his years, when Reakla realized his strength was beginning to wane, reflexes growing slower, and gray starting to sprout, he knew it was time to hang up his double-headed battleaxe and retire. For only a fool continued to adventure when youth has fled.

There have been many theories as to why a warrior of great renown would settle in such a place. One suggested it was because he wanted the quiet solace he never had in his youth. Another put forth that he had fallen in love with a woman who lived there. But whatever the reason, this great warrior came to live among the residents at the edge of Keot's Swamp.

As time went on, word spread of his whereabouts and fellow adventurers whom he had known would come to share a pint of ale, and a tale or two of past exploits. Eventually, Reakla's shack was enlarged and grew into a tavern, then an inn.

A few of Reakla's cronies retired there as well, desiring to continue being in the same company as the great warrior. A few brought families with them, others slaves, and this collection of ramshackle dwellings began to turn into a bona fide village. The place began to be called Reakla's Place, Reakla's Inn, and others that have now been lost to the past. It was a century or more after Reakla's death that the elders gathered and stated that forevermore, their village would be called Reakla. They were proud their home would bear the name of the great warrior.

Year after year, it seemed more and more adventurers gravitated to Reakla. The camaraderie of fellow warriors, the sharing of mutual histories, drew men and women alike from all over. It seemed that whenever an adventurer grew too old, or too infirm to continue, they would stake a claim, build a house, and hang out at Reakla's Inn.

The earliest records indicate that the first real construction on what is now known as the Adventurer's Guild didn't begin until the third century after Reakla's death. By this time, his original inn had undergone many additions to accommodate the influx of people. Rooms were added, a courtyard built, and areas began to be designated for the main classes of the day; fighters, thieves, and magic users.

Magic users didn't start coming until the great magic user Meyk built his tower not far from Reakla's Inn. Brother to a fighter by the name of Breyki, whom you may recall from such sagas as *"Breyki and the Troll's Head"* and *"Breyki Atop the Goblin's Mound,"* Meyk settled in Reakla when his brother lost a leg to an overzealous Giant of the Clan Dirtclout. Ordinarily, a simple healing spell would have taken care of his leg, but the loss had occurred far from such aid, and by the time he reached civilization, the stump had healed to such an extent that the healers were unable to affect a restorative cure.

After Meyk built his tower, he began accumulating a great collection of books that to this day can be found at the Great Library within the Adventurer's Guild. Scholars, and up-and-coming magic users, came from all over to research spells. For one who walked the Arcane Path, Meyk was unusually friendly and helpful.

Now, the catalyst for the initial construction of the Adventurer's Guild that we know today didn't come from a desire to create such a complex, but rather due to a massive migration of Trolls from out of the Swamp. Overrunning the town in a spree of killing and destruction that resulted in more than a third of the buildings being either outright destroyed, or burnt to the ground, it took every able-bodied man and a few women to throw the horde back. Unfortunately, Reakla's Inn which had stood for five hundred years, fell during the onslaught. Little more than charred beams and shattered stone remained, some of which can be viewed in the Gallery of Fallen Heroes, a room within the Guild dedicated to those members who personified courage, resourcefulness, and success.

Plans were drawn up in the months following the end of what came to be called *The Troll Invasion*. At first, the new building was going to follow the same lines as the previous one, only on a slightly larger scale. But the idea was proposed, by whom the histories fail to mention, to make the new construction into a centralized place where adventurers could come and find more than just a room, a good meal, and stories of past exploits.

It became a place where heroes past their prime could still find value in their lives by teaching the younger, newer crop of adventurers. Other crafts came as well; fletchers and master crafters of bows, blacksmiths, and more whose services were in demand. Very soon this new place was dubbed *The Adventurer's Guild* and the name has remained to this very day.

Magic Users were always part of the Guild, ever since the time of Meyk. The joining of brain and brawn on adventures grew quite common. Thieves didn't come along until later. It has been rumored that thieves were always there anyway, hiding in the shadows, but it wasn't until about a century ago that they were officially incorporated as part of the Guild. The reasoning behind such a move depends on whom you ask. On the one hand, thieves play an important part in any adventure; disarming traps, picking locks, etc, so it only made sense to have them as part of the Guild. The other side of the coin claimed that the Thieves connived their way into the Guild in order to be in on the *"know"* about the Guild members' activities so they could beat them to the prize.

By and large, the three classes coexist together fairly harmoniously. Each class was almost always represented in Guild Parties, a Party being a group of adventurers that have banded together to hire out collectively. A few Parties are formed entirely of fighters or thieves, rarely do magic users band together as they tend to prefer having muscle-bound toughs taking the hard knocks while they fire off spells from a respectably safe distance.

In the centuries since the village of Reakla first took the name of the renowned hero, it has grown by leaps and bounds. The league of open space between the original collection of huts situated at the northern edge of Keot's Swamp and the road now called Adventurer's Way, has been completely filled in by a town to rival any in the realm. Two other trade routes now find their way to Reakla. One is the North Road which leads to the Lands of the Kittikin, a place most civilized people would just as soon keep as far away from as possible. Brigand's Way is the other, so named due to the frequent raids on caravans and travelers foolish enough to attempt to pass without sufficient escort.

Adventurer wannabes come from all over in the hopes of joining the Guild, the prestige and glory which went with membership was something every lad desired. Unfortunately, only a very few ever succeeded in gaining the honor of being added to the Adventurer's Roll of Heroes. An auspicious sounding title, the Roll was merely a list of currently active members, and some who were past their prime yet still called the Guild their home away from home.

Before anyone is allowed to join, they must be able to lay claim to the successful completion of an Adventure. Of course, such an Adventure cannot be any old adventure, but one which satisfies three qualifications.

The first qualification is that there must have been some element of risk to life and limb. Finding a lost cat that strayed too far from home would hardly count toward Guild Membership. Unless, of course, the cat in question weighed five hundred pounds, had a mean disposition, and liked nothing better than to chew a man's head off. Then perhaps it would qualify as a bona fide Adventure.

The second qualification is for the Adventure to be successfully concluded. If the whole point of the quest was to retrieve a specific item, that item had better be in hand when all was said and done.

Lastly, and perhaps most important of all, a reward of some kind had to have been given. After all, what good was an Adventure if you didn't get paid for your troubles? A man's got to eat.

Very few wannabes are able to satisfy the requirements since most have no experience or training for such a life. The bones of many a lad can be found in out of the way places where their misguided hopes to complete an Adventure had led to an untimely end.

There *are* those who have friends or relatives in the Guild and merely tag along on an Adventure with a seasoned Party to satisfy the requirements. For others without such connections within the Guild, membership can be as elusive as a five-legged dog. Their recourses were few indeed, and all held a high rate of mortality.

But for those who make it, the rewards are great: fame, gold, and the chance to become a power in the realm. All are waiting for the one strong enough, smart enough, and especially lucky enough to survive.

—1—

It was a day like any other in the great city of Reakla. The hustle and bustle of everyday life continuing as it had for many a year, though in this city, what constituted everyday life could at times seem extraordinary if it were to be encountered anywhere else. But in Reakla, the sight of three trolls being led through the streets by a party of adventurers was hardly worth a second look.

Ye's Band of Thugs, a party of five that had been adventuring together for the better part of a decade, were herding six of the great beasts toward the Adventurer's Guild. Trolls were in demand at the Guild, being as they were very hardy and regenerated well. They gave the up and coming newbies something to practice on. Each of the three Classes that called the Guild their home had a courtyard in which they could hone and fine tune their skills between adventures. Within the courtyard, fighters fought, mages worked on spells, and thieves, well, they did what thieves always do and were not about to explain themselves to others. If you're a thief, you know what goes on. If not, it's best not to pry.

Below the Guild lies a network of pens which house beasts that for a price, were made available to its members. There were the usual sorts of animals one would expect, such as cows, dogs, cats, rats, etc. Then there were the more exotic beasts such as the trolls, and if the rumors could be believed, even a green dragon held in a great cavern far below the rest, but such was most likely nothing more than rumor.

Ye's Band of Thugs tended to receive the commissions to acquire trolls for the Guild as they have had much success at it and almost always returned with good specimens that had little in the way of damage. Of course, the regenerative nature of trolls could in no small measure account for that as well.

For the lads of Reakla, those too young or not predisposed for adventuring, the sight of Trolls being marched to the Guild pens was the closest they could get to the excitement, and glory that was Adventuring.

Two of the onlookers that stood in awe of the seasoned band of adventurers herding the trolls, were relatively new to Reakla. Having arrived only the night before, they gaped at the massive beasts passing by.

"Would you look at the size of them!" Jaikus remarked.

Reneeke was much too enthralled by the sight to respond.

"Only three this time?" one onlooker shouted.

The man walking at the head of the procession glanced toward the shout. "That's all they wanted," responded the seasoned fighter. He bore a longsword and shield, his helm was silver with an erect bright blue plume sticking six inches straight up, while his chainmail, though looking well-worn, shone in the afternoon sun.

As the men and trolls moved on, Jaikus slapped his friend Reneeke on the back. "Just think. One of these days, that's going to be us."

Reneeke turned his gaze from the departing trolls to his friend. "Yup."

"Tomorrow we'll go down and join."

"If they'll have us," countered his friend. "We don't exactly look the adventuring type."

Which was true. Jaikus was but five feet seven, slight of build, and not exactly muscular. Reneeke on the other hand stood a hair over six feet, had worked on a farm all his life and thus had built up a sizeable set of muscles. Chopping wood will do that to a lad. But despite his build, dressed as he was in hand-me-down homespun, he looked anything but someone ready to face the evil in the world.

"Of course they'll have us," asserted Jaikus. "Do you think every adventurer started out with a set of armor, swords, and all that stuff? No, of course not. They were like us. Full of energy and raring to go."

"If you say so." To be honest, Reneeke preferred life on the farm to that of adventuring. It was good work, you knew what each day would bring, and perhaps best of all, you weren't risking your life on a daily basis. Jaikus had talked him into coming to Reakla to join the Guild with him. If they turned them away without so much as a how-do-you-do, that would suit him just fine. He definitely felt out of place among such company.

"Come on," said Jaikus as he grabbed his friend's arm. "Let's follow them to the Guild."

"Okay."

They had gone to the Guild upon first arriving in town, but hadn't worked up the nerve to approach the front door. Several rather intimidating individuals had been standing before the entrance and the two lads thought that perhaps coming the following morning would prove better.

But such had not been the case. They again lost their nerve when they went down earlier that day, Jaikus being the one to balk at approaching.

For all his enthusiasm to join the Guild, he was afraid they would turn him away. And he feared such a fate.

They and others, mainly kids, tagged along behind the procession of men and trolls until the Guild came into sight. It was an impressive structure at three stories high with a box tower rising on the eastern edge that extended for another four levels. The tower, they knew, was the province of the magic users. At times, strange noises could be heard coming from the windows of the upper levels, as well as mysterious flashes of light. Arcane powers beyond the ken of the average man were manipulated within.

Ever since he was a lad sitting on the wooden floor of the inn listening to the bards spin tales of daring-do, Jaikus had his heart set on being a fighter. Back home, he and Reneeke used to practice with wooden swords they crafted from the remains of an old oak tree. It had been split in two by lightning and they imagined special properties imbuing the wood when they sparred. Jaikus could usually whomp Reneeke and felt pretty good about his prowess with a blade. Reneeke didn't really care what he would be, he was only there so Jaikus wouldn't have to go it alone.

There was a hunger in Jaikus' eyes, a longing to be a part of such a close-knit society. To be an Adventurer! What greater thing could there be? "Let's do it."

"What?" asked Reneeke. Glancing down to his friend, he saw that look in his eyes, one he had seen before. It said his friend had found his spine. "Are you sure?"

"Yes." Then, as the men and trolls disappeared around the corner of the Guild, Jaikus stalked toward the Guild's entrance with Reneeke close behind.

A rather large individual stood near the entrance, Jaikus judged him to be a fighter by the way he was armed, one who had seen better days; the man's left arm was missing. His eyes tracked the two lads on their approach, and as they stepped upon the bottom of three steps leading to the entrance, moved to block their entry.

"Only Guild members are allowed in, boys," the man said in a raspy, though not entirely unfriendly, voice.

"Boys?" declared Jaikus. Coming to a stop, he stood all of his five feet seven with hands on hips. "We are not boys, but men."

A grin spread across the man's face. "Be that as it may, you can't come in. Unless...you were invited by someone?"

Jaikus' bravado began oozing away now that he stood toe to toe with a real Adventurer. A serious case of self-consciousness and doubt came over him. "No," he replied. Being in the situation, he had no other recourse but to see it through to its end. About to continue, he was forestalled by Reneeke.

"We are here to join the Guild."

Looking the pair up and down, the man replied, "Go home, boys. You have more the farm than fame about you. It would be a shame for your mothers to lose you so early in life." Scoring upon Jaikus with the jab about the farm, the man saw the wannabe Adventurer's face turn red.

"We will have you know that we are not the bumpkins you make us out to be. Reneeke and I are no strangers to the sword, and…" But he was again forestalled by laughter.

"Boys, boys, boys. Thank you. I haven't had a good laugh like that in many a moon. *No strangers to the sword.* Why, you two don't even *have* swords. Go home."

"Are you turning us away?"

"It looks like it, *boy.* You can't just walk up to the Guild, announce your desire to become an Adventurer, and be one." He then gestured to the open entryway behind him. "You must earn the right to walk through this door."

Reneeke laid a hand on his friend's shoulder. "Let's go home. You tried."

Jaikus knocked the hand from him. He would not give up so easily. "How can we earn the right?"

"Go on an Adventure, boy. Do something brave, something worthy of the Guild. Then we'll see."

"What kind of an Adventure?"

The man shrugged. "How about slay a dragon? The Guild's always looking for exotic beasts for its members, go find something unique and bring it back."

"How?" asked Reneeke.

Rolling his eyes heavenward, the man replied, "If you have to be told, then there isn't much point in trying to join the Guild now, is there?"

"But Adventurers go on adventures all the time," argued Jaikus. "How is it they know what is going on in the world?"

"What are you, stupid? Don't you know anything about the Guild? People come to the Guild, or send word, of tasks that need doing. They hire out a party to resolve whatever problem or task needs to be addressed."

Before Jaikus could reply, Reneeke asked, "Are there any that we could do?"

"Sorry, kid. But those are for members only."

Jaikus could see he was going to get nowhere with this fellow. "We'll be back."

"I'll be here," the man assured them.

Jaikus stalked off in a huff.

"Let's go home," stated Reneeke yet again.

Jaikus shook his head. "Rene, I simply cannot resign myself to the life of my father. Work all day long and into the night in an attempt to scratch a living off the land. Watch my youth and dreams fade as year after year passes with no change in sight. No Rene, I cannot do it."

"But you heard what the man at the Guild said. We have to do something worthy of the Guild. And to be honest, we don't exactly have any skills that would be useful in such an endeavor."

"Nevertheless, I shall not give up."

Reneeke sighed. Relaxing in the common room of the Inn of the Silver Spoon, he downed his mug of ale and signaled the barmaid for another. His friend could be headstrong at times, and to his chagrin, this was one of them.

He liked Jaikus. Being raised in the same backwater farming community of Running Brook had produced a bond between them that he could not simply ignore. But there were times when his friend was exasperating. Like the time when he thought a gnome had set up shop in Tilly's bakery. Two weeks of sneaking about and spying were spent in watching the place only to discover the gnome to be Tilly's baby nephew who had come to visit. Thank goodness they kept their suspicions to themselves or they would have been the laughingstocks of their village.

"He did have a point, however," Reneeke announced.

"What was that?"

"We might want to think about getting a couple swords. Those at the Guild might take us more seriously if we were armed."

Jaikus nodded. "Good thought." Pulling out his coin purse, he dumped two silvers and five coppers onto the table. The seven coins represented everything he had in the world.

Without bothering to check his, Reneeke said, "I've another silver, two coppers."

Meeting his friend's eye, Jaikus asked, "Think this will be enough?"

Reneeke shrugged. "Don't know. Never priced a sword before."

"Well, I guess we can at least make inquiries at the local weapons dealer."

Bright and early the following morning, the two wannabe adventurers found their way to *The Keen Blade*, a weapon shop reputed to be the best in town. Within they gazed upon a wide variety of weapons: battleaxes, longswords, pikes, maces, flails, and other death dealing instruments.

Jaikus' eyes gleamed when they fell upon a longsword sporting silver filigree delicately interwoven across the face of the guard. About to reach out and touch it, he was interrupted by the emergence of a man from the back.

"Can I help you, lads?"

Five-foot four and thin as a rail, the man was one of the few Jaikus had ever encountered shorter than himself. He had fiery red hair that was neatly trimmed, and was dressed in a plain jerkin. He looked nothing like a smith should.

"We're looking for a couple swords," Reneeke piped up.

The man's eyes narrowed. "Looking to join the Guild are you?"

"How did you know?" asked Jaikus.

"Every other week or so, I get one or two young folks such as you lads who think the adventuring life is for them. Let me tell you, it isn't all it's cracked up to be. After long stretches of boring monotony, there's a short duration in which your lives are hanging by a thread, then back to boring monotony. You're better off returning to the farm."

"No farm, thank you," replied Jaikus. "I'll try my luck with the Guild."

Shrugging, the man said, "It's your life."

"You bet."

Taking in the two lads before him, the man didn't seem to think too much of them. "How much are you looking to spend?"

"Three silvers," answered Reneeke.

"*Three silvers?*" asked the man with a laugh. "Three silvers won't even get you a scabbard, and a used one at that."

"How about a spear?" asked Reneeke. Turning to his friend, he said, "We're pretty good with those."

"Son, there is nothing in this shop that can be had for three silvers. Not for both of you at any rate."

"But we need a weapon if we're to join the Guild," complained Jaikus.

"True." Growing thoughtful for a moment, the man said, "You might try over at Keeler's. He has a smithy located on the eastern edge of town. Adventurers often dump their unwanted and extra items off on him."

"Thank you," said Jaikus. He took another longing look at the longsword he desperately wanted before leaving the shop. One day, he vowed to himself, he was going to have a sword like that.

Keeler's was easy to find. A quick question of a local and they were soon hearing the ringing hammer of a smith at work. Unlike the man back at *The Keen Blade*, the man doing the hammering had the thick arms and broad back of a smith.

When the smith noted their approach, he plunged the piece of metal he worked on into a bucket of water. Steam rose as he held it there for a second before removing it. Then he gave the metal bar a brief inspection before setting it on a worktable close to hand.

"Need a weapon?" the smith asked before the two lads had come to a stop.

"What makes you ask that?" questioned Jaikus.

Giving them a grin, the man replied, "Okay then, what can I do for you?"

"We need a weapon," stated Reneeke.

Laughing, the smith shook his head and Jaikus grew a bit red about the ears. "Pay me no mind boys, just a jest at your expense."

"We were told you might have weapons on the cheap," stated Jaikus, overcoming his irritation.

"That I do. What sort are you interested in?"

"Swords."

"Of course, how silly of me. You all want swords. Don't even think about a mace or a halberd, or any other type of weapon. Everyone wants a sword."

"Aren't swords the best?" asked Reneeke.

"Not for everyone, son. It all depends on what you want to do. A good mace can pulp an opponent's internal organs quite readily. A spear or halberd gives you reach which allows you to strike your opponent before they can come close."

"I still want a sword," asserted Jaikus. "And so does my friend."

"As you wish," shrugged the smith. Extending his hand, the man said, "Name's Keeler. I have half a dozen or so out back that a party disposed of just yesterday." After shaking hands and hearing their names, Keeler indicated for them to follow. He then turned about and headed for a side door, beyond which lay a room with many different weapons, swords included, displayed upon the walls and lying atop tables. One longsword within a scabbard bearing a dragon design caught Jaikus' eye.

"How much for this one?"

"*Too* much I'm sure," replied the smith. "The equipment you two can afford I keep out back."

Bristling under the smith's comment, Jaikus remained silent and followed him from the room. His mood didn't improve when he saw the selection of weapons that, according to the smith, was within their means.

These weapons were hardly what one would call worthy of a member of the Guild. Perhaps that was why they had found their way to Keeler's back room. Lying in uneven stacks upon the floor, jammed into barrels, leaning against the wall, these weapons were in a sad state of upkeep.

Many were either chipped or broken, a couple had complete holes scored through that when Reneeke asked, Keeler explained the party had run into an acid trap. "It took out two of their members and ruined most of their equipment." Gesturing to the hodgepodge of adventuring cast-offs, he added, "What you see here are weapons no longer deemed serviceable.

A few aren't too bad." Moving over to a barrel with a score of sword hilts sticking out the top, he inspected them for a moment before pulling out one with minimal disfigurement.

"This one is still serviceable," he explained, bringing it over to the pair. "Not great, but it'll only cost you a silver."

Jaikus looked at the sword with undisguised disgust. It didn't have a shine to it, rust covered much of its surface, and there were two nicks near the end. "Isn't there anything better?"

"Son, fresh from the farm as you two are, I'm assuming you don't have a great deal of coins. Am I right?"

Miserably, Jaikus had to nod affirmative.

Turning the sword over, the smith then waved it back and forth. "Though it doesn't look first-rate, it has a good balance and can still hold an edge. It'll take a bit of work to make it serviceable once again. But once sharpened and cleaned, it will do the job."

"I'll take it," offered Reneeke. "If you will also throw in a whetstone and some oil?"

Keeler nodded. "Done."

"But I still need something," stated Jaikus. These were hardly the weapons of heroes.

"So you do," agreed Keeler. He returned to the barrel and pulled forth a second blade, equally as disreputable as the first. "This one is in fair condition and will serve."

The last thing Jaikus wanted to do was to be seen sporting such a sword. Glancing around, he saw one that looked in much better condition lying on a nearby table. The blade had a shine and the few nicks marring its surface were hardly noticeable. Not only that, but there was an archaic design engraved in the crossbar that gave it a mysterious quality. "How about this one?" Crossing over to it, he gripped the hilt and held it up.

"Nice," said Reneeke, approvingly.

"You don't want that one son."

Turning to Keeler, Jaikus replied, "Why not?"

"It's not that good."

"*Not that good?* Why, this sword is much better than that pig-sticker you're holding." Taking out a silver, he flipped it over the smith. "I'll take it."

Keeler snatched the coin out of the air and slipped it into his pocket. "As you wish."

Satisfied with his sword, Jaikus turned to go when Keeler stopped him by saying, "Just one more thing."

"What?"

Striking out with the sword Jaikus had called a "pig-sticker", the smith struck his newly purchased blade, and the metal shattered.

Reneeke stood amazed. The blade didn't just break in two, it shattered into over a dozen, separate pieces. "Wow."

"Don't you *ever* ignore wisdom from one who knows better, son," the smith said sternly. "It may just cost you your life."

With but three inches of blade still attached to the hilt, Jaikus stared at what was left of his new sword in disbelief. "You broke my sword."

"Yep. It sure looks that way."

"I want my silver back." Tossing down the stub of a blade, Jaikus stood with hand outstretched to receive his coin.

"No."

"*No?*" Growing irate, Jaikus was about to shout a few choice words at the smith when the smith laughed.

"I just saved your life, boy. Days from now, or maybe a week or two if you were lucky, you'd have been in dire straits when that sword shattered during your very first fight leaving you defenseless. Let this be a lesson. When advice is given on something as important as a sword, especially when it comes from a smith such as myself, listen. Or die. In the line of work you are seeking to embark upon, life is tenuous at best."

"Good idea," agreed Reneeke.

Jaikus seethed, but could understand the wisdom of what Keeler was saying.

Holding out the "pig-sticker" to Jaikus, the smith asked, "Do you want this?"

He glanced at Reneeke, who nodded for him to take it. Turning his gaze back upon the "pig-sticker," Jaikus shuddered and said, "Yes." Taking out his last silver, he handed it to the smith and took the sword.

At no extra charge, Keeler supplied each with a scabbard as worn as the blades, then gave Reneeke the whetstone and the oil, which Reneeke promised Jaikus he would share. "Now all we need to do is find a way to join the Guild," Reneeke told his friend.

"Yeah."

"You're not even part of the Guild yet?" Keeler shook his head. "How do you plan to join? You two know someone?"

Jaikus shook his head. "I wish we did, but no."

Reneeke asked, "You wouldn't know where we could get an exotic animal for the Guild?"

"Who told you that you needed one?"

"The man out front of the Guild we met yesterday."

The smith eyed the two before him. Raising his hand to just above his head, he said, "About this height with only one arm?"

Reneeke nodded. "That's him."

"And I suppose he failed to mention the Scrolls?" Two blank looks were all the answer he needed. "Damn, Jeral. Ever since he lost his arm two years ago due to a Springer's carelessness, he's had it in for anyone looking to join the Guild. Though that's probably why they stationed him outside, sort of like a first line of defense to keep away those who truly don't have the grit to be part of the Guild."

"What are the Scrolls?" asked Jaikus.

"Well, in case you didn't notice, not more than ten feet to the right of where you met Jeral, are the Scrolls listing Adventures that have gone unresolved."

"Unresolved? Why would they not be completed?" wondered Reneeke.

"Several reasons. First and foremost is the reward not being worth the risk or time invested. Most Adventurers are mercenaries at heart, and unless there is some serious gain to be had, they will pass it over. Another reason would be it is too dangerous. Once an Adventure has claimed a party or two, few are willing to sign on."

"So, if we take on one of these Adventures and resolve it, we're in?" asked Jaikus.

"Not being part of the Guild, I wouldn't know for sure. But it's your best bet. I've heard of some current Guild members having gone that route."

Eyes agleam with possibilities, Jaikus said, "Thank you, master smith." Then to Reneeke, he said, "Let's return to the Guild and take a look at those Scrolls." Assuredly, there must be some task considered beneath the average Guild member that they could accomplish without too much threat to life and limb. Then, they would be in!

—2—

"Remove a Specter..."
"Ice Giant stealing cattle..."
"Recover family heirloom from cursed crypt..."
Reneeke turned to Jaikus. "I'm not sure about these."

Seven scrolls, each detailing over a score of tasks needing completion were nailed to the side of the Guild. They had gone through six thus far and hadn't found anything their meager talents could handle.

"Here's one that doesn't look overly dangerous. A Mr. Phats requests leaves of the Atalas plant." Glancing from the scroll to his friend, Jaikus asked, "Maybe we could find some in an apothecary?"

Reneeke shook his head. "If they could be had so readily, I doubt if Mr. Phats would have sought the services of the Guild."

"You have a point, Rene." Further reading revealed that the nearest location of the leaves was some leagues within the Keota Swamp. "Maybe not." To travel such a distance into the Swamp would almost ensure encountering trolls. A prospect neither relished.

Flipping to the last scroll, Jaikus' eyes were drawn to a scrawl written across the bottom.

Lost ring. See Matron Grantha—Reakla. 5 GP

"A lost ring. What do you think?"

Reneeke nodded. "Sure. She's in Reakla too." Most of the tasks listed ranged throughout the realm, even to places neither of them were in the least bit familiar. It was fortuitous that this one was near.

"Five gold pieces would come in handy," added Jaikus. "We spent all but our last few coppers at Keeler's."

"Then let's find this Matron Grantha and see what we can do."

Setting out from the Guild with but a name to go on, they asked passersby as to this lady's whereabouts. It wasn't until the sky was growing dark and they had wandered up near Adventurer's Way that someone knew who they were asking about.

"Matron Grantha?" questioned a lad of about seven. "Sure I know her. She lives by herself in the house next to Chondy's Outfitters. You can't miss it."

"Thanks." After finding out the general direction in which her home lay, they quickly came across Chondy's Outfitters and the two-storied home that shared its south wall. To the right of the outfitters was a small open plaza, so the house on the left had to belong to Matron Grantha.

The door of the home bore ornate scrolling with faded varnish. Jaikus rapped on the door with the round brass knocker, paused, then rapped again. There was no response. He was about to rap a third time when they heard a bolt being thrown and the door swung inward a few inches before halting.

An elderly woman squinted through the crack at the two on her doorstep. "Yes?"

"Good afternoon," began Jaikus. "Are you Matron Grantha?"

Squinting harder, the woman asked, "Is that you, Booba?"

Jaikus glanced to Reneeke who only shrugged. Turning back to the lady, he replied, "Uh, no ma'am. My name is Jaikus and this is my friend Reneeke. We saw that you were in need of someone to locate a…ring?"

"Oh my, yes," she replied. "My husband gave me that ring during our seventeenth year together." Face pursing, she cursed, "He was a drunken lout, but I did dearly love that ring." Opening the door wider, she gestured for them to enter. "Won't you come in?"

"Yes, ma'am." Passing through the door, they entered a nice, if not lavish, outer room one would expect to find in the home of an elderly lady. Frilly lace abounded. The door closed behind them and Matron Grantha indicated for them to have a seat upon the divan. She sat in a plush chair directly across from them.

"Could you tell us about the ring, ma'am? When did you last see it and most importantly, what does it look like?"

"Well, I do seem to recall wearing it last month when I went to Clara's for dinner. Clara of course is the wife of my first son. He's been gone these many years and we find comfort in each other's company. She runs the bakery now with the help of my two granddaughters, Mara and Chari. Lovely girls both. Soon it will be time to pick out a husband for Mara, she's the oldest."

She eyed the two seated before her. "I don't think either of you are right for her. Perhaps you should go and I'll try to find someone who is better well-off." She squinted at them for a moment. "From the looks of you two, coins don't find their way into your pockets very often."

"Ma'am, we're not here about your granddaughters," Reneeke explained. "We're here to help you find your ring."

"My ring? Oh, yes, that's right. It went missing. Did you find it? You know you don't get the reward until you do."

"Yes, ma'am, we understand that. But we have only just arrived and you haven't told us what it looked like or where you may have lost it."

"Didn't I? I was pretty sure I had. Well, it is a gold ring with a large diamond set in the middle with two red sapphires, one to either side. Those are supposed to represent my granddaughters Mara and Chari. Mara is set to be betrothed to a miller's son, but he seems a bit shiftless to me. I cautioned her mother as to his ways but she doesn't seem to care."

"I thought you said a husband had yet to be picked out for Mara?" asked Reneeke.

She then launched into an exhaustive explanation of why-tos and wherefores, and Jaikus turned an annoyed glance to Reneeke. "Let's try to keep her on the ring, shall we?" he whispered.

"Sorry."

When a break finally came in her convoluted rendition of Mara's betrothal prospects, final disposition, and so forth, Jaikus interrupted her with, "Now, about your ring. Could you..." A nudge from Reneeke caused him to leave the sentence unfinished. His friend was pointing across the room toward where a vase decorated with pictures of violets sat on a small table against the wall.

"On the table behind it," whispered his friend.

It was the ring. From where they sat, they could readily make out the diamond and two sapphires placed to either side of the ring just as she had described.

Reneeke turned his attention back to Matron Grantha. "Ma'am, your ring...*oof!*"

A quick jab in the ribs silenced his friend. "...will be in your hands by morning," finished Jaikus.

"Thank you, young man," she said with a smile. "It means so much to me. Not because of my late, layabout husband you understand, but because it represents my darling granddaughters."

Jaikus came to his feet. "Have nothing to fear. Jaikus and Reneeke are on the job."

"Wonderful."

As she turned to see them to the door, Jaikus moved toward the vase and the ring partially hidden behind it. Then when her back was turned while opening the door, he snagged the ring and slipped it into his pocket.

Reneeke frowned and shook his head. *That's stealing,* he mouthed to his friend.

Heading to the door, Jaikus ignored Reneeke and slipped through to the street beyond.

"You boys have a good time finding my ring," she said.

"We will, ma'am."

Once Reneeke had joined him out on the street and Matron Grantha closed the door, Jaikus turned to his friend. "Tomorrow, bright and early, we'll return with the ring and collect our reward."

"But this is not right," argued Reneeke.

"What do you mean? She didn't know where it was, we found it and are going to return it to her."

"Jaik, she didn't lose it, merely misplaced it."

"Look, we need to complete an Adventure before we get into the Guild, right?"

Reneeke nodded.

"We do this, and we get in."

"I still don't think this is the right way to go about it," asserted Reneeke. "We are taking advantage of an old lady whose mind and eyesight are going." A pause, then, "What if it was your grandmother in there?"

"Which one?" Waving off the answer, Jaikus continued, "Besides, we need the coins. We are not stealing, merely satisfying a need that she has requested we fill. Namely, returning her precious ring to her. We're down to coppers, Rene!"

Reneeke did not look convinced.

"Trust me. This will all work out."

Bright and early the next morning, Jaikus and Reneeke were once again knocking upon Matron Grantha's door. When the elderly woman answered, she squinted at the two of them. "Booba?"

"No, ma'am," replied Jaikus. "We are not Booba. My friend and I were here yesterday and said that we would help you find your ring."

"My ring? Did I lose that ring again?"

"Apparently. You posted a notice at the Guild and we came in answer."

"Oh, yes. That's right, my ring is missing again. When you find it, let me know."

She started to close the door and Jaikus quickly stepped forward. He laid a strong hand upon it to prevent the door from closing, then said, "We have already found your ring."

"You did? You boys are quick."

Jaikus pulled the ring from his pocket and held it out to her. "Here you go, ma'am."

Taking it, she said, "Thank you, young gentlemen."

When she again began to close the door, Jaikus said, "I believe there was a reward?"

"Oh that's right. I almost forgot. Wait here a moment." She closed the door until there was only a crack left through which Jaikus and Reneeke could peer.

"You shouldn't take any reward," stated Reneeke. "We didn't do anything."

"Look Rene, we need the gold. Without it, we'll be without resources all too soon. Besides, did you see the look on her face? We brought her happiness."

"By taking a ring from her home and returning it the next day. It isn't right."

Jaikus rolled his eyes and sighed. Reneeke would never understand.

Seconds ticked by and the woman failed to return. Peering through the crack, Jaikus tried to discover where she had gone, but couldn't see her. He nudged the door open a little bit so he could get a better view of the interior. From the back of the house came soft, melodic singing.

Frowning, he hollered, "Hello?" When nothing happened, he hollered once more, this time louder. "Matron Grantha?"

The old woman appeared from the back. "Is that you Booba?"

"No, ma'am. We are the ones who returned your ring." Slightly exasperated, there was an edge to Jaikus' voice.

"My ring?" she asked. Holding her hand up, she showed them where the ring rode on her finger. "But my ring is here. I'm afraid you must have me confused with someone else."

"Look, we are from the Guild. You posted a request for someone to recover your ring. We came here yesterday and took on the task. Not more than ten minutes ago we returned the ring to you."

"Did you?" she asked. "Why, that was awfully nice of you young man."

"Yes. And now we would like the reward of five gold pieces you offered."

"I don't know anything about that. You'll have to take it up with Booba."

"Who is this Booba, and where can we find him?"

Growing thoughtful, Matron Grantha acquired a faraway look. Then she said, "Now I remember. He's usually in front of the Guild. Lost his arm awhile back, poor boy. He comes around here every now and then to check on me. Seems he feels I should move in with him and my youngest daughter Belle, but I simply can't bring myself to leave my home."

Reneeke gave her a warm grin. "We understand. We shall take this up with Booba."

"If you do speak with him, tell him I am well."

"It would be our pleasure." Then to Jaikus, Reneeke said, "Let's go."

As Matron Grantha closed the door, Jaikus turned to Reneeke. "We'll never get our money out of *Booba!* You heard what Keeler said, that man has it in for those of us who want to join the Guild."

"Relax, Jaik. You get too anxious about things."

"Rene, we have little in the way of coins remaining. What are we to do?"

Reneeke shrugged. "Something will come up."

Jaikus didn't share his friend's optimism.

Two locals shared their table that night. One was a rather stocky man, a candle maker by the name of Jenki. The other was Jenki's oldest son, Jenkimar. The common room being rather packed as it was that evening, a rare occurrence if what Jenki alleged was any indication. He and his son had asked the two would-be adventurers if they could share their table. Of course, Reneeke acquiesced before Jaikus could formulate a reasonable excuse why they couldn't. But, the father and son turned out to be a jovial pair and Jaikus was quickly put at ease.

"We saw the trolls being marched to the Guild yesterday," Reneeke told the pair. "I had never seen such beasts in all my life."

Jenkimar nodded with a grin. "Then you must not be from around here?"

"No. We hail from Running Brook, a small farming community many days to the east."

"Such sights are quite common," the son explained. "Why, just last week, *Treglae's Fearsome Four* actually brought in a Fire Drake. Seeing that beast paraded through the streets was something let me tell you."

"Isn't bringing such dangerous animals into the city, well, dangerous?" asked Reneeke.

"For the most part, no," Jenki replied. "Of course, there are those instances when less skilled adventurers try to bag a beast that's more than they can handle." Turning to his son, he asked, "Remember when *Teeth of Hell* brought in those devil bears?" When his son nodded, he turned his attention back to the two friends. "They hadn't made it halfway to the Guild before the bears broke the holding spells and started running amok. Ten died that day and another score will never walk again."

"People tend to be wary whenever a new band is marching their prize through the streets," added the son.

"They didn't seem concerned when those trolls were passing through," stated Reneeke.

"That's because it was *Ye's Band of Thugs*. Everyone knows Ye and his crew know how to handle the beasts."

"Quite the colorful names these parties have," commented Jaikus.

Jenki nodded. "They tend to. If you boys are thinking about joining the Guild, you'll probably want to join one of the existing parties, at least until you get some experience under your belt."

"Why?" asked Reneeke. "Jaik and I thought we could, you know, go it alone?"

"I suppose you could, but you'll survive much better if you have a few extra swords with you, not to mention a spell caster or two."

Reneeke turned to his friend, "What do you think, Jaik?"

"I doubt if anyone would have us," his friend replied.

"They might. We won't know until we ask."

The prospect of going hat in hand from party to party in the hopes someone would deign to allow them to tag along just didn't sit well with them.

Downing his ale, the father stood and motioned for his son to do likewise. "This will have to be goodnight, gentlemen," he announced. "We've an early morning ahead of us."

"Have an order for the Guild to complete before noon," explained the son. "Thank you for allowing us to share your table."

"You are welcomed," Reneeke assured him.

"Good night," Jenki said then led his son across the common room and to the door.

Once the pair had left the inn, Reneeke signaled their server for another round of ale. "They were nice."

Jaikus nodded.

They didn't have long to wait until two frothy mugs sat before them. Reneeke picked up his and knocked back half of it.

"Excuse me," said a voice from a neighboring table.

Turning toward the hail, Jaikus saw that it was a dark haired lad slightly younger than himself and Reneeke. He sat with five others of similar age. "Yes?"

"We couldn't help but overhear what you and those other fellows were talking about."

"Kind of rude, isn't it? Listening in on other people's conversations?" Jaikus didn't care for such behavior.

The kid shrugged. "Probably. But thought you might like to know of a Guild party leaving on the morrow that may be interested in taking along a couple Springers."

"Springers?" asked Jaikus. "What do you mean by, '*Springer*'?"

"Didn't Keeler mention something about Springers?" queried Reneeke.

The lad glanced to his buddies and gave them a grin. "A Springer is what they call a new adventurer. You know, because in the spring, the world reawakens and becomes new again. A beginning as it were."

"What party?" asked Jaikus.

"*Charka's Troupe*. I heard they are escorting Hymal the Apothecary into the Swamp to collect rare reagents. They usually have a Springer or two on these trips, or so I heard."

"Why would they want someone along who would be next to useless?" asked Reneeke. Jaikus flashed his friend an annoyed look at being referred to as useless.

"Charka's pretty nice about such things," the lad explained. "Always one to help out the new guy."

Reneeke turned to Jaikus. "What do you think?"

"We don't know anything about this Charka, or his Troupe. How can we know he'll do right by us?"

"Hey, I wouldn't steer you wrong," the lad assured him. "I just thought I'd let you know. Take it or leave it as you will. If you're interested, Charka can usually be found at *The Dented Helm*, a hangout for fighter types located near the Guild."

"I suppose it can't hurt to check it out," stated Jaikus. Then to the lad he said, "Thanks."

"You're welcome." Turning back to his friends, they began talking in hushed tones.

Jaikus rose to his feet and told Reneeke, "Let's head over to *The Dented Helm*."

Two men stood conversing near the entrance. Both were obviously fighters of the Guild. One had twin blades strapped to his back while the other had a mace hanging from his belt. Both gave the two wannabe adventures a cursory glance. Bobbing their heads in greeting, Jaikus and Reneeke walked past without a word and entered *The Dented Helm*.

It turned out to be a rather large tavern with two floors of sleeping areas above the drinking area. Raucous laughter could be heard coming from within. Hanging on a rusty old chain attached to a beam near the entrance was an old war helm. Its left side was completely caved in.

It was a busy night and there wasn't an empty table left to be had in the common room. A bard was setting up on the small stage in the far corner and no less than three barmaids worked their way through the tables delivering mugs of ale and platters of food.

Jaikus scanned the sea of faces. "Which one is Charka?"

"I don't know," replied Reneeke. Flagging down one of the barmaids, a comely lass with long flowing auburn hair and a well rounded figure, he waited until she drew near then said, "My friend and I would like to buy a drink for Charka. You wouldn't know what he favors would you?"

"He usually drinks the Black Syderkult."

"Black Syderkult?"

"It's brewed locally from a plant grown on the edge of the Swamp. I've never tried it but have heard it could knock a troll back a step or two."

"Very well then." Pulling two coppers from his pouch, he handed them to the barmaid. "Will this do?"

She shook her head. "No. Two more."

Producing another two, he gave them to her.

"I'll get it to him right away."

"Thank you."

As she walked away Jaikus asked, "What did you do that for? We don't have many coins left you know."

"Just wait." He kept an eye on the door through which the barmaid had disappeared. Then when she reappeared with a tall flagon on her tray, he directed Jaikus' gaze toward her. "Look there." They watched as she crossed the common room and set the flagon before a large bear of a man. Clad in skins with a beard as full as a tree in spring, the man looked questioning to the girl. Then, when she pointed over to where Jaikus and Reneeke waited, Reneeke said, "We have found Charka."

The big man waved for them to come over and join him. When they reached his table, he said, "Many thanks, lads. I do appreciate a flagon of the 'kult."

"Our pleasure."

Charka's two comrades, one a woman as thin as a rail and dressed in a green gown, and the other a fighter dressed in leathers with a simple looking sword hanging at his hip, nodded greeting as well.

"Please, sit," Charka offered.

"Thank you, the common room seems a bit full this evening." Taking a seat, Jaikus gave the big man a grin. Reneeke took the seat next to his.

"Now, what do you want?" Charka eyed the two newcomers from behind the flagon as he took another drink.

"We understand you may be in need of a couple Springers," explained Jaikus.

The big man looked surprised. "And you are volunteering your services in that capacity?"

"Absolutely," Jaikus replied.

"We wish to join the Guild, and it appears this may be the only way."

"Well, it's true we do prefer to have a Springer or two, though the last one didn't work out so well."

"Oh?"

The woman sitting beside Charka nodded. "He didn't make it."

"Well, let me put your minds at ease. My friend and I are no strangers to the sword and we would be a great asset to have along."

"Do you have supplies and equipment to last a fortnight in the Swamp?" When he saw how their faces turned crestfallen, he knew they hadn't. "You'll need to get some."

Jaikus was about to reply, but was forestalled by Reneeke, who said, "We spent all but a few coppers to just get here and in purchasing our swords." Jaikus flashed him an annoyed look.

"Not a problem. Do you know where The Dirt Road is?" asked the man dressed in leathers.

"Aren't all the roads in Reakla dirt?" asked Jaikus.

"No, it's a chandler's shop called *The Dirt Road*. Bella sells travel supplies and equipment. His place is near the Swamp Wall just off Keota Plaza. If in the morning you are still serious about accompanying us as Springers, seek him out and tell him Charka sent you and that you need the 'regular' supplies. You tell him that, and he'll set you up with everything you need."

"But, we won't be able to afford it," stated Reneeke.

"Don't worry, it'll come out of your share of the commission."

"What is our share?" asked Jaikus, very interested now that the possibility of receiving gold or treasure was mentioned.

"Five percent, and a like share of any treasure we may come across and bring back. That's standard for Springers."

"If we do this, would we be allowed to join the Guild?" asked Jaikus.

Charka nodded. "I shall put your names forward upon our return, provided you acquit yourselves honorably and abide by the contract."

Jaikus nodded.

"Very well then. We leave at noon tomorrow. Meet us in front of the Guild an hour before. Make sure you stop by Bella's first and have your equipment with you."

"Yes, sir," responded Jaikus. "We will do that." Coming to his feet, he motioned for Reneeke to do the same.

Reneeke bobbed his head and mumbled, "Thank you."

"See you tomorrow," the woman said. The man in leathers merely eyed them and remained silent.

"That you will," affirmed Jaikus.

Then turning from the table, he and Reneeke headed for the door. Once outside, Jaikus was practically jumping up and down in his excitement. "An Adventure, Rene! We're going on an Adventure!" Meeting his friend's gaze, he added, "And after we return, we'll be in the Guild. Isn't that great?"

"Yeah, sure," replied Reneeke as he followed his friend back to their room at *Inn of the Silver Spoon*. Though if the truth be told, he *had* been kind of hoping their bid to get into the Guild would have fallen through.

For some reason, he thought life on the farm may be much preferable than what they were about to embark upon.

—3—

The following morning before the sun was barely above the horizon, Jaikus and Reneeke were on their way to find *The Dirt Road* and acquire the equipment needed for the impending journey.

Jaikus had hardly been able to sleep through the night, so excited was he at the prospect of embarking upon an Adventure with real adventurers. Reneeke, on the other hand, had slept the night away.

It was easy enough to find Keota Plaza, it comprised the open area before the gate leading to the Swamp. The wall had been built some time after *The Troll Invasion*; mostly to keep the trolls and other creatures of the Swamp from wandering into town and creating a ruckus, but also in part to stem the settling of the Swamp.

Newcomers to Reakla who staked a claim within the Swamp often came up missing a short time afterward. There were more than trolls inhabiting the Swamp, though trolls were by and large the most common creatures encountered. So the wall was built.

It stood over fifteen feet high with a platform running along the inner lip where members of the City Guard patrolled to keep watch for any creatures that may wander too close. When one was spotted, they notified the Guild who then sent out some of its members to either kill, or more preferably, capture the creature and bring it back to the Guild's pens beneath its grounds.

Though the plaza was bordered by many shops, it was a simple matter to find *The Dirt Road*. Within, they discovered Bella who had to be one of the tallest people either of them ever met. Standing easily a head and a half taller than Reneeke, the man practically towered over both of them. Either he was a tall human or a small giant, which, was hard to tell. He looked every bit the human, though around the eyes he had a slightly different build. Later they would discover he was half-ice giant and half-human. How such a thing came to be was something Bella had never fully explained to anyone.

"Ah, welcome sirs," boomed a voice as deep as the deepest cave.

"We are...that is, Charka said to tell you we need the *'regular'* supplies. Do you know what he meant?" stammered Jaikus. Being in the presence of such a tall person made him feel small, and slightly unnerved him.

"Ah, yes. If you will but wait for a moment, I shall gather your items."

"Thank you," said Reneeke.

They watched as Bella accumulated a pile of goods upon the counter. Ropes, blankets, bedrolls, two sacks bulging with dried beef and hardtack, as well as a dozen other items useful for camping in the open. He also added two bundles of six torches each. When the tall man placed two large, finely woven mesh nets upon the stack, Reneeke asked him about them.

"They keep the bugs off of you at night," explained Bella. "The Swamp is full of little nasties that come out once the sun goes down."

Once the items had been accumulated, he glanced at Charka's newest companions. "I take it you will also need packs sufficiently large to carry all this?"

Jaikus nodded. "If you please."

Bella shrugged and produced two large backpacks, laying them atop the pile. "There you go."

"Don't we need to sign something?" asked Reneeke.

"No. Charka will take care of it next time he comes in."

They each came to the counter and took a backpack and began filling it. Not completely familiar with that particular style of backpack, Bella had to instruct them in the proper placing of items so as to get it all to fit. Some were intended to attach to the outside such as the bedroll and blanket, once they were rolled to the proper size.

"You tell Charka that if he comes across any Pyra Stones, that I have a buyer and will give him two golds each."

"We'll do that," agreed Jaikus. With pack now fully loaded, he slung it on his back. Reneeke did the same.

"You boys take care of yourselves," cautioned the Chandler as the two left his shop.

"This is heavy," groaned Jaikus.

"It's not that bad. I'm sure you will get used to it."

Making their way through the streets, they reached the Guild a couple hours before the appointed time when they were to meet Charka. They moved down from the entrance a ways so as not to be in the way while they waited.

After removing their packs and leaning them against the side of the Guild, they sat on the ground beside them. "Wonder what a Pyra Stone is?" asked Reneeke after they were settled.

"I don't know," replied Jaikus. "Who cares?"

"Do you think maybe they have something to do with magic?"

"Quite likely, Rene."

An hour went by and Jaikus was growing impatient for the arrival of Charka and the Adventure to begin. Unable to simply sit and wait any longer, he started pacing back and forth.

"Relax," said his friend. "They will be here when they do."

"I know, Rene. I just hate having to wait. I want to get going!"

Reneeke shook his head and sighed. For as long as he had known Jaikus, his friend had always been impatient. When he wanted something, he wanted it right then.

During his pacing, Jaikus' attention continued roving up and down the street passing before the Guild for any sign of Charka. So engrossed was he in scanning the people passing on the street, that when a voice, seeming to come out of the very air before him boomed, "Watch where you are going, you lout!" he jumped back in startlement.

Glancing around, he sought the source of the deep, thunderous voice.

"Down here," rumbled a voice as deep as the mountains.

His initial shock quickly gave way to humor when he discovered the owner of the voice to be no more than half a foot in height.

Looking for all the world like a miniature human male dressed in armor with a mace that couldn't have been more than two inches in length hanging from its tiny belt, the little guy stood glaring up at Jaikus with hands on hips.

"What the heck are you?" Jaikus chuckled.

Not bothering to reply, the little guy instead demanded, "Step aside."

"Hey Rene," Jaikus said, ignoring the miniature human, "get a look at this."

As Rene got to his feet and began to walk over, Jaikus turned back to the little guy with an amused grin and saw that all six inches of the miniature man was now at eye level. Seeming to hover in the air, face red with anger, the little guy pulled back his arm and struck Jaikus right between the eyes.

The blow hit him like a ton of bricks and Jaikus was knocked backward off his feet. Sailing through the air, he came to land flat on his back in a cloud of dust several feet away.

Reneeke drew his sword to come to his friend's aid.

"I wouldn't do that, lad." Charka and his two companions from the night before were approaching from down the street. The man with Charka led three mules loaded with supplies and equipment.

"But he attacked Jaikus!"

As the little man stalked off toward the entrance to the Adventurer's Guild, Charka shook his head. "If Lord Teritus had seriously meant to attack your friend, he'd be dead. As it was, he was only annoyed."

The little guy turned his gaze upon Charka who nodded his head respectfully. "Milord."

"Who is he?" asked Reneeke.

"Someone you don't want to mess with," Charka's lady companion replied. The other man with them merely nodded agreement.

Glancing to where Jaikus was slowly regaining consciousness, Charka said, "So, you two were serious about signing on as Springers?"

"Yes, sir," said Reneeke.

"We have already been to *The Dirt Road* and have our supplies."

"Excellent."

Lending his friend a hand, Reneeke helped Jaikus to his feet.

Taking in the man who wore the same leathers as the night before only today had a longsword and shield, and the woman now in a dark blue gown, Jaikus asked, "Is this your *Troupe?*"

"You bet," affirmed Charka. Gesturing to the lady, he said, "Lady Kate, a magic user of terrible power."

The woman gave them a small smile and bowed her head slightly.

Reneeke grinned back. "Nice to meet you, ma'am."

"And the sour looking individual next to her is Seward, fighter of modest accomplishments."

"Modest? Humph!" The man scowled at Charka who only grinned.

"So what's the mission?" asked Jaikus.

"We'll tell you that once we're in the Swamp," replied Charka. "After we take care of some business here, we'll meet our patron in Keota Plaza near the gate."

Jaikus looked at the *Troupe* leader with skepticism. "What business?"

"Before we begin, you and your friend must sign contracts stating that you are coming along as Springers. It's standard practice. That way when we return, I can put you forward for Guild membership."

Reneeke looked to Jaikus. "What do we have to lose?"

"Exactly. Where do we sign?"

Going to one of his mules, Charka pulled out a piece of parchment covered with writing. At the bottom were five lines. "Just sign your names on one of those and I'll do the same. Then Seward will take it in to the Guild Clerk and we can be on our way." Producing a quill and small vial of ink, he offered them to Jaikus.

After only giving the parchment a very cursory examination, Jaikus readily signed his name. Then giving the quill to Reneeke, he waited while his friend gave the contract a more thorough once over.

...duties of a Springer as set forth in Guild Bylaw Twelve...

...mutual pact of defense and rescue...
...proper burial if body is recovered...
"Proper burial?" he asked, glancing up from the contract.
"It simply means that we won't leave you to rot in the Swamp if we can help it."
"Why would you not be able to help it?" asked Jaikus.
"Situations where you are eaten, or dragged to the bottom of the Swamp. Such occurrences make it difficult to recover the body for burial."
"Just sign it," urged Jaikus.
Not seeing anything indicating life long servitude or extended indebtedness, he signed.
Charka took the parchment, signed, and then handed it to Seward. "We'll meet you at the gate." Seward merely nodded. Then as he headed for the Guild's entrance, Charka had them grab their packs and follow him to Keota Plaza.
A man waited for them there, the reins of his packhorse held in hand. Rather nondescript, and one who would easily blend into a crowd, Charka introduced him as Hymal the Apothecary. Hymal took in the two newcomers with a raised eyebrow.
"More Springers?" he asked. "After the last time I thought you had given up on them."
Charka shrugged. "I was, but they volunteered."
"To be Springers?" Hymal shook his head.
Jaikus frowned as he followed their discourse. *What was wrong with being Springers?*
"Good to see you again, Lady Kate."
"A pleasure, Master Hymal."
"I don't see Seward..."
"He's at the Guild taking care of their Springer contract," explained Charka. "He should be along shortly."
They waited another ten minutes for Seward to arrive, during which Jaikus and Reneeke exchanged questioning glances, wondering just what they may have gotten themselves into. When Seward finally arrived, he and Hymal exchanged silent nods, then Charka announced it was time to go.
The gate through which one gained access to the Swamp was merely ten feet wide, barely sufficient to allow a wagon to pass though such an occurrence rarely happened any more. Once in a while, a local might forage the fringe of the Swamp under the watchful eyes of the guards atop the wall for firewood, herbs, and other things the Swamp provided. But by and large, the only ones to pass through the gate were adventuring parties such as *Charka's Troupe*.

At their approach, guards entered the gatehouse and threw the lever unlocking the gate. Then another pair pushed the gate open to allow the party to pass. What met them on the other side was not what Jaikus had been expecting. Thinking to find marshland, dead trees, and bogs, he instead discovered a lush growth of vibrant vegetation that started two hundred feet or so from the wall. Trees soared high, bushes were full, all being very much what one would find anywhere.

"Good luck, Charka," hailed one guard. "See you in a couple weeks."

The *Troupe* leader waved in reply as he led the others forward.

Directly before the gate, in the midst of the foliage, was the beginning of a trail that wound its way deep into the Swamp. Upon reaching the trailhead, Charka paused and turned back to his two Springers. "From this point on, our lives are dependant on each other. Keep silent, do what we tell you, and you'll live to see Reakla again."

"Give us trouble and we will dump your bodies in the nearest bog," mumbled Seward beneath his breath. Charka gave him a silencing glare.

"You can count on us, sir," Jaikus assured him. Reneeke nodded.

"Good. Now, stay close. Master Hymal, you're behind me, then Kate. Seward, take the rear." The man merely nodded and moved to place himself and the mules behind Reneeke.

Entering the Swamp was kind of anti-climactic for Jaikus. The night before he imagined having to battle their way through hordes of trolls, ghouls, and other nightmarish creatures with which his over active imagination had filled the Swamp. But, now that the moment was upon him, he had to admit this was much preferable.

Once they were upon the trail and the wall was no longer visible through the Swamp's undergrowth and trees, Lady Kate moved to walk next to Jaikus.

"Don't let Seward's mood bother you. He's always a bit sour after a night of hard drinking. Charka doesn't allow more than a single pint to be consumed a day, and the night before any Adventure, Seward goes a little overboard."

"We won't, ma'am," Jaikus assured her.

"Please, call me Kate. Such formalities have no place in the Swamp. There will be more important things to worry about than titles."

From behind, they heard Seward snort. "Not for a day or two there won't. Haven't encountered a troll or bogbeast this close to the wall in over two years."

"Still, we must be wary."

"Lady…uh…I mean, Kate, how long will it take to get to wherever it is we are going?" questioned Reneeke.

"It takes about four days to reach our destination. Then we will take a full day to poke around before starting the return trip."

"What is our purpose?"

"Your purpose is to act as Springers of course. The *Troupe*'s purpose is to see Master Hymal safely to his destination and back. We've made this trip many times with him. For the most part, it's pretty boring. We don't venture too deeply into the Swamp, and the worst of its denizens don't wander the fringe area."

"Master Hymal is going to a place older than Reakla where some of the most precious and hard to come by reagents for spells and potion making can be found. We humans were not the first race to inhabit this region. You can find ruins of an ancient people scattered throughout the Swamp area, even to points beyond."

"Who were they?" Jaikus asked.

She shrugged. "We don't know, and if Hymal does, he isn't telling. He calls the place where we are going, Sythal. It's an ancient city of the long ago race. Most of it has been swallowed by the swamp, but there are some buildings readily accessible from the surface."

"You mean we get to scrounge around for treasure?" Jaikus grew excited at the prospect.

Lady Kate nodded. "That's part of the bargain. We escort him to Sythal, and in return we get a full day to root around on our own and see what we can find."

"I bet there is lots of treasure simply waiting to be discovered."

"True, but we don't always find it. Some trips are quite profitable while others are a bust."

Charka glanced over his shoulder. "Quiet! The way you are carrying on, we'll have every troll in the vicinity coming this way to see what fools were nice enough to place themselves on the menu."

"There aren't any in this part of the Swamp," stated Seward.

"Are you willing to bet *my* life on that?" Staring his man down, Charka dared him to continue. Seward had the good sense to remain silent. "Okay, then."

"We'll talk later," Lady Kate whispered.

Charka shot her a warning-filled look. She merely gave him a grin.

"Man, we're going to be rich!" he quietly exclaimed to Reneeke who shrugged.

"We don't have it yet," his friend asserted.

"No, but we will."

The rest of the first day in the Swamp continued to be routine as the trail they had originally been following slowly disappeared until vanishing altogether. Evening found them beginning to see changes in the Swamp as it turned from lush verdant land to the quagmire/bog infested place one would expect a swamp to be.

Master Hymal and Charka often conferred as the best way to proceed. For the most part, the apothecary was content to allow Charka to determine their route. Which seemed strange to Jaikus since Lady Kate had earlier told them how Hymal was the only one who knew where this place was. Curious, but not enough to ask, Jaikus was satisfied to follow wherever they led. He was on an Adventure and there was going to be treasure. Visions of shimmering swords and piles of gold occupied his mind until they reached their first campsite.

The campsite was atop a knoll of dry ground rising above the bog around them. Insects buzzed and drove them crazy until wood was collected and a fire built in a ring of stones that had seen use as a fire-ring before. Charka instructed them to put green, or even damp, foliage onto the fire. The smoke produced by the less-than-dry fuel kept the insects down to merely an annoyance.

"Make sure the fire keeps burning all night," ordered Charka to his newest companions. "If the flame dies, we'll have visitors."

"Trolls?" asked Reneeke.

He nodded. "Trolls, bogbeasts, swamp-bats, and other nasties. Gather more fuel but stay close. If you see or hear anything…strange, return to the camp immediately."

"And don't shout," added Seward. "That only encourages the beasties to attack."

"Thanks," said Reneeke. "We'll keep that in mind." Then to his friend, "Let's go Jaik."

They spent an hour collecting wood until Charka deemed they had compiled a sufficient quantity to see them through the night. By that time, Seward had a stew going that they would be able to share.

"Save the rations you got from Bella for when we'll need them," Charka explained. "They'll last while the meat we brought won't."

"Thanks," said Jaikus.

Charka shrugged. "As long as you are part of my *Troupe*, you'll be taken care of. It's the least we can do." Seeing as the stew would take a little longer before it was ready, Charka asked to see their swords. "I'm assuming they were cheap?"

"Probably from Keeler's back room," guessed Seward.

"How did you know?" asked Reneeke.

"There isn't any place in all of Reakla where you can find a cheaper blade," explained Seward. "At least, none worth staking your life on at any rate."

Reneeke pulled his from the scabbard and handed it over. A long exercise in polishing and using the whetstone the night before had removed most of the rusty patches and left the edge moderately sharp.

Taking the blade, Charka first eyed down its length then tested the balance. Moving over to one side of the knoll, he struck the flat of the blade against the side of a gray tree whose dead limbs reached up into the sky as if for salvation.

"It'll do," he stated upon returning the blade to Reneeke. Then he turned to Jaikus.

"Mine's fine," said the Springer. Visions of his last blade shattering at Keeler's made him nervous to trust this one to Charka.

"As leader of this Troupe, it is my responsibility to ensure the safety of each of its members. I cannot allow a member to endanger the rest of us by using a blade that won't last the first passage of arms." Holding out his hand, he said, "Hand it over."

Reneeke nodded for him to do it. Still having mixed feelings about this, he handed it over. Then he watched Charka go through the same motions as he had with Reneeke's. "Keeler said it would suffice."

"And so it will," replied Charka once the ringing of the blade from being struck against the side of the tree faded away.

Reclaiming his sword, Jaikus quickly reinserted it back into the scabbard.

"Not so fast," said Charka. "Just because your blades are satisfactory doesn't mean they're good, or that you will be good with them." He then eyed both of them. "Those weapons still have a long way to go before they will cleave troll-hide. I want the rust off those blades and to have an edge you can shave with before the sun comes up."

For the rest of the evening until the stew was ready, and for a stretch afterward, Charka instructed the lads from Running Brook on the proper care and maintenance of their swords. Much of the time until they turned in was spent with rag and oil, working to remove the last of the rust. When one would polish, the other would use the whetstone to sharpen. Charka oversaw their efforts until satisfied they were doing it properly.

Reneeke was an apt pupil, willing to learn and taking to the tasks set for him well. Jaikus took to it as well, seeing in the instruction the means whereby he could become a better swordsman, and thus, one step closer to becoming the hero he always longed for.

They took turns on watch that night. Neither of the boys were allowed a turn by themselves. Being new to the *Troupe*, Charka wouldn't trust them to go it alone until they've proven themselves. Reneeke was paired with Charka while Jaikus had the dissatisfying duty with Seward.

When Seward awakened Jaikus to join him at watch, he did so with a nudge to the side of the ribs. Though nudge was a loose term, his "nudge" could in some instances have been termed a kick. "Wake up, boy."

"What?" Looking around bleary eyed, Jaikus saw the man standing over him.

"It's our turn at watch."

Jaikus nodded and climbed from his bedroll. Keeping his blanket wrapped tightly about him to ward off the chill, he moved to sit next to the fire.

"Where do you think you're going?"

"I was going to warm myself by the fire," he explained.

"No, you aren't. We're on watch boy and that means, *we watch*. First rule in guard duty, don't look into the fire. It ruins your night vision. Second rule, walk the perimeter and keep alert for any movement or strange noises coming from within the Swamp. And third, don't fall asleep. Your life, and the lives of us all, could well depend on your alertness."

"Fine." Pulling his blanket even tighter, he moved from the welcoming warmth of the fire to the less hospitable fringe of the knoll. There, he began walking along the dry ground along the bog's edge.

As his eyes began scanning the darkness, his ears picked up all sorts of noises that he hadn't been aware of before, a rustle here, the cry of a night creature there. After completing his third circuit around the knoll, it gradually began to unnerve him. Shadows seemed to be everywhere, and perhaps it was only his imagination, but he would catch movement out of the corner of his eye only to discover that upon turning his full attention toward it, nothing was there.

"Don't get jumpy," he mumbled to himself. He well remembered Charka's assurance that there were no trolls or other fell beasts in this part of the Swamp. But could there be? Back home on the farm, once in a while one of the mountain beasts would wander down to the plains where they were rarely seen. Perhaps there in the Swamp, such things could happen too?

The snapping of a twig out in the Swamp caused him to jump. Hand resting shakily on the hilt of his sword, Jaikus peered into the darkness for what had caused the twig to snap. His heart was racing. Could this be it? Could this be when his mettle would first be tested?

Then a form emerged from the Swamp. "Run!" screamed Seward. Face awash with blood, he fell to his knees before the young adventurer. "Flee for your life!" he shouted before keeling over completely.

Jaikus' eyes were wide and fear rose up inside him like a volcanic eruption. Reaching out to see if Seward still lived, a roar splitting the silence of the Swamp, forestalled him. Then the huge form of a troll with blood on its lips materialized from out of the darkness. Roaring again, it raced for Jaikus.

"Trolls!" screamed Lady Kate from the top of the knoll. "Run, you fool!"

Jaikus didn't need anymore prompting. He lit out of there like a hare with a fox on its tail.

Reneeke, brought out of a dead sleep by the troll's cry, stood with sword in hand. He looked to Lady Kate.

"You and your friend get out of here! You'll never stand against them." Then raising her arm, a ball of fire appeared in her cupped hand. "Run!" she shouted to Reneeke as she let fly the burning sphere.

Reneeke saw Jaikus hightailing it out of there and he moved to join his friend. As they fled down the far side of the knoll, the sound of an explosion came from the other side. Jaikus was in total flight and Reneeke tried desperately to catch him. He finally caught up with his friend just as the sound of Lady Kate's painful shriek came from the camp. Glancing back toward the knoll, he discovered they had passed some distance into the swamp and that their campsite was no longer visible through the undergrowth and trees.

Then, the Swamp grew deathly quiet.

—4—

Glancing up from his bedroll, Master Hymal turned sleepy eyes upon the scene unfolding at the edge of the knoll. Troll emerging, new guy screaming, more shouts for them to flee, fireball exploding, and two Springers racing for their lives. The troll moved up onto the knoll and made its way toward the camp.

"Do you have to do this *every* time?" asked Hymal.

Taking off the troll head, Charka gave him a grin. "No, but why waste the opportunity?"

Lying back down, the apothecary pulled his blanket up over his head. From beneath came, "It's gotten so a guy can't even get a good night's sleep anymore."

Charka knew Hymal was only grousing because he was tired. Most times when they enacted the troll attack on a Springer, he would play along. Sometimes he would even be one of the bloody victims. But the night before he had been up late due to a prior commitment and thus hadn't felt inclined to participate.

Seward got to his feet and looked toward where Jaikus and Reneeke had disappeared. "Think we should go get them?"

"Probably." Removing the entire mocked-up troll body, none of which was in fact constructed from what had once been an actual troll, Charka nodded. "You get cleaned up and I'll go find them."

"Just be quiet while you go about it!" exclaimed Hymal.

Two figures huddled behind a stump at the edge of a bog. Looking back toward where their comrades must assuredly have fallen to the trolls, Jaikus turned to Reneeke. "Should we return to see if anyone survived?"

"I...I don't know."

It was quiet. Light from the camp's fire could be seen through the trees and indistinct silhouettes would at times move about.

"We could try to make it back to Reakla," suggested Reneeke.

Jaikus didn't like the prospect of returning without having completed the mission. How were they supposed to get into the Guild now after having not only failed to see Hymal safely to their destination and back again, but losing the rest of their party to a troll attack?

Movement in the trees near the knoll brought all thoughts back to their present situation. They each had their hands on their swords, though flight was on their minds more than fighting.

"Come on back, lads," Charka shouted into the Swamp. "It was all just a bit of fun."

Jaikus wasn't laughing. Soiling oneself in a moment of terror wasn't something he enjoyed.

Reneeke chuckled. When Jaikus flashed him a look he knew meant his friend was mad, Reneeke slapped him on the back. "Aw, come on Jaik. It wasn't that bad. Kind of funny now that the moment is behind us."

"It wasn't funny."

Making sniffing noises, Reneeke said, "I can tell." Then he chuckled again as he slapped Jaikus' back once more. "Over here!" he hollered to their *Troupe* leader. Coming around the stump, Reneeke waved.

Charka gave them a grin. "All in good fun, lads," he said. "No hard feelings?"

Reneeke shook his head. "Naw." Jaikus glared.

"It wasn't just to make sport of you two, though there was an element of fun to it. This was also to see what sort of men you two are and how you would react."

"And?" asked Jaikus.

"You two didn't flee until after we shouted for you to. Which tells us that not only would you have remained to fight, but that you are not so prideful as to ignore directions given by those with more experience." He placed a hand on each of their shoulders. "You two are all right."

"Thank you," said Reneeke.

On their return to the camp, Jaikus got over his annoyance at the trick they played on him. And once he cleaned himself up a bit, felt better about it.

The next morning, the *Troupe* seemed much more relaxed and amiable toward the pair of newcomers. Perhaps the events of the night before had been sort of an initiation, a way for them to be drawn into the camaraderie of the others. Even Seward's attitude had softened somewhat.

"Here," he said as they sat around the fire eating their breakfast. He handed a rag and a small vial of polish to Jaikus. "Now, you won't have to share with your friend."

"I appreciate this."

Seward shrugged.

Before they got underway, Charka inspected their blades and found them to be much improved. There were still a few patches of rust adhering to each, but by and large the greatest concentration had been dealt with. "You should be able to get the rest when we make camp tonight."

Hymal took the lead from this point with Charka walking beside. The rest of the marching order was the same as the day before.

As the day wore on, the Swamp deepened, growing ever more wild. Solid ground was also becoming harder to come by as bogs and waterways took over. Hymal seemed to know where he was going, and their path somehow remained upon what little dry ground there was. At times, they navigated through bogs from which bubbles would emerge, gases coming from unknown depths.

At one point, Reneeke lost his footing and slipped a foot into the waters of the bog. Immediately, the muck began to roil with small creatures not more than a finger in length. Seward grabbed Reneeke by the collar and yanked him back, dragging his foot from the muck. "Keep to high ground," he warned.

Pulling his knife, he used the tip to pry the jaws of one little creature from where it had its teeth embedded in the heel of Reneeke's boot. "They can strip the flesh from a man in a matter of minutes."

"I'll keep that in mind," Reneeke assured him.

Jaikus came to his friend and laid a hand on his shoulder. "Are you alright?"

"Yeah." He stared at the surface of the bog which had quieted down now that his foot was no longer mired in its muck.

"Let's get going, lads," Charka hollered from where he stood with Hymal and Lady Kate.

During the noon break, Charka showed Jaikus and Reneeke the proper way in which to hold their swords. He also instructed them in the rudimentary methods of hack, slash, parry, and thrust. The sword arms of both lads were leaden by the time they resumed their progress.

Later that afternoon, Jaikus commented to Lady Kate, "Charka is certainly being nice in giving us pointers with the blade."

Turning an amused look his way, she said, "Nice has nothing to do with it. You and your friend are our greatest liabilities at present. Showing you the proper use of your swords helps to reduce that liability should swordplay be needed. He's doing it, because *that* is what a good leader does."

"Is that why you are part of his *Troupe*?" asked Reneeke who couldn't help but overhear the conversation.

"In part. He and I go way back. When I first began the *Arcane Path*, he had just entered the Guild and we both signed on with Hulga and his Stickers. A band of raiders had attacked the small town of Rock Point and taken off with five young girls. The town's elders contracted with Hulga to retrieve the captives and slaughter the raiders."

"Did you find them?" Reneeke asked.

"Hulga tracked them down in four days. Not one raider lived to see the fifth."

"And the girls?"

"One was dead, the other four were the worse for wear but we were able to return them to their families. After Hulga let go those recruited for that specific venture, Charka and I signed on together again with Ye's band. It wasn't intentional. They needed a spell caster and another sword, and we just happened to be the ones selected. It was during that trip a friendship developed between us. Then when Charka decided to form his own *Troupe*, he asked me to come along and I agreed."

"What about Seward? Was he with you from the beginning?"

She shook her head. "No, he didn't join until a year later."

"I'm going to have my own party one day," boasted Jaikus.

Giving him a smile, she said, "I'm sure you will."

Then he slapped Reneeke on the back. "And Rene here is going to be part of it, won't you?"

Nodding, Reneeke replied, "Yeah, sure."

Twice more were rest breaks called before arriving at that night's campsite. Each break entailed more drills.

Charka was a hard taskmaster who demanded perfection with every movement of the sword. If they didn't halt their blade at the right angle, or they didn't thrust far enough, he made sure they knew about it. Even when the campsite was reached, he had them practice their drills rather than set up camp.

Reneeke's form was steadily improving. Jaikus looked like he was fighting it all the way. Never quite stopping at the right angle, or would have his feet set too far apart to suit Charka, he was the focal point of the leader's tirade more often than not.

"You should be able to halt your sword at the right position by now!" he shouted when Jaikus' blade came to a stop a few degrees off center. Grabbing him by the wrist, he repositioned his hand. "Keep it in line with your elbow and the blade. Think of the area from your shoulder to the tip of your blade as one."

"I'm trying!" retorted Jaikus.

"A dead man tries, an Adventurer does. Or *don't* you want to be an Adventurer? What if your buddy's life depended on you being able to take out your opponent and come to his aid? Is he going to want you to *try* and help him? *Or would he want you **to** help him?*"

Assuming a determined look, Jaikus once again went through the motions, intent on getting this right. When his sword finally reached the ending position, he maintained the position as he flicked his eyes toward Charka.

"Hmmmm, better. But your wrist is still slightly twisted. A well placed blow against your sword could snap the bone. Another score of sets before you eat."

Arm already protesting with pain, Jaikus replied. "You got it," then returned his sword to the primary position and began again.

During watch that night, Jaikus was again paired with Seward. This time, he kept more alert, not only watching the Swamp, but also his fellow comrades. He didn't want a repeat of the night before.

The hours of his watch passed slowly. Seward kept near the fire, satisfied to allow Jaikus to do the brunt of the work. Which if truth be known, suited Jaikus just fine. The man wasn't all that friendly, and even though Seward had thawed a bit after the previous night's escapade, his company was still a bit unsettling for Jaikus.

When it came time to wake Reneeke and Charka for their turn, he woke his friend then climbed into his bedroll and quickly fell asleep.

Before leaving the campsite on their third day of travel, Charka explained to Jaikus and Reneeke that they would be entering troll territory. "Keep on your guard and speak only when necessary. It is unusual for us to encounter one of the beasts, but it does happen. If we *should*, stay together and do exactly what we tell you."

Two heads bobbed understanding.

With that, Charka signaled for Hymal to take the lead.

Dry land continued to grow less and less abundant as the day progressed. Wherever they were going must be in the middle of some great mire, or so Jaikus thought. Walking along strips of land threading between bogs on one side and stagnant pools of water on the other, he worked diligently to keep his feet from finding their way into the water and muck.

He couldn't understand how Hymal knew the way. Had Jaikus needed to return to Reakla on his own, he seriously doubted his ability to accomplish such a feat. He had no clue as to where they were, or even the way back.

During their few rest breaks, he tried to discover the method by which Hymal guided them. But with Charka still drilling them, and at times sparring with them, he was never able to figure it out.

Noon came and went with no troll sightings. At one point, they came to a long, narrow strip of dry land upon which a post was set within the ground with several skins and human skulls attached.

"Troll totem," stated Charka. He brought the *Troupe* to a halt. "This wasn't here the last time."

"A clan has claimed this area for its own?" asked Seward.

Charka nodded. "That, or one that's gone rogue."

"A rogue, troll?" asked Reneeke.

"A rogue troll is one whose clan no longer accepts it and must fend for itself."

"They're usually pretty mean," stated Seward. "More likely to attack than one claimed by a clan."

The Swamp was quiet but for the normal sounds of birds and the odd gas bubble bursting after escaping the clutches of the muck and mire. Jaikus and Reneeke scanned the surrounding area for any sign of the totem's owner.

"It may be off hunting," said Charka. "Let's get moving and pass through its territory before we are discovered." Turning his attention upon his two newest members, he added, "Keep quiet and eyes open."

Charka rode side by side with Hymal as they passed the totem and continued down the strip of land. Reneeke slowed slightly when passing the totem. Inspecting the skins, he realized that they were definitely human, probably from the same donors as the skulls adorning the totem. The sight gave him the shivers.

"Hurry up," urged Seward from his position at the rear.

Reneeke quickened his pace once more and caught up with Jaikus. "Scary," he whispered to his friend.

"You're telling me," replied Jaikus.

They had just reached the end of the widened area of land, and were about to continue along a narrow strip when the beast was spotted off to their right. Moving in the same direction as they, it traversed a similar strip of land on the far side of a stagnant pool of water. Charka brought them to a halt. Using hand gestures, he signaled for everyone to remain still and quiet.

Jaikus watched the beast lumber along, his hand rested upon the hilt of his sword, ready to draw at any sign the creature took notice of their presence. Part of him wished to face the creature toe to toe, while another hoped it would keep right on going. The former wish was granted when the troll, for whatever reason, happened to glance their way.

It came to an abrupt stop and stared, almost as if it couldn't believe what it was seeing. Then it roared. Lurching into the water, it raced across to the meal waiting on the other side.

To Jaikus and Reneeke, Charka said, "You two watch the mules. Seward, Kate, let's do this." Drawing his sword, he moved to stand shoulder to shoulder with Seward while Kate took position behind them. "Wait until he's closer."

Kate nodded.

Roaring, the troll reached the end of the water and raced onto their strip of dry land.

"Now!"

Three bolts of red fire shot forth from Lady Kate's hand to strike the creature dead center on the chest.

Howling with rage and pain, the bolts knocked it back a step before the creature recovered and charged. It's long, muscular arms struck out toward Seward only to have the man's shield knock them to the side. Again it howled as Charka and Seward's swords cut deeply into its side. Then it was slammed with another round of red fire from Lady Kate.

Eager to join the fray, Jaikus said to Reneeke, "We should help."

"They told us to watch the mules."

Suddenly, a green, web-like substance bound the troll's legs together and it fell face forward onto the ground. Immediately, Seward and Charka moved forward with swords raised to impale the creature.

But it wasn't out of the fight yet. Before the blades could fall, the claws of one hand shot forward and raked Seward's calf, shredding his pants and the flesh beneath. Crying out from the pain the blow delivered, his strike fell off center and sliced the creature through the shoulder.

Charka's blade, however, struck true. Using both hands, he impaled the creature through the spinal cord and chest cavity. Leaving the sword within the creature, he backed away.

"It doesn't look as if they need our help, Jaik," Reneeke commented as the creature lay on the ground, twitching.

"No, lads, they don't," affirmed Hymal. "Charka, Seward, and Lady Kate have been doing this for some time."

When it appeared the fight had gone out of the troll, Charka pulled his sword free and stepped back quickly. As soon as he was several feet away, Lady Kate spoke three words that made Jaikus' skin crawl.

Whoosh!

The troll went up in flames. From feet to head, fire consumed the body.

"You got to *burn* 'em, lads," Hymal stated. "If you don't, they'll regenerate and become mobile once more in a day or two."

As Lady Kate saw to the immolation of the beast, Charka helped Seward over to where their Springers watched the mules. Going to the packs one of the mules carried, he pulled out a small flask and had Seward drink from it.

"Healing potion?" asked Jaikus.

Charka nodded. "Always have half a dozen of them, just in case."

Intrigued, the two lads moved so they could observe how the healing potion worked its magic on Seward's wound. This was the first time either of them had ever seen a healing potion at work. First, the bleeding stopped. Then, the wound began to close. In less than a minute, pink skin grew to cover the damaged area.

"Does it hurt?" Reneeke questioned Seward when it looked as if the healing potion had run its course.

He shook his head. "Not anymore. Just a tingling sensation akin to how it feels after your foot falls asleep and starts waking up again."

"Good work," praised Hymal as he came up to Charka.

The *Troupe* leader shrugged, "It's what you're paying us for."

"True. Still, good work."

Seward tested his newly healed leg and found it sound with only a minor twinge in the freshly grown skin. It would take some time before it grew as flexible as the rest of his skin.

Reneeke walked over to where Lady Kate's spell was reducing the troll to ashes. "I don't suppose you could teach me that?"

She shook her head and grinned. "I'm afraid not. This particular spell took me the better part of a year to learn. And that was after already spending *two* years apprenticed to another, *three* years honing my abilities, and *lots* of healing scrolls."

"Healing scrolls?"

"You don't think learning the *Arcane Arts* is easy do you? Far easier is it to wield a blade than the forces of the universe."

"I'm sure it's not, Lady, uh, er, Kate. But what about these healing scrolls. Where does one acquire them?"

"There are two places in Reakla that specialize in scrolls for Adventurers. One of course is located within the Guild grounds. Not every Guild member has access to it I'm afraid. The other is *Travel Scrolls* operated by a Scriber named Olaf. His scrolls tend to be less expensive but quite common. The best ones can be had only in the Guild."

"Does he sell the healing scrolls?"

She nodded. "Rather inexpensive too, only two golds each for the lesser ones. He sells two kinds. One is for minor wounds similar to what Seward received during the troll attack. The other can heal much more extensive damage and costs five golds each. It won't bring you back from the dead, but will take care of just about everything else. If you plan on adventuring, and don't intend on hiring a cleric to travel with you, then you will need to have a supply of either the healing scrolls or healing potions. Since you two are new, I would advise having a *lot* of them."

Ceasing her spell, she used a stick from off the ground to poke amidst the ashes for any part of the troll she may have missed. Coming across a small piece, she used a lesser fire spell and took care of it. "I think that will do."

"How much can be left before a troll is able to come back?"

"Surprisingly little. I knew this one magic user during my apprentice years who claimed to have cut a finger off of a troll just to see if the finger would regenerate back into the troll."

"And did it?"

"According to him it did."

"Man. They are some tough beasts."

"That they are," commented Charka from over his shoulder.

Lady Kate and Reneeke glanced toward him.

"Is it finished?" the *Troupe* leader asked.

She nodded. "Nothing but ashes."

"Then let's get going. It may not have been alone."

"But, I thought you said it was a rogue?"

Charka turned an unamused grin to his Springer. "Son, never believe yourself to be safe in the Swamp. Always assume that where there is one troll, there is another. Only Mossbacks are completely solitary. Now, let's get going."

Mossbacks? What are Mossbacks? Deciding there was much to the Swamp of which he still remained ignorant, Reneeke left the questions unspoken and rejoined Jaikus.

Jaikus greeted his friend with a wide grin. "Hymal said that the *Troupe* gets a bonus for every attack thwarted."

"That's nice," replied Reneeke.

"*That's nice?* Don't you know what this means? Our share will be bigger!"

"If you say so."

Jaikus rolled his eyes as Charka took the lead with Hymal right behind pointing the way. Now that a troll had been encountered, it was no longer prudent to have the apothecary take the lead.

As they left the scene of battle, Jaikus scanned the Swamp for signs of other creatures that may deign to allow their bonus to be raised by attacking. Perhaps next time, it could be two trolls instead of one. Calculating the figures, he hoped for three.

—5—

Mid-afternoon found them traversing through a series of mounds rising from the muck. There was little in the way of firm ground upon which to walk, necessitating that each watched their step carefully.

Hymal led them alongside the mounds rather than taking what Jaikus figured to be the better path, over them. Some were quite large, almost islands in themselves, and would appear to afford safe passage from the bog.

"Why do we go around?" questioned Jaikus, as he barely avoided his foot slipping into the muck for the untold time.

"Quiet!" Charka whispered back to him. "No talking."

"I would rather be on the mounds as well, Jaik," whispered Reneeke, from where he walked just behind his friend.

"This is a cursed place," Seward told the boys in a hushed voice. "Some say the spirits of the dead walk among the mounds at night. It would be best not to anger them by treading upon their graves."

"Graves? These are graves?" Jaikus whispered back. Visions of treasure buried with the dead sprang to mind.

He must have had his thoughts written upon his face for Seward said, "Don't even think about it, boy. The dead don't take kindly to those who remove their trinkets."

"But the dead are, well, *dead,* aren't they?"

"You don't know nothing about nothing, do you?"

Just then, Charka held up his hand and brought the *Troupe* to a halt. He and Hymal were stopped at a junction where the corners of four mounds converged. Motioning the others to gather near, he knelt down and inspected the ground.

Pointing to a line of tracks running between the mounds coming from their left and disappearing to the right, he said, "Trolls." He paused a moment as he inspected the ground further. "And something else too, maybe a mossback."

"Are the trolls hunting it?" asked Seward. "Or is it hunting them?"

"Hard to tell. I make out five trolls, so I would be inclined to believe that they were after the mossback." Standing back up, he said, "Mossbacks rarely try to take on so many at one time."

"Sir?" asked Reneeke. "What is a mossback?"

"Large reptile," explained Charka, "about the size of a cow with razor sharp teeth and a mean disposition."

"It gets its name from the small patch of hair upon its back that resembles moss hanging in the trees. The younger ones are able to climb up into the trees where the moss conceals them until prey passes below, then they pounce."

Reneeke came forward and examined the tracks as well. "They look a couple hours old."

Charka nodded. "You have a good eye, boy."

Shrugging, Reneeke replied, "My father used to take me hunting in the hills."

"Handy with a bow?" asked Seward.

"Fair. I tend to hit more often than not."

"Then you should have brought one with you," Seward stated with irritation.

"We didn't have enough coins to buy one, and my father wouldn't allow me to bring the only one he had. To be honest, he didn't think our chances of getting into the Guild were very good." He grinned. "And neither did I."

"Well, you aren't in the Guild yet," Seward pointed out.

"But we will be," asserted Jaikus. "Once we return, Charka said he would put us forward for membership."

"Boy, you have to survive before that can happen."

"Enough," interjected Charka. "All this talk will surely draw the attention of creatures we don't want to meet. It appears this area is no longer as safe as we used to think. There is still a day to go and standing around here talking won't get us there any quicker. Keep alert and no talking." He eyed his two Springers meaningfully before resuming their trek through the mounds.

Later that afternoon when the sunlight was beginning to fade, Charka again brought them to a halt. He stood still with head cocked to the side. They had left the mounds behind some time ago and were now making their way through a dense forest consisting of dead trees and scraggly bushes.

"What do you hear?" asked Lady Kate, as she came up behind him.

He held his hand up for silence as he turned his head from side to side, then pointed to a position almost directly ahead. Without saying a word, he held up two fingers. Glancing back to the others, he laid a finger against his lips for silence.

So intently was Jaikus peering into the forest of dead trees before them, that he about jumped out of his skin when Seward patted him on the shoulder. Seeing the man holding out the mules' reins for him to take charge of, he took them.

Drawing his sword, Seward moved forward to stand with Charka. Lady Kate positioned herself behind them. Hymal and his horse moved to the rear with Jaikus, Reneeke, and the mules. Then they waited.

Minutes ticked by as six pairs of eyes and ears searched for any sign of what Charka had sensed. Jaikus was about to announce that he hadn't heard anything when a troll's lumbering silhouette appeared as it passed laterally through the trees before them. Then another.

Jaikus couldn't understand why Charka wasn't going on the offensive. Didn't two beasts mean a larger bonus? After all, hadn't they easily taken care of the last troll? Two shouldn't be any greater difficulty. Yet, their *Troupe* leader acted as if he didn't *want* to face the beasts. Jaikus began to wonder if the man was a bit of a coward.

As he watched the "increase in bonus" fail to take notice of their presence and continue moving off through the trees, he coughed. Charka, Lady Kate, and Seward turned angry eyes upon him as the beasts, drawn by the noise, glanced their way. Seeing dinner waiting amidst the trees, they charged.

Snarling, the pair of trolls crashed through the dead trees and withered foliage. Lady Kate shouted a single word and a myriad of miniature, dancing lights sprang into being around the first troll's ugly head. Distracted, it slowed its pace as it tried to bat the lights from out in front of its face.

The second troll paid the predicament of the first no heed. Continuing forward, it was met by Lady Kate's trio of fire bolts, each impact causing the beast to misstep and roar in pain. But her effort didn't stop it.

The two fighters stood as a wall before the charging troll, Charka on the left, Seward on the right. When the troll drew near, Seward stepped forward and met its attack with his shield, just as before. Knocking aside a forceful swipe of claws, Seward thrust forward with his sword. Blade sinking deeply into its side, he danced quickly backward as the other arm shot forward to grasp the top of his shield.

Whack!

A mighty downward hack of Charka's sword severed the arm at mid-forearm. Lady Kate's *Webs of Binding* trapped the creature's legs and down it went. Immediately, the two fighters stepped forward to impale their swords through the creature's back.

Giving the troll a second to stop twitching, Charka then pulled his sword free and glanced toward the second troll. The spell of *Dancing Lights* had run its course and the troll was once again charging forward.

"*Scroll!*" shouted the *Troupe* leader.

Prepared for the call, Lady Kate passed a bound piece of parchment to him.

As Seward moved forward to meet the attack of the second troll, Charka placed the scroll upon the first. Already, the regenerative nature of the beast had begun restoring it, and its limbs were starting to twitch. "Immolate!" Instantly, the power of the scroll caused the troll's body to burst into flame.

Fire bolts slammed into the oncoming creature, knocking it backward slightly, only enough to ruin the force of its charge. Seward moved forward to deliver a slice across the beast's chest before it could recover. Webs appeared to entrap its legs sending it crashing to the ground. Then as before, Seward and Charka moved forward to deliver the telling blows.

Lady Kate came to the beast's side and brought forth fire to consume it.

"You guys are good," praised Jaikus as he came forward with the mules. "I only hope to one…"

"Think you're pretty smart, *do you*?" Cutting him off, Charka turned a visage full of wrath and anger upon him.

"What…what do you mean?" Jaikus stammered.

"You coughed on purpose," accused Seward.

"No one coughs that loudly when danger is near, unless they intend to."

Withering beneath the two men's glares, Jaikus turned to his friend Reneeke for aid. But none was forthcoming from that quarter. He could see it in his friend's eyes that he, too, believed the legitimacy of the accusations being laid.

"I…I…"

"I'm afraid it was my fault," said Hymal. "I was foolish enough to tell him that the *Troupe* gets a bonus for any attacks." Glancing to Jaikus, he shook his head. "Boy, I didn't think you were that stupid."

Charka's eyes narrowed. "Is this true? Did you put the lives of myself and my *Troupe* in danger just to pad your share of the bonus?"

Jaikus didn't need to reply, for the answer was clearly written across his face. Trying to come up with something to say, he was flattened by a blow from Charka's fist. Breath knocked from him by the impact with the ground, he tried to rise only to find the point of Charka's sword at his throat.

"You *ever* do something like that again, and I'll leave your body to rot in the Swamp. Do you understand?"

He looked from face to face but there was no mercy, no leniency. Jaikus knew he had lost the respect of everyone there, and for what? A few more coins?

"Boy," Charka said, pressing his sword painfully into the softness of Jaikus' throat, "I asked you a question."

"*Yes!*" he shouted. "I understand."

Meeting his eyes for a few seconds more, Charka returned his sword to its scabbard. "Master Hymal, there will be no charge for this attack. It will come out of *his* share." Then he glanced back to where Jaikus was sitting up and rubbing his throat. "As well as the cost for the scroll."

Jaikus had the good sense to lower his eyes and hang his head.

For the rest of the day's march, no one so much as looked at him. Even Reneeke was giving him the silent treatment, spending most of his time in hushed conversation with Lady Kate. Jaikus felt bad for what he had done. He would take it back if he could. But what was done, was done.

Their evening's campsite, the last before reaching their destination, was again situated on top of a knoll. Jaikus tossed his pack down and immediately began collecting firewood. Much to his relief, Reneeke joined him.

"Are you okay?" his friend asked.

Jaikus nodded. "I'm sorry."

"I know you are. I think the others are getting over their resentment and by tomorrow, things may be close to as they were." He paused a moment then said, "I hope."

"So do I, Rene."

Returning with an armload of wood, he dumped it by the fire where Seward was busy preparing another batch of his stew. Their eyes met for a moment before Seward turned away. Shoulders sagging, Jaikus returned to the surrounding trees to collect more wood.

Returning with his own load of firewood, Reneeke paused as Jaikus met him halfway. "Lady Kate told me that Charka meant what he said, about the money for the scroll coming out of your share."

Turning gloomy eyes upon his friend, Jaikus asked, "Really?"

Nodding, Reneeke continued. "The scroll was fifty golds, Jaik. She doesn't think your share will amount to anything when this is said and done."

"Great," he moaned. His moment of ill-conceived greed had cost him dearly.

"And that's not all."

"There's more?"

"I'm afraid so. That stunt you pulled may have just changed his mind about putting you forward for Guild membership."

"What?"

"He considers such an act as not honorable."

"That's...he can't...."

"He *might*. She wasn't completely sure how he plans to handle it. She did say, however, that you might still have a chance if you adhere to the highest standards of honor and bravery from now, until our return to Reakla. It's a small chance only."

"How about you?" asked Jaikus. "If I'm a wash, will he still put you forward?"

"We're a team, Jaik, you and I," his friend stated. "Either we both get in, or neither of us will."

"That's awfully considerate of you, Rene. But I wouldn't want to stand in your way should you be able to join."

Reneeke put his hand on his friend's shoulder and looked him in the eye. "Why would I want to join if you weren't there with me? I'll wait until we both can join together if I must." Then he grinned and slapped him on the back. "Plenty of opportunity for two Springers such as ourselves to prove our worth in the days to come."

Jaikus gave him a half-hearted grin. "You got that right. Let's be quick about our task and see to our drills."

"That's the Jaikus I know!"

Charka required twice the wood as they had collected the previous nights. "We must keep the fire bright tonight, lads," he explained. "Came across fresh tracks from a mossback. They don't care much for fire and tend to avoid it whenever possible."

"Yes, sir," replied Jaikus with great enthusiasm.

Their *Troupe* leader eyed him but remained silent.

Once the desired amount had been accumulated, Charka set them to practicing their basic sword maneuvers until dinner. Then during the hours afterward, they spent time on oiling and sharpening their swords. "You may have need of them before the night is over."

"Will the mossback attack?" asked Reneeke.

Charka glanced to the Springer and said, "There are more than mossbacks abroad in the Swamp at night, boy. Where fire keeps mossbacks away, there are other creatures that it will attract."

"Like glow-moths," offered Seward. "They are not very big, barley larger than a gold coin. But they have stingers longer than your little finger and have no qualms about using them."

"If you see soft, pale lights moving about in the Swamp, it's the glow-moths. Did Bella give you sleeping mesh?"

Pulling the large, finely weaved mesh net from his pack, Reneeke asked, "Is this it?"

"That's it. Make sure you cover yourself with it when you sleep. It will keep the moths away."

"Yes, sir," they replied in unison.

"Jaikus, you have first watch."

"By myself?" he asked, surprised.

"Is that a problem?"

"No, sir."

"Okay then. Wake me for the second."

"Yes, sir." Glancing to his friend, Jaikus saw him shrug.

"Perhaps he's giving you a chance to prove yourself," suggested Reneeke.

"Not so," interjected Seward. "First shift is often given to those deemed the most untrustworthy."

Crestfallen, Jaikus asked, "It is?"

Seward nodded. "It's the easiest to stay awake, and most likely Charka won't even fall asleep since he has elected to follow you." The man then moved over to where he had laid out his bedroll earlier that evening on the far side of the fire near Lady Kate's.

"I still think it shows he has some faith in you," asserted Reneeke. "This is the first either of us have been allowed a solitary turn at watch."

"I hope you are right, Rene."

"Of course I am. You'll see."

"Get some sleep," Jaikus told his friend. "Your turn at watch will come all too soon."

Flashing him a grin, Reneeke replied, "Don't I know it." Pulling his blanket over him, he then maneuvered the mesh so it covered his upper body. It wasn't large enough to cover him completely. "'Ware the moths."

"I'll see you in the morning." And with that, Jaikus moved to the outer fringe of firelight and began his circuit of the perimeter.

The others settled into their bedrolls, each moving their mesh nets into position in anticipation of glow-moth incursions. Jaikus' mesh netting remained atop his bedroll as he didn't figure on needing it right away. How wrong that supposition turned out to be.

Not more than twenty minutes into his watch, the first glow appeared out in the Swamp. He paused to watch it move about amongst the trees. Even though it didn't head directly toward the camp, it did steadily draw closer in a roundabout way.

A second one appeared, then a third. By the time the fourth one began its way forward, Jaikus decided it to be time to get his mesh and drape it over his head. He felt kind of silly with the thing on him, but since everyone else seemed to believe in its effectiveness, he would trust in it.

The night was silent as more and more lights began to appear. From all directions, the glow-moths were drawn to the light of their fire. Four became eight, eight grew into sixteen, and their numbers kept increasing.

Jaikus was rather nervous when the first one came his way. He saw the stinger Seward had mentioned. Long and barbed at the end, it definitely wasn't something he wished to be impaled with. As the glow-moth came and fluttered near his face, he quickly realized that should it decide to attack, the flimsy mesh would hardly impede it.

But the glow-moth didn't attack. In fact, it veered off before coming within six inches of the mesh. Intrigued, Jaikus stood his ground and watched as a myriad of glow-moths flittered about on their way toward the fire. Very graceful and beautiful to behold, Jaikus would have tried to grab one if it hadn't been for their barbed stingers.

He had to let Reneeke see the aerial display for himself. Going over to his friend, he gently woke him. "The moths," he whispered as Reneeke started awake. "Aren't they something?"

Reneeke nodded sleepily. "Yeah. They're great, Jaik." Then after another brief glance at the flittering insects, he rolled over and immediately fell back asleep.

The display lasted for only an hour before the glow-moths departed. A few had come a bit too close to the flames and were consumed. But by and large, they appeared to have come to dance around the flames, then leave. Once the exodus began, it took only a few minutes before the last glowing moth had vanished back within the Swamp. Taking off the mesh, he went to wake Charka for his turn at watch. He approached the *Troupe* leader cautiously, wondering if he were in fact asleep.

At Jaikus' first touch, Charka's eyes snapped open. Focusing on the lad standing over him, he asked, "Everything go okay?"

"Yes, sir. The glow-moths came and departed. Everyone is fine."

"Good." Then as he came to his feet, he said, "Get some sleep."

"I'll do that."

Turning in, he placed the mesh over him in the event of the moth's return. He thought of their graceful ballet as he drifted off to sleep.

The following morning dawned with a drizzling rain. An overcast sky was spitting just enough water to make life miserable. It didn't soak. There wasn't enough moisture to do that, it just made traveling…unpleasant.

"We'll be there a little after noon," announced Charka. Taking a rope from his pack, he had everyone tie themselves to it until they were secured in tandem.

"What's this for?" asked Reneeke.

"Sythal doesn't care much for visitors," explained their leader. "As we get closer, it will try to make us turn aside. Without the rope, we would be scattered and lost in no time."

"Can't we just follow the person in front of us?" asked Jaikus.

"It isn't that simple. You'll see." And see, he did.

Tied between Lady Kate and Reneeke, Jaikus thought the whole idea of the rope to be rather foolish. After all, how hard could it be to follow the person in front of you when they were only a few feet away? But when he felt a tug on the rope behind him, and discovered Reneeke had started wandering away on a tangent, Jaikus began understanding the need for the rope.

Time and again, Jaikus would be following right behind Lady Kate only to feel the pull of the rope and discover that he, too, had begun to wander off. At the head of the line, Hymal the apothecary led them unerringly.

"How come he doesn't get misled?"

"He never does," replied Lady Kate. "In all the times we have escorted him to Sythal, he has never once become lost, or been misdirected. It's either magic or some sort of innate ability he possesses."

"Intriguing. I..." but then he felt the pull of the rope and discovered he had been moving off to the right before the rope brought him up short. *"Damn!"*

"What's the problem, Jaik?"

Jaikus glanced over his shoulder to his friend. "I was in the middle of speaking with Lady Kate when I found myself wandering off."

"I know. It's disorienting. I've been brought up short by the rope at least half a dozen times by now."

"How much farther is this place?" wondered Jaikus.

"Not much," came the reply from the front. "Maybe another league or two."

Feeling the rope pull him up short yet again, Jaikus sighed. "It can't be soon enough."

—6—

The transition from the Swamp into Sythal was rather abrupt. One moment they were trudging through a tree-filled, treacherous bog, and the next had emerged onto dry land. The broken remains of what once had been a rather large edifice loomed before them. Its columns were shattered, walls had long since collapsed leaving only a small section still remaining upright.

"We have arrived," announced Charka. "You can untie yourselves."

Jaikus looked in awe at the remains of the structure. Others could be seen farther back and to either side. None were intact, most were in similar states of ruination as the one before them.

"Fascinating," said Reneeke. Once he had untied himself from the rope, he went forward to the building. "How old is this place?"

Coming up behind him, Hymal replied, "A thousand years, maybe more. I don't think anyone knows for sure."

"What do you know of it?"

"Not much more than what you have already learned," was all the answer he was willing to give.

Coiling the rope they had used to keep from being separated, Charka said, "We don't have time to stand around talking. We still have an hour or more to go."

"Is that correct?" Jaikus asked Hymal.

The apothecary nodded. "Where I harvest the reagents is still some distance away."

"I take it Sythal is large?" asked Reneeke.

"Larger than Reakla," replied Seward. "*Much* larger."

Hymal took the lead as they continued on. Skirting around the ruined edifice, he maintained a route that took them past many of the buildings that had fallen in disrepair. When they came to a stone dome rising ten feet out of the ground, Lady Kate pointed it out to the two Springers. "See, there? Most of Sythal lies beneath our feet."

"Is there a way to reach the areas below?" asked Jaikus.

"Oh yes," she replied. "Everything above ground is but the tops of the buildings buried beneath. Sythal was a massive city in its day. You may not believe this, but once, we found a building that extended a hundred feet below the ground."

"No way," replied Reneeke. Glancing to one of the taller stone structures still partially intact, he tried to picture it extending to such a distance below. "No building could be built so high. Wouldn't the weight of the stone cause it to collapse in on itself?"

"Apparently not," said Lady Kate.

"Wow." Jaikus was impressed. If the city extended that far beneath the surface, assuredly there must be treasures down there just waiting to be discovered. He longed to ask if they could take time to investigate, but after the debacle with the trolls, decided to keep his desires to himself. Jaikus would try to remain satisfied in the knowledge that they would have an opportunity to explore the ancient city once Hymal reached his destination.

The stone dome was but one of the architectural marvels encountered during their trek through Sythal. Tall spires, other domes equally as impressive, even the top of a pyramid were found rising from the depths. One spire appeared to be solid gold, but Seward threw water on the fire of Jaikus' excitement by stating the substance was not gold, but instead was composed of another material that quickly disintegrated if removed.

"I've never seen its like anywhere," he explained. "It's hard as iron, yet can be scraped off as easily as a man's beard."

"That doesn't seem possible," argued Reneeke. "If it was that hard, how could you scrape it off?"

Seward shrugged, then gestured over to the spire. "See for yourself."

"We're not stopping," announced Charka.

Reneeke simply *had* to check it out, his innate curiosity could not be denied. So while the others continued on, he hurried over. Taking out his knife, he tapped the gold-looking plating with its butt and didn't so much as make a dent in the material. Then, using the knife's blade, he tried scraping the gold-like material off and it peeled away like butter.

"Jaik!" he hollered. "Come look at this." But by the time Jaikus joined him, the part that he scraped off had already disintegrated into dust.

"How could it do that?" asked his friend.

Reneeke shrugged. "I have no idea."

"Would you two stay with us?" shouted Charka. Having moved off, they were about to round the remains of another large building that still had two walls more-or-less intact.

The friends left the spire behind and hurried to catch the others.

For the rest of the journey, they encountered more of the same: a couple of the gold-like spires, one dome protruding from the ground covered in the stuff, and of course, a myriad of buildings of various sizes, all in advance stages of ruination.

Upon reaching a wide expanse that was bordered on one side by the tops of three columns coming out of the ground, Charka brought their group to a halt. To either side of the columns, jagged remains of what may have once been walls gave the enclosed area a boxed-in feeling. Two fire-pits were in evidence, indicating this area had previously been used.

"We shall make camp here for the duration of our stay," Charka told his two Springers.

"Lady Kate, you and Master Hymal set up camp while Seward and I take our young Springers out to secure the area."

"I didn't think there would be anything around here to worry about?" queried Jaikus.

Seward laughed. "Whatever gave you that idea?"

"Well, I just thought…"

"You thought wrong," said Charka. "While it is true that Sythal's boundary works to keep out all those who seek to enter, it isn't foolproof. Once in a while, something gets through."

"Just like us," added Seward.

"Exactly," agreed Charka. Then he pointed to the three columns and passed his hand to the left. "Seward and I will sweep this area while you two search to the right." He eyed Jaikus. "This isn't a treasure hunt. We will do that on the morrow, and when we do, we do it *together*."

"Yes, sir," replied Reneeke.

"Go out a hundred yards," Charka instructed. "Look for fresh tracks, dung, and anything else which would indicate that we are not alone. Then return."

"What if we find something?" asked Reneeke.

"Use your own judgment. But don't be heroes. Come get us if you think you two can't handle it."

Seward chuckled. "And considering the way you two handle your swords, I'd say anything larger than a rabbit would warrant calling for help."

Reneeke smiled as he knew good-natured kidding when he heard it. Jaikus on the other hand took it personally. "I think we could handle ourselves," he grumbled to himself.

"Come on, Jaik," Reneeke said, slapping his friend on the back. "Our first solo mission."

"Yeah. *Yippee!*" he said with voice dripping in sarcasm.

They made their sweep and found little to indicate the presence of impending danger. Mid-way through their sweep, they came across a ruined building that was in less a state of collapse than most.

One wall remained completely intact, two others were partially intact, and the fourth had disintegrated into rubble. Looming in the intact wall was the enticing maw of a doorway.

When Jaikus moved toward it, Reneeke said, "Charka said to wait until tomorrow."

"Ah, come on, Rene," his friend said. "Just one little peek. Who knows what could be in there?"

"Jaik, you are already on Charka's bad side. Don't make it worse."

Pausing at the door, Jaikus glanced back to his friend. It was clear by the expression on his face that he very much wanted to go take a look inside that building. Fortunately, the desire to regain the good grace of Charka won out, and he backed away. Sighing, he left the doorway unexplored.

"We'll have our time to poke around tomorrow," Reneeke assured him.

"That's true," said Jaikus. Then with a last, longing look at the doorway, he rejoined his friend and they completed their sweep of the area. Neither group found any evidence of worrisome creatures lurking about.

After the evening meal was over and a cheery fire kept the darkness and cool night air at bay, Reneeke mentioned the doorway Jaikus had almost investigated. Lady Kate nodded.

"I know the one you are talking about," she explained. "We've searched through there a couple of times. During the first, we found a few gems and a small, golden statue of a tree that fetched a few coins. Subsequent explorations failed to turn up anything else of value."

"Most of the buildings nearby have been searched repeatedly," added Charka. "There's a group of them an hour away to the north that we have yet to tackle. We'll see what they have to offer in the morning."

"Master Hymal, will you require assistance in the gathering of your reagents?" asked Reneeke.

The apothecary shook his head. "No, but thank you for asking. As long as the area is safe, I will be fine by myself."

Seward flashed him a mischievous grin then turned his attention to Reneeke. "He doesn't want anyone to know where he gets them," the fighter explained.

"Not true. It's just that none of you would wish to forego hunting for treasure to come along with me gathering herbs and other essentials."

"What kind do you harvest? I have yet to see anything that I would call out of the ordinary around here."

Master Hymal smirked. "You just have to know where to look, boy."

"I suppose you're right," agreed Reneeke.

"What sort of treasures do you typically find?" Jaikus asked, bringing the conversation back to his favorite topic: treasure hunting.

"Oh, the usual assortment one would expect to find in a place like this; scrolls, tomes, coins, gems, perhaps a weapon or two. Once we uncovered a room with seventy-seven ingots of gold. It took us three trips before we managed to haul the last one away."

"Any magical items?" asked Reneeke. "Like a ring, wand, or crystal ball?"

"Rarely, but it does happen. As for crystal balls, I've never come across one. Those are just something bards put in their tales to spice up a more mundane world."

"We did find a *Torc of Might* once," offered Lady Kate. Then she jerked a thumb toward Seward, "But *he* dropped it in the Swamp."

Seward made an annoyed sound and rolled his eyes. "Aren't you ever going to let that go? It wasn't my fault!"

"One would think, that with an item such as that, you would have found a better place to carry it than *stuffed* in your belt."

Reneeke chuckled. "In your belt?"

"Hey, it was very secure there. Besides, I didn't want it to get scuffed by the equipment in my pack."

"In Seward's defense," interjected Charka, "he lost the *Torc* during a scuffle with a mossback. Its jaws had clamped onto his leg and was beginning to pull him beneath the surface. By the time we *'persuaded'* the mossback to let go, and dragged Seward from the water, the *Torc* was gone."

Seward lifted the leg of his trousers to reveal the mossback's bite-mark that ran the length of his calf and even up onto his thigh. "They were so mad with me for losing the Torc, that all they gave me was just enough healing potion to save my life. The scar was left as a reminder."

"Needless to say, items of such worth are carried *in* packs from now on." Charka gave his man a stern gaze, then chuckled. "We live and learn." His face turned grim as he added, "Or we die."

"There is only one thing about this that I don't understand," said Reneeke.

"What's that?" asked Seward.

"If the mossback dragged you into the water, why didn't those little flesh eaters devour you?"

"I was fortunate in that, that particular stretch of water didn't have any. Those little fishes aren't in every pool of water within the Swamp."

"How can you tell?" Jaikus wondered.

"The only sure way is to throw meat into the water and see if there is a reaction," explained Lady Kate. "Alive, dead, cooked, it makes no difference to them."

"That is correct," added Charka. "They seem to leave trolls and mossbacks alone for some reason. Perhaps the taste of troll isn't to their liking."

Seward nodded. "And a mossback's hide is far too tough for their little jaws to tackle. Although I did once see a mossback emerging from the water only to shake off a score of the little critters that had tried."

Jaikus was excited over the prospect of treasure hunting. His error in judgment may have cost him his share, but that did little to dampen his enthusiasm for the hunt. Delving into hidden rooms, uncovering lost treasure, perhaps even accessing a secret treasure room filled with a king's ransom, these scenarios and more played through his mind until Charka announced it was time to turn in.

Lying awake, listening to the fire crackle while Seward moved about the area during his turn at watch, Jaikus found it hard to fall asleep. He was just *too* anxious for the morning to come, and the fun begin.

The sun's first rays woke him to a cool and dew shrouded world. Sitting up, Jaikus looked to the others and found them still asleep. Lady Kate was up as the last watch had fallen to her. He made his way over to where she stood by the fire.

"Good morning," he greeted her.

Turning, she gave him a smile. "And to you as well."

Noticing their number was one less than the night before, he asked, "Where's Master Hymal?"

"Gone. He will be back tomorrow morning."

"Isn't going off on his own a little…dangerous?"

She shook her head. "It's his way. And besides, he *is* the patron. If he wants to go alone to collect his reagents, who are we to gainsay him?"

Jaikus noticed that the apothecary's horse was missing as well. Turning back to Lady Kate, he asked, "When are we to get going?"

"Charka likes to sleep late in the morning after our arrival. It's best not to speak too loudly or you may wake him."

Nodding, Jaikus glanced over to where their leader still lay asleep. "Do you think he would mind if I looked around some?"

"Not if you stay nearby. Should you come across any valuables, be sure to let him know. After all, you are working for him."

"Of course," he replied, though doing such was the last thing he wanted to do. But if it would aid him in regaining Charka's good grace, and thus be put forward for Guild membership, he would do so.

Reneeke still slept and Jaikus was loathe to awaken him since his friend had just come off his turn at watch. Pointing over to where he and Reneeke had found the building that remained mostly intact with the enticing, opened doorway, he said, "I'll be over there."

Lady Kate glanced in that direction then turned another smile his way. "Going to investigate the building you mentioned last night?"

"Yes. I thought I might poke about for a bit."

"Very well. Just be careful." As he was about to depart, she laid a hand on his arm. "I'll send your friend after you once he awakens."

Jaikus nodded and headed off toward the building.

Oh, man, this was going to be good. Rooting around in an ancient building had long been something he has desired to do. Ever since his days spent on the wooden floorboards of *The Creaking Tap* (the sole tavern of his hometown, Running Brook) as a lad, listening to itinerant bards weave their tales of daring-do.

He stepped lively as he headed toward the building. The opened doorway gaped just as tantalizingly as the day before. Giddy with excitement, he hurried to the doorway where he paused a moment to peer within. Not seeing much of interest in the room on the other side, he entered and crossed to the opening in the far wall leading to the room beyond.

"Where's Jaik?" asked Reneeke shortly after awakening. In the quiet of the morning, the sound of Seward preparing the morning meal provided a home-like air. Naught more than flour cakes and jerked beef, it was still better than the trail rations he and Jaikus had stashed away in their packs. He was beginning to wonder why Bella had given them so much.

"Off exploring the building you two came across yesterday," replied Lady Kate. A glance to the position of the sun and she added, "He has been gone almost an hour."

Charka sat up in his bedroll. "You might want to go get him, Reneeke. We'll be eating shortly."

"Sure thing," he replied.

Getting up, he stretched then made his way through the ruins toward the building Jaikus had gone to explore. When he drew near, he hollered, **"*Jaik*!"** No answer came back as he reached the doorway. Stepping within the room, he hollered, *"Jaik! Time to eat!"*

Then from deeper within the building, he heard Jaikus reply, "Rene, you've got to come here and see this." Entering the room, he walked across to the doorway on the other side of the room. "Charka wants you to return," he said.

Reneeke found Jaikus standing before a mural depicting a great battle of some distant past. A walled keep was encircled by armored beasts of hellish vision. Siegecraft rained stones and fire over the walls to devastating affect upon the defenders. From the way the part of the keep's wall was in mid-collapse, it was apparent the attackers were winning.

Jaikus cast a grin to his friend. "Pretty cool, huh?"

"Yes, it is. But that still doesn't alter the fact that our leader wishes you to return. You are in enough trouble already without giving him more reason to dislike you." Glancing around the barren room, Reneeke asked, "Did you find anything?"

Disappointment tinged his friend's words when he replied. "Not yet." Then he indicated an opening located on the far side of the room. "There is a whole series of rooms further down that way I explored until the light grew too dim. The only thing interesting I came across was this mural. There was a patch of darkness even further in that I thought might have been a stairway leading down. I would dearly love to go check it out."

"Maybe tonight. But right now, I think it best for us to return."

"You're right, of course."

The two friends left the room with the mural and headed back through the ruins to the *Troupe's* campsite. Breakfast was ready. It wasn't the most flavorful of meals, but it did fill one's stomach.

"We're going to leave most of the equipment and two of the mules," Charka explained while they ate. "Travel light on the way there…"

"And heavy on the way back," finished Seward.

"That's the plan," agreed Charka.

Seward glanced over to the two Springers with a grin. "Are you boys ready?"

"Ready for what?" asked Jaikus. Mouth full of flour cake, he turned a questioning stare to the man.

"To be Springers of course," the man replied.

Two faces gazed at him in confusion.

"Don't know what that means?" he asked.

"Of course they do," interjected Charka. "They volunteered for the job, didn't they?"

"*Springer*…is a…*job title*?" asked Reneeke.

"Yes. What did you think a Springer was?"

Reneeke glanced over to Jaikus. "We thought it meant someone new to the Guild. You know, like a new adventurer."

Swallowing the flour cake, Jaikus nodded agreement.

Seward laughed. "Where did you hear that?"

Before they could answer, Charka stepped forward and held his hand up to just below his chin. "Was it from a boy about yea high?" When Jaikus nodded, he asked, "Dark hair, and probably hanging out with another five or six others just like him?"

"Yeah," answered Reneeke. "That's the kid. He mentioned you usually take along a couple of new adventurers such as Jaik and me."

"Why, in the name of all the gods, would I want a pair of useless lads along on a trip through the Swamp?"

"He...uh," clearing his throat, Jaikus grew a bit red in the face when he said, "said that you were...uh, *'pretty nice about such things'*."

"That's right," nodded Reneeke. "That you were *'always one to help out the new guy.'*"

Seward doubled over in laughter. "Oh, man. That's *funny!*"

"Quiet," Charka ordered his man.

"Yurki?" questioned Lady Kate.

Charka nodded. "Sounds like something he would do." Turning to his two Springers, he explained. "Yurki is the leader of a pack of young'ens that hangs around the Guild. It seems he played a small joke on you boys."

Jaikus looked at their Troupe leader with growing apprehension. "What...*kind* of joke?"

"You aren't going to hold them to the contract are you?" asked Lady Kate. "They didn't know."

Charka nodded. "A contract is a contract. Besides which, if not for their volunteering, we would have contracted a thief for this venture."

"What kind of joke?" reiterated Jaikus for a second time.

Seward smirked. "Springer is *not* the term for a new adventurer."

From Lady Kate's expression, Reneeke was certain it wouldn't be good. "What *does* it mean?"

She sighed. "A *Springer* is someone that we at the Guild use in lieu of a thief."

Jaikus was even more confused. "I don't get what you're saying."

"Springers *'spring the trap,'*" explained Charka.

"You mean...?" questioned Jaikus with growing horror.

The Troupe leader nodded. "That's right, lad. If we feel there is an element of danger, you and your friend go first. A chest to be opened, you open it."

"But, we'll be *killed*," objected Reneeke.

"Most likely," agreed Seward. "Only about one out of three Springers makes it back alive."

"We're not going to die just so you can get rich!" exclaimed Jaikus.

Charka stepped right in his face. "I'm not going to lose out on recovering treasure just because you didn't know what you were agreeing to. You *are* our Springers. You **will** be Springers! And if you fail to uphold your end of the contract that you signed so readily signed before we left Reakla, you can forget about accompanying us back through the Swamp. And you will *never*, **ever**, be admitted into the Guild!"

—7—

Under the withering glare of their *Troupe* leader, Jaikus and Reneeke moved off a ways to discuss this latest development.

"We're going to die," moaned Jaikus.

"Everyone dies, Jaik."

Flashing his friend an annoyed look, Jaikus spat, "*Don't* start in on one of your philosophical musings. Not now." A glance back to the others revealed them waiting for their answer impatiently.

"There is no way he's going to put me forward for Guild membership anyway."

"I think you are correct, Jaik. But that still doesn't alter the fact that we are in a dire situation."

"Rene, I don't want to die on my first adventure!"

"Neither do I; nor on any other for that matter."

"And for what? Just so they can get rich?"

Reneeke was silent a moment as he pondered various courses of action. Finally, he said, "I see that we have only two choices before us. First, we agree to be Springers and possibly die some grisly death at the hands of a long dead trap-setter."

"You put that so *well*!"

He ignored his friend's outburst. "Or, tell them that we renege on the contract and forge our way back to Reakla through the Swamp on our own." He met his friend's eyes. "You know there is *no way* we could even begin to make it back on our own. The Swamp would swallow us up as sure as anything."

"So what are you saying?"

"Being Springers may be a death sentence, but at least there is the possibility, however small, that one or both of us might actually survive to see Running Brook again."

At mention of the village where they had grown to manhood, Jaikus envisioned the worry his mother would experience should he fail to return. The thought saddened him greatly.

"It's better than nothing," Reneeke said.

"I don't like it."

"Sometimes, Jaik, life only gives you the choice between bad, and worse."

Sighing, Jaikus nodded. "You are correct, as usual."

Reneeke laid a hand on his friend's back. "Come on. We may as well get this over with."

Resolved to face the unenviable task of being Springers, the pair walked back to where the others waited.

"So? What's your decision?" asked Seward. "Are you going to die here, or in the Swamp?"

Reneeke shot the fighter a look of annoyance. "Neither." Then to Charka, he asked, "What do we have to do?"

The trip through the skeletal remains of Sythal took a little under the hour foretold by Charka. During the trek, Lady Kate walked with the forlorn, and despondent, Springers.

"It isn't nearly as bad as what you two are thinking," she announced.

"What isn't? The chance of us surviving this ordeal?"

"The fact that you are Springers does not relieve us of the obligation to do everything in our power to see that you survive. We have a score of healing potions and scrolls with us for no other reason than because you two are along."

Hope glimmered. "Really?" asked Jaikus, almost afraid to believe it to be true.

"Of course. We are not heartless mercenaries. What Yurki said is partly true. Charka takes care of those under his command. And that means you two, too."

"Don't let him hear you say that," commented Seward. Glancing ahead to where their leader led the way, he said. "He isn't *that* nice."

"Perhaps not," she agreed. "Although, a leader who habitually returns with fewer than what he left with, quickly finds it difficult to recruit more when the need arises."

Reneeke gave Jaikus a glance and grinned. Perhaps their situation was not completely hopeless as they had thought.

"You see, Jaik? We're going to be fine."

Seward couldn't resist one last barb. "Springers are considered expendable. It goes with the territory. So should he come back with one, or none, very few would think much about it."

Lady Kate turned a withering gaze upon her cohort. "Perhaps you could curb your tongue and leave these boys alone?"

He gave her a bow with half a dozen flourishes. "As you wish, milady."

Rolling her eyes, she shook her head.

Their destination turned out to be a group of buildings that, somewhere far below the surface, may have formed the four sides of a plaza. The northern side was rubble, while the east and south sides each had a few walls jutting upward out of the ground, but held very little in the way of areas in which to explore. Three buildings were still relatively intact on the west side, though *intact* was a generous term.

The building on the left had three walls still in place, with the fourth having disintegrated into a pile of rubble. The one on the right boasted two walls still proudly standing, while the other two were in various stages of collapse. In the center, four sturdy walls rose in almost perfect majesty for a span of two floors before quickly tapering to a point. It was to the center building that Charka led his people.

An opening loomed in the side. The interior was lit by intermittent rays of sunlight making their way through cracks and other imperfections in the structure.

"A doorway," commented Jaikus.

"No, a window," corrected Lady Kate. "Remember, the bulk of Sythal lies buried deep below our feet."

"So that means it wasn't a doorway I entered earlier when I went exploring. It was a window?"

"Hey, we got ourselves a smart one here." Seward flashed Jaikus a humorless grin.

"Ignore him."

"I'll try," Jaikus assured her.

Charka brought them to a halt before the window. "We will explore the upper areas first. After that, we will descend into the depths."

"Shouldn't we explore the lower areas first?" asked Reneeke. "It would seem that there is where treasure would most likely be found."

"No. You're thinking about this all wrong. If you were on the ground before a tall building, where would you expect the treasure to be secreted away? In the uppermost reaches, of course. People tend to stash their really good items as far from the entrance as possible. Before Sythal was buried…" he pointed toward the edifice rising before them, "this was the area furthest from the entrance. And thus, more likely to still contain items of value."

Jaikus nodded. "That makes sense."

"Okay, then." Glancing to his two Springers, he said, "Who wants to be first?"

Exchanging glances with Reneeke, he was about to volunteer when Reneeke said, "I will." Relief flowed over him, but so too did concern for his friend.

"You two will rotate the duty." Turning to Jaikus, he said, "Until I say otherwise, stay back with Lady Kate."

"Yes, sir." Moving to stand beside the magic user, he watched as Charka removed a rope from his pack.

Passing one end to Reneeke, Charka said, "Tie this around your middle."

About to ask why, Reneeke stopped the urge and took the end of the rope. While he secured it around his waist, Seward removed a lantern from his pack. It was a bulls-eye lantern, one that shined its light through a single opening in one side. There was a shutter whereby the light could be reduced in smaller increments to a tighter, more focused, beam. By the time Reneeke was securely bound, the lantern was lit and its light was being directed in through the window. With the shutter opened to its widest, the light filled the room.

Charka motioned for Reneeke to precede him into the room. "You first."

Seward handed Reneeke the lantern before the Springer carefully made his way through the window.

Following ten feet behind came Seward and Charka, both keeping a firm grip upon the rope. After them came Lady Kate, with Jaikus bringing up the rear.

A single doorway broke the empty monotony of the room. Other than dust and dried leaves that had been blown in by the wind, there was nothing else of note. Reneeke paused and turned back to where Seward and Charka still stood on the other side of the window. "Should I go through the doorway?"

"Go ahead."

Moving forward, Reneeke heard the others begin making their way through the window and into the room.

A hallway extended from the other side of the doorway. Further openings appeared in the walls on either side at staggered intervals. The first one was on his left and opened onto a room similar to the one behind him.

"If you don't see anything," Charka instructed, "continue to the next."

Keeping that in mind, Reneeke moved from doorway to doorway. At each, he would pause to inspect the room by directing the lantern's light from one side to the other. When he failed to see anything of interest, he would continue on.

As he approached the fifth doorway, his eyes caught sight of a flash of light coming from within the room. He immediately came to a stop. "I think I see something?"

"What?" asked Jaikus. Despite the possible lethality of the situation his friend was in, Jaikus found himself drawn into the excitement of the moment.

"I'm not sure," replied Reneeke. Moving to the doorway, he paused and slowly roved the light across the room's interior. When the edge of the light reached the far right, the flash appeared again. A closer look revealed that whatever it was, was partially hidden amidst a pile of debris.

He sensed someone had come up behind him and glanced back to find Charka peering over his shoulder. "It might be a coin. Go find out." As Reneeke entered the room, the *Troupe* leader added, "Be careful."

The debris held bones, stones, and tufts of fur which may have once belonged to an animal. "Looks like this may have been a predator's den."

"If it was," replied Charka, "then that would mean the room is safe."

Crossing the room, Reneeke aimed the lantern directly toward the pile. He could see that there was more than a single item glittering within. Upon reaching it, he used the toe of his boot to disperse the pile and revealed two round, golden disks, each the size of his palm. There was also a silver one of the same size tucked beneath the two golden ones.

"Three disks," he announced. "Two golden, and one silver." He then bent over to pick them up.

"Wait," ordered Charka. Turning to his magic user, he motioned for her to enter and check it out. "We've encountered these before," he told his Springer. "Most are harmless. Others are not."

Reneeke stepped back as Lady Kate came forward to kneel by the three disks. A moment later, they glowed a soft blue. The glow lasted for only two seconds.

She glanced to Reneeke. "They are safe," she told him then collected the disks and slipped them into her pack.

"What happens when they are not safe?"

"Of the two we have encountered that were not, one exploded, and the other caused a colony of warts to appear and spread across Seward's face." She gave the Springer a grin. "Lucky for him, Charka was willing to foot the bill for a curse removal at the temple upon our return."

"Why would it do that?"

She shrugged. "Who knows? There are all kinds of magical items out there of which the intrepid adventurer should be leery. In the Tower back at the Guild, there is an entire room devoted to the weird and odd."

From the doorway, Charka said, "If that is all, then we should continue."

"Yes, sir," Reneeke said, then made his way from the room and headed down to the sixth door.

Therein they discovered a small room with a narrow, winding stairwell extending to both the floor above and the floor below.

"Let's finish this level first before heading for the next."

"Yes, sir." Continuing down the hallway, Reneeke came to where it ended at another hallway moving perpendicular to theirs. Down to the right, this new hallway ended with a pair of doors, one to either side. To the left, the hallway extended for a good thirty feet before the first doorway appeared. Relaying the information to the others, he waited until Charka instructed him to investigate down to the right first.

The doorways where the hallway came to an end sat directly across from each other, and like the others, didn't have doors. Reneeke thought that odd until the notion occurred to him that had the doors been constructed of wood, they would have succumbed to rot long ago. Given the age of Sythal, such was a very good possibility.

Coming to the doorways, he shined the light through the one on the right first. The room beyond was small and devoid of anything of interest. Turning to the other, a brief scan revealed it was just as barren.

"There's not much in here," he commented to Charka upon returning to the hallway junction whereat the others waited.

"Sometimes it's like that," the *Troupe* leader replied. "There have been trips in the past where we've come away with only Hymal's gold for accompanying him here."

"At least we have the three disks," piped up Jaikus.

Charka nodded. "Yes, indeed."

Moving down to the left this time, Reneeke made his way toward the doorway thirty feet away. When he had gone ten feet past the junction of passageways, the lantern's light revealed something past the doorway that protruded from the side of the wall. Directing the beam toward it, he discovered the protrusion to be a face.

Constructed of stone, the face stuck out several inches from the wall with a diameter of a foot and a half. It was human, sort of. There was an odd slant to the eyes, and the ears seemed a bit bigger than they should be, as was the nose. Its mouth was open and appeared to be a hollow cavity.

Giving the room only a cursory examination before continuing to the mask, Reneeke shone the light within the mouth. "There's an opening here," he explained to the others. "It looks like it extends for over a foot before coming to an end."

"We've come across these before as well," said Charka. "I would be extra careful from this point on."

Glancing back to his leader, Reneeke asked, "Why?"

"They are quite often found in the proximity of a trap," explained Lady Kate.

Charka nodded. "More times than not we've discovered."

Backing away from the face, Reneeke stared uncertainly at it. "What should I do?"

"Avoid the mouth for starters. Keep as far from it as possible as you make your way past. If nothing happens before you reach the other side, it's safe."

"And if it does?"

"That's part of being a Springer," piped up Seward.

"Good luck, Rene," Jaik said to his friend.

"Yeah. Thanks."

Reneeke sidestepped to the wall opposite the face. There he pressed his back against its hard, cold surface and began to shuffle his feet as he started working his way past.

Eyes glued to the mouth opening, heart racing, expecting at any moment some dreadful, painful fate to befall him, the young Springer worked his way down the hallway until he was directly opposite the face. For a brief moment he stood frozen, transfixed by the imminent doom weighing down upon him. But then his feet started working again and carried him past.

"I made it!" he hollered back to the others.

"Yes," replied Seward, "we see that."

"Great job, Rene," Jaikus praised from his position at the rear.

"Great job?" Seward asked as he turned to him. "He didn't do anything other than walk down a hallway."

Jaikus met the man's eyes and would have liked nothing better than to close them for him.

"You really are annoying sometimes," commented Lady Kate.

Seward broke off the gaze with Jaikus to give her a crooked smile. "It is but part of my charm."

"Charm of a snake," Jaikus murmured under his breath.

"What was that?" asked Seward.

Once again being the focal point of the man's attention, Jaikus murmured, "Nothing."

"Can we continue now?" asked Charka.

"Certainly," replied Seward.

Charka eyed his man disapprovingly a second before signaling Reneeke to continue.

Following along beside Lady Kate, Jaikus asked her, "Why does Charka put up with him?"

"His father was a cartographer," she explained. "And aside from being able to read a map with ease, Seward has an unusual ability where the area of a building is concerned. Practically every secret room we have uncovered has been due to his ability to tell when there is less space being used than there should be. After we make sure a level is safe, he goes back through it and determines if there is a hidden area or not."

"How?" asked Jaikus.

She only shrugged. "He's never been able to satisfactorily explain it to me. Claims he just *'knows'*, that his years as a youth working at his father's elbow instilled it in him."

"So what happens when he thinks there is a hidden area?"

"We search for the opening mechanism."

Further discussion was curtailed when a shout from Reneeke announced he had found something.

He stood at the end of the hallway. Before him loomed an opening wider than the doorways previously encountered. "It looks like some kind of hall."

The others came up behind him and saw by the lantern's light that the *"hall"* was quite large, large enough in fact so that the home Jaikus had grown up in could comfortably fit within, with room to spare. Two staircases located against the walls to the left and right rose toward a balcony that completely encircled the upper reaches.

"A ballroom perhaps?" suggested Reneeke.

"Perhaps," said Charka.

There were five other doorways spaced around the room, each granting access to parts unknown. Vacant recesses dotted the walls in fifteen foot intervals where statuary or other items could have been placed for display. A pair of torch sconces haloed each of the recesses.

After a brief visual examination, Charka announced that the room would most likely be safe. "Snares in such a place would run the risk of catching the unwary as well as the unwanted." Even though he felt it was safe to enter, he still had Reneeke lead the way.

Seward removed two torches from his pack. Then using flint and steel, he lit the brands and placed them in torch sconces near where they emerged from the hallway. The light did much to dispel the darkness filling the room.

Jaikus came to his friend. "How is it going?"

Reneeke gave him a nervous smile and shrugged. "I still live. So, not *too* bad I guess."

"Let's check out those other rooms." Charka directed Reneeke toward the closest.

"I'll come with you," offered Jaikus.

"We'll *all* go," asserted Seward. "If we start getting separated in a place like this, someone is apt to come up missing."

"True," agreed Charka. "We stick together."

"Understood," replied Jaikus.

The first doorway led down a short hallway and ended at another small, empty room. They checked two more and found similar areas, each holding nothing of interest. The fourth doorway entered onto a room a third the size of the hall. Its walls were as dark as night and seemed to absorb the light coming from the lantern. In the center of the room was a dais rising two feet from the floor. A pair of steps led to the top. Reneeke directed the lantern toward the top of the dais and saw a square, stone block. The block was not black like the walls of the room. Instead, it looked to be constructed of the same material as was the building. The dais, and the stone block resting upon it, were the only items of interest within the room.

"Better check it out," Charka told his Springer.

As Reneeke moved toward the dais, Jaikus asked Lady Kate, "Ever come across anything like this before?"

She shook her head. "No. This is something new."

Upon approaching the dais' steps, Reneeke paused to pass the light across the surface of the dais, and of the stone block. Both appeared rather nondescript. Hesitantly, he moved his foot to the first step. Quickly putting his weight upon the step, he jerked his foot back, fully expecting something bad to happen. When nothing did, he tried the second one. When still nothing happened, he took the steps up to the dais top and came to a stop.

A feeling came over him, something that was completely alien to him. Unsure what it could be, he *was,* however, fairly certain that the feeling emanated from the stone block. "I feel something."

"What?" asked Lady Kate. Things magical and *weird* were her bailiwick.

Reneeke glanced over his shoulder toward her. "I don't know. I've never felt anything like it before."

She came forward until she stood at the dais' edge. "I don't feel anything."

"Neither did I, until I stood up here." He pointed to the stone block. "It's coming from that."

"Is it a good feeling, or bad?"

"Do you mean, like, does it make me afraid?"

She nodded.

He thought for a moment. "I...it, uh..." Then he shook his head. "I wouldn't call it either, actually. Merely a strange sensation."

"Don't move any closer to it," Charka told him. To Lady Kate he asked, "What do you think?"

Not taking her eyes from the stone block, she said, "We should leave it alone. If he feels something, then it is either magical in nature, or spiritual. In either case, it would be best not to tempt fate."

"Spiritual?" queried Jaikus. "Like a ghost?"

"Perhaps. A cleric might be able to make a more accurate assessment if such were the case. But, seeing as we don't have one..."

"Can't magic users cast spells to learn about items?"

"If I felt the situation warranted it, I could," she replied.

Suddenly, everyone in the room felt a momentary pulse radiate from the dais. Jaikus was just beginning to think that the odd sensation of the pulse must be similar to what Reneeke was feeling when darkness surged outward from the dais's surface. His friend quickly vanished from sight as the darkness rose to engulf him, forming a shimmering dome that completely enshrouded the area above the dais.

"Reneeke!" he shouted.

"Pull!" yelled Charka as he and Seward yanked on the rope attached to the young Springer. The line snapped taut and budged no further. Jaikus and Lady Kate were quick to take up the rope and lend their aid. Yet despite their added strength, they were unable to bring Reneeke from the darkness.

Jaikus feared for his friend. "We have to get him out of there!"

Then in an instant, all tension on the rope vanished. Snapping back like a coiled serpent, the rope came free as the darkness which had risen to swallow Reneeke, returned back into the dais.

"Where is he?"

When the darkness vanished, Reneeke was gone.

—8—

Making a dash for the dais, Jaikus was abruptly brought to a halt when Charka grabbed him about the chest.

"Let me go!"

"He's *gone*, son."

Jaikus struck him across the chin in an effort to loosen Charka's grip. "I have to get to him." Squirming, he had almost wriggled from the *Troupe* leader's grasp when he heard Charka say, "Ready?" To which Lady Kate responded, "Yes."

Then he was free, but only for a moment. He took all of one step toward the dais before Lady Kate's *Webs of Binding* encased his lower half in their sticky, immobilizing mass.

"No!" As he toppled over, he broke his fall with his hands, then used them in an attempt to crawl forward, but the webbing adhered him tightly to the floor.

"Son, listen to me."

Twisting, he turned to look back with tear-laden eyes.

"He's gone."

"No. He can't be!"

"Yes, he is."

"We can get him back!"

"You don't know that he went anywhere," reasoned Charka.

"That's right," added Seward. "For all we know, that blackness could have simply dissolved him into nothing."

Charka eyed his man with unvoiced retribution. "You let me handle this."

Seward merely shrugged.

Returning his attention back to the lad on the floor before him, Charka said, "Kate will see if she can determine what that thing is, and maybe even a way to get your friend back. If that is even possible."

Casting a hopeful gaze toward the magic user, he asked, "Will you?"

"I shall do my best," she affirmed.

"But first, you are going to have to calm down," the *Troupe* leader insisted. "I am *not* going to lose both of you. Not if I can help it." He paused a moment to let that sink in. "No one goes near that thing until she says it is safe to do so. Understand?"

Wracked with worry and fear, it was hard for him to see the logic in doing nothing. But he quickly understood that Lady Kate may be the best shot they had of finding out what had happened to his friend.

Miserable, yet resigned to waiting, he nodded. "Yes."

Charka nodded to Lady Kate who then dispelled the webbing binding Jaikus' legs. He watched him rise, ensuring his remaining Springer wouldn't do anything foolish, then signaled Lady Kate to begin.

Jaikus remained sitting on the floor. With knees brought up to form a rest for his chin, he wrapped his arms around them tightly for comfort. He watched Lady Kate as she cast her first spell. At any other time, he would have been greatly intrigued by the workings of magic. But now, all he could think of was that Reneeke was lost, or maybe even gone forever. Either way, it was his fault. He had been the one to drag Reneeke into being an adventurer. And if his friend never returned... Jaikus couldn't bear to contemplate such a thought. Lady Kate *would* be successful, and they *would* be reunited!

"Jaik?"

The sudden immersion in darkness had completely unnerved him. *"Charka?"*

Not even the barest hint of light could be made out. *"Lady Kate? Seward?"*

Reaching outward with his hands, he sought the comforting feel of another human being. But all he encountered was the cold, hard surface of the stone block that rested upon the dais. Had he gone deaf as well as blind? If so, the others should have taken charge of him by now. Yet they hadn't.

Checking his waist, he found the rope to still be there, with a little over a yard hanging from where it knotted about his middle. Feeling the rope's end, he discovered that it had been severed cleanly. He couldn't feel so much as a single, frayed strand.

"Jaik!"

Shouting at the top of his lungs, he was rewarded with an echoing of his cry. "At least I'm not deaf." By the sound of the echo, he was in a large, enclosed area. Back home near Running Brook, there had been a series of caves high in the hills that he and Jaikus often explored. Their voices had echoed there in a similar manner.

Concentrating less on sight and sound, he focused more on his sense of smell. Detecting the odor of earth and mustiness reminiscent of the caves back home, he nodded. Somehow, he had been relocated. It was the only explanation. Unless he had gone mad, a supposition to which he gave little credence.

In his pack was the bundle of torches acquired at Bella's, as well as his flint. Kneeling down on one knee, he took off his pack and rummaged within until feeling the hard surface of the flint. Praying to see sparks, he took out the flint and scraped it across the side of the square stone.

A line of sparks appeared in the darkness. Seeing them greatly eased his sense of unsettledness, for it meant he wasn't blind. Reneeke then removed one of the torches from his pack and worked to set fire to its business end. Several strikes of flint later, the combustible material ignited.

As the torch grew to full brilliance, Reneeke stood and looked around at his new surroundings. Though he still stood upon the dais, he was no longer in the hall, that much was certain. Rather, this new locale was located, as he had earlier suspected, within a large, underground cavern.

Gazing about his new environs, he saw another of those stony faces carved into the cavern's wall not far from the dais. Ones that Charka said often indicated the presence of a trap. Fortunately, the cavern grew wider as it extended outward from where he stood, and the face's vicinity could readily be avoided should further exploration be required.

The cavern itself wasn't remarkable in any way, at least not the corner of it illuminated by his torch. Rock growths dotted the floor as well as cascading down from the ceiling. The floor was uneven as a cavern's should be, though there was a narrow area moving away from the dais that looked slightly worn down, quite possibly due to the passage of many feet.

How did he get there?

The answer to that in some way dealt with the dais. Being the only similarity between where he had been, and where he was now, it had to mean something. Reneeke put the fear he felt aside as he considered the problem.

He had been there with the others one moment, then here in the dark the next. *Magic?* Had to be. Bards often spoke of devices used to travel far distances in a blink of an eye. They were rumored to be rare and powerful, and not to be trifled with. It was also said that such devices were jealously guarded by those who created them. That thought brought him no peace of mind. Alone as he was in an unfamiliar place, the last thing he wanted to think about was having to fend off an attack of some kind.

"I have to do something," he murmured to himself. Recalling the earlier shouts for Jaikus, he worried that perhaps he had inadvertently alerted someone, or some *thing* to his presence. He scanned the darkness surrounding his small radius of light. Should he remain where he was in the hopes that the others could find him? Or would he have to make his own way back? As he struggled to determine which course of action would best suit the situation, he again started to feel that odd sensation he had felt when first he climbed onto the dais before arriving in the cavern. Nervousness filled him as he didn't know what it could mean.

Before he was able to decide on a course of action, the darkness took him once again.

"It is very powerful," Lady Kate said after several minutes of magically examining the dais and stone block.

"Can you tell what it did to Reneeke?" Jaikus asked anxiously. He stood back a ways with Charka and Seward while they waited for Lady Kate to finish.

She turned her attention onto the young, worried Springer. "It wasn't so much that it did something *to* him. Rather, it sent him somewhere." Gesturing to the dais, she said, "This, is a teleporter."

"A teleporter?" asked Jaikus and Charka simultaneously.

Jaikus glanced to his leader and could see the man had a certain gleam in his eye.

She nodded. "I'm not sure how he activated it, but your friend was sent somewhere."

"Can we follow?" Again, Jaikus and Charka spoke in unison.

Nodding again, she said, "I would think so. Most devices like this need to recharge their magical energies before a second teleportation can take place."

"How long?" questioned Charka.

"That, I don't know. It could take a minute, or even a week before the magical energies are refreshed."

Charka slapped Jaikus on the back. "Boy, you may see your friend again!"

"You mean to follow, then?" questioned Seward.

"By the gods, I do!" He gazed at the teleporter with undisguised avarice. "Something like that has to lead to a treasure horde, or some other place of importance. There's no telling what we'll find on the other side."

"But, oh fearless leader," began Seward, "we must be back to meet Hymal by the time the sun rises. And as our Lady of the Arcane Arts has just said, it could take longer than that before this teleporter thing is ready."

"Let's try it now," Jaikus suggested. "I'm the Springer, so it is my job to test it first." Such an offer would never have left his lips, had it not been for his need to discover the fate of Reneeke.

Charka glanced questioningly to Lady Kate. "What do you think?"

She shrugged. "Either it is ready and he will be sent to wherever his friend went, or nothing will happen." Turning her gaze toward Jaikus, she said, "Reneeke claimed to have felt something strange when he stood upon the dais. It would be reasonable to assume that what he felt was the power of the device."

"So if I feel something, it might be ready?" He waited only long enough for her to nod before dashing for the steps. Vaulting to the top, he moved to the exact spot where Reneeke had stood prior to disappearing.

"What now?"

"Do you feel anything?" asked Charka.

Jaikus closed his eyes. Not sure exactly *what* he was searching for, it didn't take him but a moment before he felt…something. He nodded. "Yes. There is something here."

Lady Kate moved closer until she almost came into contact with the dais, then stopped. "Can you describe it?"

"No. It's just like Reneeke said, *a strange sensation*."

Then just as the first time, a quick pulse radiated outward from the dais followed immediately afterward by the rising of the darkness.

"It's working," observed Charka as his last Springer was swallowed by the dark field until a shimmering dome covered the area above the dais. He and the other two watched as the dome remained in position for several seconds, then quickly sank back down into the dais.

The vanishing of the dome left behind a person, but it wasn't Jaikus.

"Hey!" exclaimed Reneeke in jubilation. "I'm back!" Torch held aloft, he turned toward the trio of onlookers. It didn't take him long to realize they were one short. "Where's Jaik?"

"Are you okay?" asked Lady Kate.

"Yes." Hopping from the dais he asked again, this time with more urgency tingeing his voice, "Where's Jaik?"

"Wherever it was the dais took you," replied Charka. "He was trying to reach wherever it was you had been sent."

Seward laughed. "Now the other one is missing."

"Quiet," ordered Charka and his man tried to rein in his amusement.

Lady Kate came and looked into his eyes. "Where did the teleporter take you?" Seeing nothing untoward about them, she relaxed.

"Yes, lad," Charka asked, "Where did it take you? Was there treasure?"

"Treasure? No. It was a normal cavern. Jaik's there?"

"He was on the teleporter when it activated," explained Lady Kate. "You came here, he went there."

Turning back toward the teleporter, he said, "Then I have to go back and get him."

"We *all* will," said Charka. "I think that cavern may be a good place to continue our search for treasure."

Taking the steps, Reneeke returned to his spot while the others gathered in about him. "There wasn't any treasure there."

"Are you sure? Did you check every nook and cranny?"

"Well, no. I was more concerned about how to return." Pausing a moment, he then added, "But I did see one of those stone faces carved into the cavern wall."

"I knew it!"

They had to wait several minutes before they began to feel the strange sensation.

"Magic," Lady Kate told the others. "This is magic that you are feeling. Very...powerful...magic."

"Interesting," commented Charka just before the teleporter activated and they were no longer in the room.

"Rene!"

Jaikus' cry drew his friend's attention to where he stood next to a tall stalagmite. Face alight with happiness at seeing his friend, Jaikus hurried his way. "I was getting worried there for a moment."

Reneeke hopped off the dais and met Jaikus halfway. "You know I wouldn't leave without you." Giving his friend a brief, fierce hug, he heard Jaikus say, "Neither would I."

Seward had the lantern in hand and was beginning to investigate the vicinity surrounding the dais.

"Don't go too far," Charka said to his man. "That's a Springer's job." Turning to Jaikus, he held out the now shortened rope and said, "Your turn."

Resigned to the inevitable, Jaikus nodded and took the rope. After tying it securely around his middle, he gave Reneeke a half-grin. "I hope it goes as well as your stint did."

"It will," his friend assured him. "Adventure awaits."

Jaikus nodded. "Adventure awaits."

Charka indicated for him to proceed along the narrow, slightly worn path Reneeke had earlier discovered leading away from the dais. Jaikus held the lantern and panned the light to the left and right as he continued along.

The path led through a forest of stalactites and stalagmites, some actually having come together to form magnificent columns that stretched from the cavern floor all the way to the ceiling high above. For a hundred feet or more the path remained discernible upon the cavern floor. It wasn't until the cavern began to narrow that a man-made construct came into view from out of the darkness ahead. Five feet tall and obviously made of stone, an obelisk rose from a squat, box-like base to a tapered peak at the top. Runes were etched into the surface.

"Hold up a second," Charka said to Jaikus. As his Springer came to a stop, the *Troupe* leader asked his magic user, "Is it a threat?"

After speaking a single word and making a gesture toward the obelisk, she shook her head. "It holds no magic and I detect nothing malignant in its nature."

"Have you seen these before?" asked Jaikus.

"A few," Charka replied. "But none bearing this writing." Returning his gaze toward the obelisk before them, he added, "It must mean something special."

"Like turn back or you're dead?" quipped Seward.

"Quite possibly," agreed Charka in all seriousness.

Jaikus gave the obelisk a thorough once-over, then turned the lantern's light toward the cavern ahead. The well worn path continued through the illuminated area and disappeared into the dark. Considering how the walls of the cavern continued drawing closer together the farther they went, he figured they should be fairly close to reaching the end.

Glancing back to Charka, he asked, "Shall I continue?"

"By all means."

Once past the obelisk, the cavern diminished rapidly as the walls and ceiling steadily grew closer together. When the light at last reached the end of the cavern, Jaikus was greeted by the sight of two massive columns of rock, three feet in diameter, that stood a mere two feet apart, just before the rock wall. The path continued through the columns and into a dark opening beyond.

Jaikus came to a stop. "Something ahead," he hollered back to the others.

Charka saw the twin rock formations and had him continue on. "My guess would be that once past yon pillars, things will get more interesting."

"You think so?" questioned Reneeke.

"Yes, I do." Then to Jaikus he hollered, "Keep on your guard."

"Yes, sir," he replied. But then under his breath he added, "What do you think I have been doing?"

A rough-hewn passage extended past the twin columns and made its way deeper into rock. Jaikus eyed the opening with suspicion, but as he could discern no tangible threat, continued forward.

Charka's words prophesying that things would *"get interesting"* were ever present upon his mind. A sense of foreboding settled over him that increased with every step he took. Twenty paces past the pillar, he found himself placing every step carefully before him, dreading some unpleasant repercussion to descend upon him for daring to defy the totem's warning.

Maybe it wasn't a warning? It could have been nothing more than a marker, such as the one the elders of Running Brook had put in place to inform visitors of the village's name. His edginess slackened off somewhat as he began thinking of alternate, non-lethal meanings behind the totem and its enigmatic etchings.

Another thirty paces passed before an abrupt widening of the passage became visible in the lantern's light. Not rough-hewn as was the passage they had been following, it instead was constructed of worked stone. Ceiling, walls, and floor were all crafted of stone blocks set one atop the other, or side by side as was the case in the floor and ceiling. So well did they fit together that there were hardly any seams. Not far from where this new area started, it came to a dead end.

Jaikus paused at the end of the narrow passage just before the new area of worked stone. "We can't go any farther."

"What?" queried Charka. Coming to stand beside his Springer, he saw where the new passage ended. "There must be a hidden door."

"Do you think so?" asked Jaikus.

Giving his young Springer a grin, he replied, "I'd stake Seward's life on it." Patting Jaikus on the back he indicated for him to continue. "Walk to the wall, then back. If nothing happens, I'll send Seward in. This is his area of expertise."

"I wouldn't exactly call myself an expert," came the reply from back in the narrow passage.

"You're the best we have," replied Charka. Then to Jaikus, he jerked his head toward the dead end and said, "Go ahead."

This is it, he thought to himself. *I'm going to die.* After first taking a calming breath, he stepped forward. Recalling tales of adventure spun by bards, Jaikus made sure to place his foot on only single blocks of stone. One tale in particular came to mind about a thief that had infiltrated a demon's lair. He remembered how the bard had described the way a thief had stepped on single blocks of stone in an attempt to make his way through a trapped area. Jaikus wasn't sure if such a strategy would be effective, but he wasn't about to take the chance.

Two steps, then three. He carefully made his way toward the wall at the far end.

"Do you see anything strange or out of place?" asked Seward.

Pausing, he glanced back. "Like what?"

"One stone not sitting flush to its neighbor. Or maybe of a slightly different color?"

Panning the light about the walls, he shook his head. "I don't see anything."

"Okay," said Charka. "Continue."

A quick count of the stone rows making up the floor revealed he had nine more to cross. Nine steps before he could turn around and return to safety. *Let's do this quick.*

Picking out the most stable looking stone in the row before him, he stepped forward.

One.

When that was easily accomplished, he did two more in quick succession.

Two. Three.

Then...

Four. Five. Six.

At *seven*, Jaikus froze when he felt the stone shift beneath his foot.

Reneeke saw his friend come to a sudden stop. "What's wrong, Jaik?"

"The stone!" he shrieked. *"It moved!"*

"It's probably just loose," his friend hollered back.

"Don't count on it," said Charka.

"What do I do?"

"Does it move up and down, or side to side?" questioned Seward.

"Both, I think." A pause, then... "There's more side to side movement."

Charka glanced to his man. "What do you think?"

His gaze lingered on the stone floor beneath Jaikus' foot. "The fact that the stone is near the center of the passage would tend to make me believe it's a trap. But it *is* possible he could have found the way to access the hidden areas."

Thinking for a moment, Charka then asked, "Did you put all your weight on the stone?"

"No. I had barely touched it when I felt movement."

"Remove your foot," suggested Seward.

"Are you crazy?" asked Jaikus.

"For good or bad, you are going to have to take your foot off sometime," explained Charka. "It may as well be now."

"O...okay."

They watched as Jaikus simultaneously lifted his foot from the stone floor and leaped backward with a powerful thrust from his other leg. He stumbled upon landing, but kept his balance by placing a hand against the wall.

Reneeke came to his side. "Pretty snazzy footwork there." He couldn't help but chuckle.

Knees and arms shaking, Jaikus leaned upon the shoulder of his friend.

Amusement turned immediately to concern. "Are you okay?"

Jaikus nodded. "Just a little shaky."

"He'll be all right."

Turning they saw Charka standing behind them.

"Seward, see if you can see what that stone is about."

"Are you sure you wouldn't rather have the Springers mess with it first?"

"Not this time."

Shrugging, Seward took the lantern from Jaikus and went to investigate the loose stone that had caused Jaikus such anxiety.

Lady Kate offered the shaky Springer her water flask.

Taking the proffered flask, he said, "Thank you," then drained it dry. The water helped calm his nerves. As Seward knelt down to inspect the floor stone, Jaikus whispered to Reneeke, "I don't think I can keep doing this."

His friend eyed him with compassion. "I know it's nerve-wracking. But we have only the one day and it will be over. On the morrow we head back to Reakla." Glancing over to where Charka now stood watching Seward's efforts, he said, "Why don't you sit down until he's finished?"

Jaikus nodded. Putting his back against the wall, he slid down to the floor. Reneeke followed suit.

"You two are doing a wonderful job," praised Lady Kate.

"Thank you, Lady," replied Reneeke.

Turning his attention toward her, Jaikus asked, "Do you think Charka will put me forward for Guild membership?"

She was quiet for a moment before answering. "I don't know. He did smile at you earlier, so I think your chances are better than they were. Just keep doing the best you can and cause no problems."

"I will," he asserted.

Reneeke nodded. "We *both* will."

They sat quietly while Seward worked. Jaikus had his eyes closed and head leaned back, resting against the wall. He had almost fallen asleep when Reneeke jostled his shoulder.

"He's done."

Coming awake, Jaikus saw Seward and Charka walking toward them.

"It wasn't a trap," Seward explained. "At least, I don't believe it to be. There are three loose stones, not just the one. I believe them to be the triggering mechanism that will open the secret way."

"Did it work?" asked Jaikus.

Seward gave him a half-grin. "We won't know that until *you* try."

"Me?"

"You *are* the Springer, after all."

The look Charka gave Jaikus indicated he agreed with Seward.

"Fine. What do I have to do?"

"It's simple really. Press the stones in the correct order, and the way should be opened."

"*Should* be opened?" queried Reneeke.

Seward nodded. "Of course, if you get the order wrong, the results could be disastrous."

"*Of course,*" Jaikus said, copying Seward's tone in a less than flattering way. Seward merely grinned. "Any idea what the correct order may be?"

"Nope. You're going to have to trust in your luck."

Reneeke laid a hand on his friend's shoulder. "Do you want me to do it?"

Jaikus shook his head. He would be ashamed if he allowed his best friend to assume a risk that he feared to face. And if Reneeke were to be hurt due to his cowardice, the guilt would be unendurable. "Thanks. But I'll do it."

"All you need to do, is put pressure on the stones until you feel a click."

"Are you certain this will work?"

"No."

Jaikus paused and glanced at the man to see if he was messing with him. To his distress, it didn't look like he was. Unable to escape this fate, he steadied his nerve, took the lantern and walked down to where the loose floor stones waited.

Three stones bore charcoal lines, markers placed by Seward to indicate which stones to press. Each looked identical to the next. Jaikus had hoped that perhaps there would be some tell-tale marking or deformation which might offer a clue, but was sadly disappointed. Picking one at random, he placed his foot upon it, and braced himself for the unexpected. Then he slowly transferred his weight to the stone and felt it shift under him.

With a quick, downward thrust, he stomped on the stone and stepped back quickly. When he looked, the stone was now recessed half an inch into the floor.

"Good work," praised Charka. "Now, pick the next one."

"Be careful," he heard Reneeke holler from where his friend waited with the others. He cast a glance back over his shoulder and saw Reneeke's encouraging expression. Jaikus nodded, then returned his attention to the task at hand.

One more to go. Either it will be the right one, and all will be fine. Or it won't, and he may not live much longer. Moving to in front of the charcoal-striped stone nearest the end of the passage, he gently placed his foot upon it. Then just as before, he stomped on it hard while a fraction of a second later, jumped back.

Again, he completed the maneuver without eliciting a response. The second stone was now recessed into the floor half an inch same as the first.

"I think you got it," said Charka. "Now do the third."

As he moved into position, he heard Seward say, "I hope this works."

Having successfully depressed the first two stones, he had some confidence in his chances of surviving the third. Setting his foot atop the stone, he put his full weight upon it, this time without the leap backward. Beneath his foot, he felt a click and a rumbling sound came from before him.

The wall opened.

—9—

"Lucky guess."

Seward's voice could not negate the feelings of relief and satisfaction Jaikus felt at seeing the wall slide aside.

"Way to go, Jaik!" Reneeke's shout of congratulations, on the other hand, did much to bolster those feelings.

"Yes. Well done indeed." Charka came up from behind and slapped him on the back. Gazing into the opening, he asked, "Now, what do we have here?"

The sliding of the door revealed a passage equally as large and well formed as the one in which they now stood. A pair of torch sconces sat as sentinels several feet from the opening, one to either side. Both were empty.

"Looks like a passageway," replied Jaikus.

Charka nodded. "Let's see where it goes." He then gave Jaikus a slight nudge to get him moving.

Relief and satisfaction quickly gave way to nervousness and fear as he once again proceeded into the unknown. Shining the light before him, he moved to, and then through, the newly formed opening.

After his last experience, he gave the floor a much greater scrutiny. Though how to tell if there were more loose pressure plates similar to those encountered before was something about which he hadn't the faintest clue.

Upon reaching the pair of sconces, the light from the lantern revealed another pair farther down. He was beginning to wonder if similar pairs would be encountered at regular intervals when the floor dropped out from beneath him.

A cry of fear escaped him as he started to plummet. Arms and legs flailing to find any means by which to halt his fall, he felt the rope tied about his middle snap taut. The abrupt halt caused him to slam into the side of the shaft. Then he heard from above. "Look out, Jaik!"

Horror filled him as he glanced up toward the call. Small sections of the walls to which the torch sconces were attached, were rotating outward and down. He had but a moment to ponder this new development before, from out of one sconce, a liquid gushed forth.

Twisting and pushing himself along the side of the shaft, Jaikus fought to avoid coming into contact with the liquid. Was it acid? Poison? An image flashed into his mind of the equipment in Keeler's back room, the ones the smith had claimed an acid trap had destroyed.

Despite his best efforts, some of the liquid hit him as it passed. An involuntary cry and much contorted thrashing later, he realized it was not acid at all, but oil. Possibly lamp oil.

"Catch it!" he heard Charka yell.

Something else fell from above. Its basic shape was spherical, but misshapen. He tried to do as instructed and catch it, but the object slipped through his grip and vanished into the darkness below. Two seconds later, he heard the object strike the bottom. There was a flash, then fire sprang to life forty feet below. As the smoke began to rise, he felt a tug on the rope. The others were drawing him from the shaft like a bucket from a well. When he reached the top, Reneeke was there to grab him by the hand and pull him the rest of the way out.

"Are you okay?" his friend asked, concern evident in his voice.

Smoke issuing from out of the shaft caused him to cough, but he nodded. "Yeah, Rene. I'm fine. Now I understand the need for the rope."

Reneeke grinned. If Jaikus was able to quip a response like that, he would be fine.

Jaikus glanced back to where a good section of the passageway had fallen away. "Another trap?"

"Looks that way," affirmed Charka. "You must have tripped it when you passed through."

Reneeke shook his head. "I don't think so."

"You don't?" asked Charka.

"No, sir." Gesturing back to the hole bellowing smoke, he said, "It doesn't feel right. I think that Jaikus tripped the trap when he pressed the stones to access this secret area. They opened the way, true, but they also triggered this trap to catch the intruder after he passed through. By lulling us into believing any wards had been circumvented, we stumbled into the trap quite readily. Without the rope, Jaikus would assuredly be dead."

"True enough," agreed Jaikus.

"I don't know about that," argued Charka, then shrugged. "Anything's possible."

"It was a nasty one, too," added Seward, appreciatively. "Not only was it designed to drop the intruder down a pit, but it poured oil and dropped a Pyra stone to finish the job."

"Is that what that was?" questioned Jaikus. "A Pyra stone?" He recalled someone shouting for him to catch the falling object, which he had failed to do.

Charka nodded. "That it was. Strike a Pyra stone hard enough, and it will ignite."

"So that was how the oil caught fire?"

"Exactly. When the Pyra stone hit the bottom, it did so with enough force to cause it to ignite and the oil went up in flames."

Jaikus swallowed hard. "If it hadn't been for the rope…"

"You would have been roasted alive. Provided of course that the fall didn't kill you first."

"Wicked," exclaimed Reneeke. "Oh, that reminds me, Bella said he would take any Pyra stones you found. Claimed to have a buyer wanting some."

Charka grinned. "I'm sure he would. They are in high demand by the magic users. Am I not right, Kate?"

"You are, and the Tower always pays well for such."

"Maybe there are more where that one came from?" suggested Reneeke. Glancing toward where the section of the walls had settled before dropping their lethal cargo, he couldn't see any means to access the inner workings of the trap.

Seward shook his head. "You would have to find the trap's back side. The stones are worth some gold to be sure, but not enough to warrant us wasting our time trying to get to them."

"Indeed," agreed Charka. Coming to Jaikus, the *Troupe* leader asked, "Are you able to continue?"

Jaikus nodded. "I think so. Just a little shaky."

"I'll continue as Springer for the next bit," offered Reneeke.

"Very well. That may be for the best."

"Thanks," Jaikus said as he untied the rope from around his middle and handed it to his friend.

"No problem."

Once the rope was securely in place, Reneeke moved to the edge of the shaft. He could readily leap the four foot gap to the other side. But before he did, he couldn't help but look down at what was left of the fire burning far below. Gauging the distance to the bottom at around sixty feet, he was glad that Charka had insisted they use the rope. Without it, Jaikus wouldn't have fared nearly so well.

About to leap across, he paused when a thought occurred to him. Glancing over his shoulder toward Charka, he said, "I wonder if there is anything at the bottom of this pit."

Seward laughed. "They wouldn't stash their treasure in such a place."

"That's not what I was thinking," he explained. "Perhaps Jaikus wasn't the first to run afoul of this trap. Could it be possible that someone else happened this way in the past? What's left of them could be lying down below."

"They'd be nothing but dust by now," replied Charka. "It would have to be centuries since the last person wandered these passages."

"I wasn't thinking about their body, but what they may have had *on* them; treasure, and what-not."

A calculating look appeared in Charka's eyes. "Can you see anything down there?"

Reneeke glanced back down the shaft. "I can see shadows in the firelight, but nothing definite." Grabbing hold of the rope already tied to him, he shook it then asked, "Want me to take a look?"

Charka nodded. "Might be worth the time. Go ahead."

Seward joined him on holding the rope as Reneeke moved into position. With one hand holding the rope, and the other gripping the lantern, Reneeke scooted over the edge. As his weight came full upon the rope, he glanced to the two holding him secure and nodded.

Down into the shaft he went. Charka and Seward let out the rope slowly, keeping his descent steady and manageable. Jaikus stood at the lip with Lady Kate to observe his progress.

Smoke continued rising from the shaft, though it was beginning to taper off now that most of the oil had been burned away. In the light of the dying fires, Jaikus and Lady Kate could see that the bottom of the shaft was littered with debris.

"Your friend has a good head for this business."

Jaikus nodded. "Reneeke has always been smart. Or perhaps *creative* would be a better way to describe him. You can always count on him to approach a problem in a way unexpected. Often, advantageously."

Below, Reneeke had reached the halfway point. "He's halfway there," she told the two playing out the rope. "How is the rope holding out?"

"I think we may have enough," Charka replied. Panning out more, he and Seward kept lowering the young Springer closer to the bottom.

In the shaft, Reneeke was close enough now to direct the lantern's light downward to reveal what treasures might await at the shaft's bottom. The smoke had continued dissipating until now, it was barely a hindrance.

Three sets of bones lay in various states of repose across the bottom. Two were human, one was not. Of the humans, one had a cracked skull while the other looked to have broken his leg upon impact. He wasn't sure what the non human one may have been, but there was a sword lying across its midsection indicating the creature had been sentient. Reneeke was fairly certain the sword did not belong to the two human skeletons as they each had swords of their own.

His feet alighted upon the stone bottom and the rope grew slack. "I'm here!" he hollered.

"Anything?" came Charka's question.

"Yes! Give me a moment and I'll give you a full inventory." He looked at the glitter of coins and jewels that lay scattered about, as well as several other items that he wasn't sure what they were. "Toss down my pack!" A moment later, he saw the brown leather pack freefalling toward him. Once he had it, he began scooping up valuables.

The human skeleton's swords were in bad repair. As pitted and rusted as they were, Reneeke thought that even Keeler would refuse them. He stepped on the blade of one and felt it crumble beneath his foot. *How long would it take for a blade to be reduced to such a state? Centuries? Longer?* He may never know.

On the other hand, the blade of the non-human was still in good shape. It looked rather plain with a simple, unadorned crossguard. There was no filigree or anything else that might indicate it to be more than a simple blade. Taking the sword, he noticed that it felt lighter and better balanced than the one he carried. Running his finger down the business end he discovered that it still held an edge. Reneeke removed his blade from its scabbard and slid the new one in. The fit was a bit loose as this new blade was slightly narrower, but it would work. Since his old sword wasn't worth much, he left it lying on the floor of the shaft. He felt certain Charka would not begrudge him this new blade.

The glitter of gold drew his attention to the skeletal hand of one of the humans. Two rings rested upon the bony appendages. One was a plain, golden band, and the other was silver bearing a ruby set in white gold. He knew Charka would like the second one.

Once he had gleaned everything of value from among the misfortunate trio that had long ago succumbed to the trap far above, he hollered that he was ready to be pulled up.

"Excellent job," praised Charka when Reneeke emptied the contents of the pack onto the passageway floor. And as he had thought, Charka zeroed in on the ring with the ruby. "Yes. Excellent indeed."

Lady Kate on the other hand was more interested in the objects gathered along with the coins and jewels. There were four: a six inch stick that looked like it had been taken from a willow tree; a crystal orb whose center was the color of aquamarine; and a pair of black, onyx-like spheres that had irises etched into their surfaces. What her supposition may have been as to the properties, or lack thereof, of the items was forestalled by Charka's announcement that it was time they continued on.

"We can give this all a more thorough examination upon our return to camp."

Nodding, Lady Kate put her items into her pack while Charka and Seward divvied the rest between theirs.

"Doesn't Reneeke get something?" queried Jaikus. He knew better than to ask about himself.

"Your shares will be given upon our return to Reakla."

Jaikus was less than thrilled, but Reneeke took it in stride.

Pulling his new-found sword from the scabbard, he said, "I also found this." Reneeke held it out for Charka's inspection. "It was better than my previous one, so I took it."

Charka nodded to Lady Kate who took possession of the sword. After the metal glowed blue for a brief time, she said, "There is a definite aura to it."

"Magical?" asked Jaikus.

"To some degree, yes." She handed it back to Reneeke. "I detect nothing malignant about its prowess."

Reneeke glanced to Charka before taking the sword back.

"Keep it," the *Troupe* leader said. "For without your insightful proposal of investigating the shaft, it would have remained there along with these other treasures. Consider it a bonus. It will not be accounted against your share of the profits."

"Thank you." Taking back the sword, he flashed Jaikus a grin before resheathing it. His friend was green with envy.

Charka shrugged.

"Can you tell what the, uh, *aura* does?" Jaikus asked Lady Kate.

"Not without expending much more time and effort. If he wishes to know more, he will have to do that on his own. Olaf's would have scrolls to do the trick, though they are a bit pricey. It might be wiser to invest your take from this venture in armor and other items. Or maybe even training at the Guild should you become a member."

"*Other items?* You mean like healing scrolls?"

She nodded. "Exactly. Olaf has something he calls the Basic Pack. It's a dozen scrolls for less than it would cost to buy singly."

"Thanks. We'll keep that in mind."

Over by the shaft, Reneeke leapt across the opening to land safely on the far side. Moving down only a short distance, he waited for the others to cross before continuing further. Once Charka and Seward made the crossing, he directed the lantern's light to shine down the passageway, then proceeded into the unknown.

The passageway continued straight for fifty feet before it was clear they were approaching another room. Slowing his pace, Reneeke scanned the floor ahead for any irregularities as he went. He reached the room without incident.

"Got a room up here," he hollered over his shoulder.

"Anything in it?" Hurrying forward, Charka came to stand behind his Springer.

Starting on the right, Reneeke panned the light slowly across the room. Midway through, he paused when a square, iron bound wooden box entered the field of light. Its sides were composed of wood, though the wood was in an advanced state of decay. The box's left side sagged noticeably.

"Well, well, well. What do we have here?"

"A chest, maybe?" queried Reneeke.

"Definitely." He then had Reneeke finish panning the light through the rest of the room, whose effort revealed another doorway in the wall to their left. The sagging, iron bound box was the sole occupant of the room.

Bringing the light back to settle upon the chest, Reneeke asked, "Want me to check it out?"

"If you wouldn't mind?"

Reneeke directed the light toward the floor before him, gave it a once over, then carefully began making his way across to the chest.

"It will be your turn when we continue on," Charka told his other Springer.

Jaikus merely nodded as he watched his friend's progress.

It's a trap!

That thought was very much on Reneeke's mind. He may not have been a thief, but something like this chest, left all by itself out in the open, said something was not quite right. Logically, he couldn't fathom why it would be left in such an exposed way, except perhaps, to tempt the unwary into doing something fatal. Like what he was doing right now.

As his proximity to the chest narrowed, so too did his pace slow. He rotated the iris of the bulls-eye lantern in order to focus a more direct beam of light upon the chest. There were definite cracks in the wood, some large enough to expose that which was contained within. The lantern's light was being reflected off of something metallic and bright from the inside.

The lock was an internal one with a keyhole waiting invitingly. He had no great desire to try and open the chest. To do so would most likely be extreme folly. Reneeke pictured himself being sprayed with acid, or perhaps struck by a dart covered in the most deadly of poisons, along with a dozen other situations bards had filled their stories with. Each tale contained a more gruesome outcome than the one before.

He hadn't realized he had remained motionless for an extended time until Seward hollered, "Are you going to open it or not?"

"Yeah!" he hollered back. Gazing at the keyhole, he added silently, *but not this way.*

Taking in the advanced decay and rot undermining the integrity of the chest, an idea came to mind. Moving around to the side of the chest, he kicked the rotten wood with as much strength as he could muster.

Splintering under the blow, the wood of the chest collapsed, but not entirely as the iron bands held bits and pieces of it together. He could now clearly see items of gold and silver forming a small pile within. Another kick completely obliterated what remained of the wooden chest. Simultaneously, a liquid spray exploded outward from the chest's front to coat a sizeable area of the floor.

Reneeke began sifting through the remains of the chest as the others entered the room and approached. He glanced to Charka, grinned, and asked, "Did I do that right?"

Laughing, Charka nodded. "Boy, you did that perfectly. We'll make an adventurer out of you yet."

There were five more of the golden disks, six gems of varying sizes and colors, what once had been a book but all that was left was the hard, leather binding that had bound the pages together, and a dagger long succumbed to the ravages of time and rust.

Charka divided the booty between himself, Seward and Lady Kate. Jaikus couldn't help but look longingly at the treasure his earlier misjudgment would probably keep him from ever sharing. He knew that at least Reneeke would receive a part, and that his friend would share with him.

Coming to Reneeke's side, he started untying the rope from around his friend. "My turn."

"You know, Jaik, this is easier than they led us to believe."

"So far, I would have to agree with you. But we aren't out of it yet." He glanced to the dark doorway he would be leading the others through. "The worst could be yet to come."

"If we keep our wits and do nothing stupid, I believe we will survive this."

"Rene, I sure hope so."

Securing the rope around his middle, he then waited for the signal from Charka for him to get going. When it came, Reneeke moved to the rear with Lady Kate, and Jaikus headed for the doorway.

Another passageway made a quick left turn not far from the room, then continued unabated for only a short distance before coming to where it widened to twice its former size. Three pedestals sat centered in the passageway, three feet apart. Made from gray marble, they were but two feet in height. Atop each sat a small statuette. The one atop the first pedestal was of a miniature, naked man; its face similar to that of the faces carved on the walls. The second statuette was of a little tree, possibly oak.

On the last pedestal rested a simple, three inch silver cylinder. Dark runes were inscribed upon its surface.

Jaikus came to a stop a good six feet before the first pedestal. "What do you make of this?"

The others came up behind him and looked at the naked man, the tree, and the cylinder.

"Decorations perhaps?" asked Reneeke.

Charka didn't immediately answer. "It's possible. Kate?"

"There is definitely magic at work here," she replied after a moment of spell casting.

"I don't suppose it's the good, helpful kind of magic?" asked Jaikus.

"No, it isn't." Turning her attention upon the young Springer, she said, "To put it bluntly, it's more the *'You come close and I'll fry you'* kind."

"Wonderful," Jaikus groaned.

Shining the light so it illuminated the passageway beyond the three, statue bearing pedestals, he could see where the walls again narrowed, bringing the passageway back to its original width.

Charka kept silent as he contemplated what they should do. The words of Lady Kate weighed heavily upon him. He desperately desired to find out what lay at the end of this passageway, but he didn't want to needlessly throw away the lives of his Springers. True, that's what they were there for, but he had just enough of a conscience not to do so simply because he could.

Turning to Lady Kate, he asked, "Is it passive?"

"The magic?" she asked. When he nodded, she said, "I can't be sure. What I can be certain of is that it's strong, and that it permeates the area in and around the three pedestals. It may react if we try to pass, or it may react only if we move the statuettes, or it may not react at all. But I get the feeling, that should the magic react, it will be bad. *Very* bad."

Face turning grim, he struggled with vying emotions: greed and caution. In the end, greed won out. He glanced to Lady Kate and she could see the decision in his eyes.

"You can't."

"It's what we are here for," he replied. Turning to Jaikus, he indicated for the Springer to continue down the passageway.

Jaikus looked at him with undisguised horror. "You can't be serious. After what she just said?"

"Merely pass through," Charka instructed. "Touch nothing."

"But…"

"But nothing. Fulfill your contract, or leave." He met Jaikus' gaze with one of grim determination.

A quick glance to Reneeke showed him to be just as fearful as was Jaikus. "Good luck," he said.

"Thanks." Mouth dry from nervousness and fear, Jaikus almost hadn't been able to get that single word out. Turning toward the pedestals, he could feel his legs trembling.

"...it's more the 'You come close and I'll fry you' kind."

The words of Lady Kate kept running through his mind. Doing his best to shove them back to the nethermost recesses, he took a step forward.

"Hug the wall," she advised. "Keep as far away from them as you can."

"I...I'll do that," he stammered, without bothering to glance back.

He took another step forward, moving closer to the wall at the same time. Eyes glued to the statue of the naked man, he cautiously took a third.

Was it his imagination, or were the naked man's eyes tracking his movements? His fourth step brought him within arm's reach of the pedestal. The overactiveness of his imagination was dispelled when he moved out of the naked man's line of sight. Having made it this far with no ill affects, he took two more quick steps, then paused.

Glancing back to where the others waited, he saw Charka, Seward, and Reneeke all maintaining a grip on the rope. Just behind them stood Lady Kate. In her right hand she held a black, rune-inscribed wand.

"You're doing great," said Reneeke encouragingly.

Moving once again, he quickly came abreast of the tree statuette. Back when he stood with the others, it had looked like a regular, normal tree. But now that he was closer, could see that the leaves of the tree were in an advanced state of wilting. Slightly curled in on themselves, each leaf looked like a hand, frozen in the act of curling in on itself to form a fist. The entire aspect of the diminutive tree disturbed him far more than had the naked little man.

Several rapid steps took him past the tree and brought him near the final pedestal atop which rested the silver cylinder. Passing his eyes over the dark runes marring its surface made his skin crawl. Of the three, the little cylinder unnerved him the most. Why it should be so, he couldn't even hazard a guess. Moving past, he was just glad the three pedestals and their objects were behind him. And that he was still alive.

"I made it!" he cried.

Back at the other end, Charka had Seward follow, with Reneeke waiting until Seward traversed the pedestaled area and joined Jaikus, before following.

While waiting for the others, Jaikus directed the lantern's light into the as yet unplumbed section of the passageway, curious to see what may lie ahead. He was surprised to discover that the light was being reflected, or rather refracted, by a glittering circle just beyond the lantern's reach.

"Look at this," he said to Seward when the man reached his side.

"Hmmm, interesting," was all the reply he received.

The circle drew his gaze. Curiosity impelled him to take a step forward. But the rope drew taut, preventing him from proceeding.

Seward jerked the rope another two times. "Wait for the others."

Charka was the last to pass through the pedestaled area. When he arrived and saw the circle glittering farther down the passageway, he indicated for Jaikus to continue.

His Springer nodded, took two steps forward, then collapsed.

"Jaik!"

Reneeke shouted his friend's name as he raced forward to render what aid he could. Charka grabbed him by one of his pack straps and jerked him back. "Hold up there, lad."

"But Jaik needs me!"

Ignoring him, the *Troupe* leader signaled Lady Kate who cast a spell toward their unconscious Springer. "Dart," she announced.

"Haul him back." Pulling the rope quickly, Charka, Seward, and Reneeke dragged Jaikus back to where they stood.

Lady Kate had already drawn forth a small flask from her pack by then and knelt down next to Jaikus' head. Seward knelt on the other side and held open the Springer's mouth while she poured a portion of the flask's contents through the parted lips. She then stoppered the flask and set it aside.

"Here's the culprit," Charka said as he drew forth a small dart from where it lay embedded within Jaikus' neck. "He must have triggered some sort of trap." To Seward he said, "See if you can find it."

Seward nodded then moved to carry out his leader's request.

Reneeke knelt beside Lady Kate. "Will he die?"

"Not if I can help it. I gave him a powerful antidote, which negates the effects of almost all poisons."

He looked to her with great anxiety. "What if the poison isn't one of the ones it negates?"

She turned a serious look upon him. "Let us hope that is not the case." Returning her attention to the one lying before her, she moved his head to expose the area just below his left ear that had been struck, and gasped.

It was swollen an angry red with a single, dark vein gradually making its way downward along his neck. They watched as it drew ever closer to where the neck merged with the upper body.

"Give him the rest of it," said Charka.

This time, Reneeke parted Jaikus' lips while Lady Kate emptied the flask into him. Again, they turned his head to the side. The line of red had stopped its downward progression.

"It's working," announced Reneeke with glee.

Lady Kate wasn't so assured of the potion's effectiveness, but kept her concerns to herself.

"Come on, Jaik," said Reneeke.

Then, the line slowly began to fade and the swelling to subside. In a matter of minutes, all redness was gone. When his eyes fluttered open, Lady Kate said, "Thank the gods."

Feeling weak as a kitten, Jaikus glanced from face to face, uncertain as to how he came to be lying on the passageway floor. "What happened?"

"You were hit by a poisoned dart," explained Lady Kate.

"Yeah, man. It was ugly. But she fixed you up with an antidote. Now you're right as rain." Reneeke couldn't help but smile.

"We'll take a short break so you can recover your strength," said Charka. To Lady Kate he added, "If he hasn't recovered in that time, give him a healing draught as well."

She nodded, then had Reneeke help her in moving Jaikus against the wall where he could sit in greater comfort. Producing the less than appetizing trail rations, she handed them to her two Springers and they ate while Seward worked to discover the mechanism by which Jaikus had triggered the dart.

—10—

"It was just another pressure plate beneath a floor stone," Seward explained. "There are three. I marked each with a bit of charcoal. Make sure you don't step on them."

The dart that had laid Jaikus low was now nestled safely within a bit of rolled leather at the bottom of Charka's pack. He informed his two Springers about how thieves back at the Guild often paid for samples of hitherto unknown substances.

"Poisons, you mean?" asked Reneeke.

"Yes, lad. Poisons. And considering the way it brought your friend down, this one should fetch quite a bit."

Ever the killjoy, Seward added, "Unless they already know about it."

Charka shrugged. "Still, it won't hurt to bring it back."

Reneeke took the Springer duty as Jaikus was still in no condition to adequately perform the function. Rope now tied about his middle, he stood before the stones marked with lines of charcoal. He made sure to avoid them as he navigated the trapped area and continued down the passageway.

The first thing he became aware of, was the circle of refracted light Jaikus had seen shortly before being struck by the dart. It glittered in an explosion of rainbow color that gradually increased in luminosity the closer he came.

Unlike Jaikus before him, he didn't fail to pay attention to the floor as he went. Good thing, too, as he came across another two stones that shifted beneath his feet. In neither case had he put any great amount of weight upon the stones, and thus, avoided tripping the trap. He signaled the stones' position to those that followed, then continued on.

Reds, greens, blues, every color imaginable seemed to be part of the dazzling circle. It wasn't until coming to within ten feet that he saw how the circle was composed of a myriad of tiny gems, and that it surrounded another stony face. This one, however, was different. Its eye sockets were vacant cavities, as was the mouth.

Intent as he was on watching the floor and viewing the display of color, he failed to realize they had reached another dead end until he was almost upon it. Reneeke glanced back to his leader. "Dead end," he announced.

Charka came to stand next to his Springer and contemplated the gem encircled face before them.

"I would advise against removing any of those gems," warned Lady Kate.

"Magic?" asked Reneeke.

"Yes."

"Is there another hidden way to uncover?"

Lady Kate nodded. "It looks that way."

Reneeke gazed at the face on the wall. Every face previously encountered had been identical from one to the next. The fact that this one was not could in no way be a coincidence.

As if they were thinking the same thing, Charka said, "Accessing the next area must have something to do with the face."

"I thought that as well," commented Reneeke.

"Maybe we should put a gem in its mouth or something," suggested Jaikus.

"Don't be foolish," argued Seward.

"I agree," said Charka. "Such a course of action would provide little in the way of results."

"No," said Reneeke as he turned to his friend. "Probably not." Then he glanced toward Lady Kate. "But maybe something else…"

"Such as?" she queried.

"If I'm not mistaken, two of those items in your possession that were recovered from the bottom of the shaft bore the etching of irises? And wouldn't those same items fit perfectly within the empty sockets of the face?"

Unshouldering her pack, she said, "You may be right." Once she had it opened, she reached in and pulled out a small, velvet pouch. Untying the golden, velvety thong keeping it closed, she poured the two marble sized objects onto her palm.

"Yes, indeed," said Charka. Glancing from the face, to the two items, then back again, he nodded. "They would fit perfectly."

Jaikus looked confused. "How did they get down at the bottom of that trap?"

The Troupe leader shrugged. "Could have been a thief who had acquired the items, yet ran afoul of the trap before being able to use them."

"If that's the case," began Seward, "then the third item, that uh, *orb*, may fit in the mouth."

Lady Kate reached into her pack and removed the crystal orb whose heart was aquamarine. Stepping close to the face, she held the orb before its oral cavity. It was a perfect fit.

"But the question is, should we?" Turning her attention toward Charka, she added, "These items, the eyes and the orb, are imbued with magic. Setting them within the face could start something we would be in no position to stop."

"Or, by doing so, we could gain access to a treasure trove," he argued.

"That is true." Lady Kate continued to meet the *Troupe* leader's gaze. "Is the reward, worth the risk?"

"We don't even know if there is anything worthwhile to be had," stated Reneeke. "For all we know, we could be opening a long lost prison of some demonic monster that upon release, will kill us and then lay waste to the world."

Seward shook his head. "Boy, you've been listening to too many bards."

"I am simply saying that we should proceed with caution," explained Reneeke.

"I agree," chimed in Jaikus. "With being cautious that is."

Lady Kate still held Charka's gaze. Moving the orb closer to the face's mouth, she asked, "Shall I?"

There was only the briefest hesitation on his part before Charka nodded his head. "Yes."

Then she glanced to Reneeke who shook his. "It's a bad idea. Better to leave with nothing, than die a rich man."

Seward nodded when her eyes came to him. "It's what we are here for. Let's see what happens."

Then she turned toward Jaikus. "I say no. So it is now two for it, and two against." She gave him a grin. "It's all up to you."

"This ain't up to him," argued Charka.

"His life hangs in the balance as does the rest of ours. He will be allowed his vote."

Charka scowled, but knew it would do no good arguing with her once her mind was made up.

Jaikus saw Reneeke shake his head for him to declare negatively. But then Charka said, "Boy, if you say yes, I'll forget all that's gone before. When we return, I will do everything in my power to see that you are allowed to join the Guild."

He couldn't believe it. Glancing to Lady Kate, he asked, "Does he mean it?"

"Oh, yes. I'm sure he does."

Reneeke shook his head vehemently. "Don't you do it, Jaik."

A Guild member! Dashed hopes were made new. How could he do otherwise? "Sorry, Rene. Let's do it."

"So be it."

Lady Kate slowly moved the crystal orb toward the mouth. When it was but a hair's breadth away, a force from within the face's mouth drew the orb out of her hand and sucked it into the opening. Such unexpectedness startled her, but when nothing further developed, she calmed.

Next were the two round objects with irises etched upon their surfaces. This was against her best judgment. Unfortunately, she couldn't come up with a valid reason *not* to go through with it. Moving the two objects before the face's eyes, she again felt a force reach out and pluck them from her hand, only to draw them into the empty sockets.

Aquamarine began to swirl deep within the orb that now resided within the mouth of the face. The color within began to spiral.

"It didn't open anything," observed Jaikus.

She shook her head. "No, it didn't." Unable to take her eyes from the color fluxation within the orb, she slowly pulled her wand from out of her sleeve.

"Then what...?"

A sudden burst of color from the gems surrounding the face cut short his inquiry. Taking a step backward in apprehension, he cried out when a wave of color exploded outward from the gem shrouded face, then was drawn back into it. He gasped when he saw the eyes *move*. The irises turned upon him and he knew that the face understood he was there. Then they passed from him and took in each of the others in turn. Charka was the last, and when the eyes left him, the mouth began to speak.

The orb was no longer present within the mouth. Stony lips moved with perfect fluidity as words of a long dead language issued forth.

Lady Kate was quick to react. Speaking arcane words, her hands moved swiftly in accompanying gestures as she cast a *Spell of Understanding*, and the face's words were no longer incomprehensible.

> **...*or you will surely perish as had Nevinixi in the last days of Koetha. Let darkness arise and light to fall, before death comes to call.***

As the last vestiges of the word *"call"* faded away, the gems around the face once more flashed in brilliance, this time expanding outward to completely envelope the humans before it. One moment they were engulfed by intense color, and the next, found themselves standing in a dark room.

Shocked to say the least, Reneeke turned about but found nothing but a stone wall behind him.

Charka drew his sword, as did Seward. Seeing the pair with blades in hand, Jaikus followed suit. "Wh...where *are* we?" Jaikus asked, his tremulous voice cutting through the silence of the room.

"Be quiet!" commanded Charka, his tone indicating that he wasn't about to put up with being disobeyed.

Four pillars in the middle of the room rose to form the points of a square. Centered within the pillared square was a golden statue that easily stood a head and a half taller than any of them. Its hands were outstretched to either side with palms up. Upon the right palm rested a diamond the size of a man's fist, on the left was a crudely formed stone of blackest night.

Set around the room were a dozen pedestals, each bearing a bowl made of precious metals and decked out with gems. When Reneeke panned the lantern's light toward the nearest of the bowls, its light was refracted back by the myriad of gems contained within.

"We found it!" cried Charka.

"Yes, we did," agreed Seward. Moving toward the bowl of gems which Reneeke's light illuminated, he reached in and scooped out a handful. Rubies, emeralds, sapphires, and more were gripped within his fist. That single handful could ensure a man lived to the end of his days in grand style. And there was more, oh so much more, still within the room. ""We're rich!"

At sight of the treasure, Jaikus lost what nervousness their sudden translocation had produced. Sheathing his sword, he quickly joined Seward next to the bowl. About to reach in, he felt Reneeke place his hand upon his shoulder and pull him back. Glancing back, quite ready to berate his friend for undue caution, Jaikus' retort died on his tongue when he saw the expression on Reneeke's face. His friend wasn't looking at him, but at Seward. Turning his gaze upon the focus of Reneeke's attention, he gasped and backed quickly away.

"What?" asked Seward. Then he glanced toward the hand holding the gems, it was the color of gray ash. He looked on in growing fear as the grayness steadily darkened toward black. *"Cursed!"*

It wasn't only his hand that had been affected, but his face as well.

As Charka cried *"Scroll!"* and raced forward, the whites of Seward's eyes began to darken, and the pupils flattened into ovals.

Gems fell to the floor as the hand grasping them spasmed. Seward looked in abject terror at the hand as its transformation from gray to black quickened from one heartbeat to the next. Then in a voice a full octave deeper than it should have been, cried, "What's...happening to me?"

"Don't touch him!" shouted Lady Kate to the others. Scroll now in hand, she came forward and held it out so Seward could grasp the other end. As soon as his fingers tightened around the parchment, she spoke the activation word.

A burst of white light exploded outward from the scroll, its energy being immediately drawn into Seward's hand. Jaikus watched in wonder as the surface of Seward's skin grew luminous as light traveled beneath his skin from the hand, up his forearm, until finally disappearing beneath his tunic. A heartbeat later, the sub-dermal light appeared throughout the rest of his body, giving his skin a subtle, luminous glow wherever it was exposed. When the luminosity reached his face, he collapsed.

Charka was there to catch him and laid him out upon the floor. "Is it working?" he asked.

"Hard to tell," she explained. "What has hold of him is far more powerful than anything we've previously encountered." There was a second scroll in her hand.

The two Springers looked on in horror. Neither of them, even in their darkest dreams, could ever have envisioned something akin to what they were witnessing unfold before them.

"Hang in there, Seward," encouraged Reneeke. But it didn't appear as if the power of the scroll was going to be sufficient to counteract whatever it was that afflicted Seward. Patches of darkness began fighting off the encroaching luminosity faster than it could spread. Areas that once had glowed with the power of the scroll, were gradually returning to their darkened state.

"Use the other one," said Charka.

"It's our last," warned Lady Kate. "I told you before we left that we needed more of these."

"I don't care." His man was dying before him. "Do it."

Lady Kate nodded. This time, she placed the scroll beneath Seward's tunic so it would touch his skin before activating it. Light flared again. Instead of the luminosity the first scroll had produced, the second application caused Seward's skin to glow a ghostly white.

Battles of light and dark waged across the surface of Seward's skin, only this time, it appeared as if the light was winning. Areas of darkness fell beneath the onslaught of light and didn't reappear.

"It's working," Lady Kate announced.

Seward's skin slowly began regaining its normal, healthy appearance. Even his eyes started returning to normal. The final part of his body to be free of the curse, was the hand where it had begun. Once the scrolls had run their course and he had been completely restored to normalcy, Lady Kate administered a few drops of a healing potion to give his body a boost in repairing any lingering damage.

She glanced up from her patient to Charka and the two Springers. "I wouldn't touch anything in here if I were you."

Jaikus swallowed hard as he nodded. Reneeke simply said, "I didn't plan to."

Charka wasn't at all happy. Bowls of gems, enough to last several lifetimes of extensive debauchery, were simply waiting to be harvested. *And none of it could be touched!*

Looking down at the still comatose Seward, Reneeke asked, "What was it, exactly, that happened to him?"

"Stupidity," replied Charka. "All this wealth made him forget the cardinal rule of adventuring."

"And that would be?"

"Never assume anything is safe. Usually, he's rather smart about such things."

Gesturing to the room about them, Lady Kate added, "Quite often, places like these are warded by curses. They act fast and are almost always lethal to the one who runs afoul of it.

"Seward was lucky in that we never start an adventure without scrolls blessed by priests to counteract the curses of their evil counterparts." She then flashed Charka a glance. "*Usually,* we have more than just, two."

"Time was short and we had to get our Springers before rendezvousing with Hymal."

"Time wouldn't have been short if you and Seward hadn't tied one on the night before," she said accusingly.

Jaikus interrupted what was sure to be a rehashing of an old argument by asking, "Will Seward be okay?" Bringing everyone's focus back to their recently afflicted comrade, he said, "Reneeke and I can carry him if we need to."

Lady Kate gave him a smile. "Thank you for the offer, but I think he will come around in a little bit."

"In the meantime..." said Charka, "let's take a look at where we are." To Lady Kate he added, "Cast your *Spell of Detection* on the room, if you please, so we may see where the hot spots are located."

"You can do that?" questioned Jaikus.

She merely nodded. "Keep an eye on Seward until I'm done."

"Sure thing."

Coming to her feet, Lady Kate moved as close to the four columns as she could without entering the area between. Then as arcane words flowed from her, she slowly rotated until she had faced every part of the room. Upon coming full circle, she raised her hands.

Jaikus watched as her hands clapped three times, and then heard her exclaim, *"Ey-uhd."* Instantly, blue lights flared into being throughout the room. Each of the bowls and their contents glowed brightly, as did the diamond and dark stone resting upon the statue's hands.

Charka nodded. "At least we know." Glancing around the room, he frowned as everything of value glowed blue, indicating they were cursed in one way or another. It was at that time that another detail of the room, one that had been overlooked before, finally registered. The room lacked an egress. There was no way out!

A slap brought his attention back to his man upon the floor. Having struck him across the face in the hopes of awakening him, Laky Kate now gently shook his shoulder.

"Seward?" she asked. About to strike him again, she saw his chest suddenly rise and fall as he took a deep breath.

Eyes popping open, they settled into a half-open state. "Am I dead?" he asked.

"Yes, you are," she replied with a grin. "Or at least, you almost were."

Very weakly, he raised his hand and was greatly relieved to see the normal skin tone.

"It took *two* scrolls," she explained, "but I think you will recover." Then taking his hand, she squeezed gently and asked, "Can you feel this?"

He nodded. "Yes. It's a bit tingly, kind of like it feels after having fallen asleep and is trying to wake up again."

"That's good." When he tried to sit up, she placed a hand upon his chest to keep him down. She didn't have to exert much pressure to have her way. "Lie down and rest while you can. You are weak as a kitten."

Seward ceased his attempt to rise, grinned, then laid back down. "If you say so."

"I do."

Glad to see Seward recovering from the curse's effects, Reneeke brought the lamp over to where Charka now stood gazing at the statue of the naked, golden man.

"Seward's going to be all right," he said.

Charka nodded. "Glad to hear it," he replied without moving his gaze from the statue.

"It's just like the miniature one we passed earlier."

"Almost. This one has its arms raised."

"Do you think it represents a god of some kind?" asked Reneeke.

"I haven't a clue," he shrugged. "I've never seen the likeness before."

"It could have been meant to represent nothing more than just a man," offered Jaikus. Having come up behind them, he too took in the golden man.

"We have a problem, lads," Charka told his Springers. "There appears to be no avenue by which we can leave this room."

Jaikus quickly glanced toward each of the four walls. Each appeared quite solid with no evidence of doorway, or any other form of egress. "How are we to get out?"

"Same as we came in," answered Reneeke. "If magic was the means by which we arrived, it stands to reason that magic should be the means by which we depart."

Charka nodded. "Quite possibly."

"I wish we could have heard the entire message given by the face," Reneeke said. "The parts we missed may have divulged the means of our escape."

"What *did* it say, exactly?" asked Jaikus. "Something about death, wasn't it?"

In a close approximation to the voice of the face, Reneeke said, *"...or you will surely perish as had Nevinixi in the last days of Koetha. Let darkness arise, and light to fall, before death comes to call."*

"Obviously, there is a chance of our perishing. If only Lady Kate had cast her spell quicker."

"What about that part where *'darkness arises and light falls'*? Could that refer to the end of the day when the sun goes down?" Jaikus looked to his friend, more than to Charka, for an answer. Years of habit were difficult to overcome.

"It doesn't feel right," his friend replied with a shake of his head.

"I agree," said their leader.

"Or the curse?" asked Jaikus. "Seward turned awfully dark after scooping up those gems."

"That wouldn't make much sense, Jaik. The people who built this place wouldn't want to go through being cursed just to leave. No, there must be another meaning to it."

"Or none at all," added Charka. "It wouldn't be the first time when the sole purpose of an age-old message like that was to mislead intruders."

"You mean, give them the wrong clue so they make a fatal mistake?" asked Jaikus. He was shocked by such a revelation.

"It's been known to happen."

Reneeke paid their conversation little heed. He loved a good riddle, and this sure was a dilly. The part *'before death comes to call'*, seemed to indicate that if they didn't figure out what darkness must arise and which light will fall, they wouldn't live to see the outside world.

Light...Darkness...

Those two words *had* to be the key to getting out of there. He just knew it. The room offered little in the way of clues. Aside from the golden man, there were only the four columns, and pedestals bearing the cursed bowls full of gems. No inscriptions, pictographs, or any other markings were in evidence anywhere. The room, for all its grandeur, was rather plain.

Charka wandered over to where Seward lay. "How are you doing?"

"Aside from the fact I'm 'weak as a kitten', to use Lady Kate's words, I'm feeling good and glad to be alive."

"I thought you were a goner for sure."

"So did I when I saw my hand."

"That should teach you to help yourself to another person's treasure."

Seward gave him a grin. "At least before Lady Kate has said it to be safe."

She harrumphed. "Like you are ever going to be so cautious." Glancing over to the two Springers, she saw that Reneeke had entered the column area and stood very close to the side of the statue as he gazed up toward the golden man's left armpit.

To Charka she said, "You better go see what trouble your Springers are about to get into."

"What?" he asked as he turned to look. As soon as he saw where Reneeke stood, he shouted, *"Get away from there!"* and stalked forward.

"They pivot, Jaik," Reneeke said, just before Charka's outcry.

Seeing their leader enroute to administer a good tongue-lashing, both lads stepped away from the statue.

"What in the name of all the gods do you think you are doing?" Gaze directed upon Reneeke, his ire at the perceived lack of judgment was quite evident.

"Trying to figure a few things."

Charka eyed him quizzically. "Such as?"

"For one, both of the statue's arms are hinged." When he saw that their leader failed to understand the significance, he added, "The arms can move up and down."

"So?"

Reneeke directed Charka's gaze to the hands of the statue. "If you will notice, a diamond sits upon the statue's right palm, while on the left is a stone of blackest night." He paused a moment to let that sink in. "One is light, one is dark, and the arms upon which they rest move up and down. Or in other words, they *rise* and *fall*."

Nodding, Charka replied, "I see where you are going with this. But both the diamond and the stone are cursed, same as the gems."

"True, the stone and diamond are cursed, but the arms are not." Which was true, the glow from Lady Kate's spell was not apparent on any part of the golden appendages. "We should be able to raise one and lower the other without risk of meeting a fate similar to what Seward experienced. In doing so, *darkness* will rise and *light* shall fall."

"Providing your assumption is correct."

"True enough."

Charka contemplated the situation. "If you are wrong, simply touching the arms could curse the one making the attempt."

"I don't think that will happen."

"Are you willing to take that risk?"

Reneeke glanced over to where Lady Kate sat with Seward.

"Understand lad, that if the curse afflicts you, we have no more scrolls to counter it."

"I know." Then he shrugged. "But this is what a Springer does, right? Be the one to tempt fate?"

Jaikus was not happy about the course of action his friend was contemplating. Turning to their leader, he asked, "Isn't there anything else we can try?"

"None that readily comes to mind," replied Charka. "Your friend's logic is sound." Then he glanced to Reneeke. "But before you try, perhaps we could examine the walls of the room in greater detail. There may be a switch, or something else, that might open a hidden way."

"Time thus spent would also allow Seward to further recuperate," added Lady Kate from her position at Seward's side.

"I'm not that bad off," he objected.

Laying her hand upon his chest, she applied gentle pressure before saying, "Fine, then. Get up."

He tried to rise, but the minimal pressure her hand exerted kept him down. Struggle though he may, Seward could not produce enough force to overcome her efforts. Finally giving up, he resigned himself to further rest.

She merely chuckled and took her hand from off his chest.

Charka led his two Springers to the nearest wall. Gesturing to their right, he said, "You two check that way. Be careful, and if you find something, let me know before doing anything."

"Yes, sir," replied Jaikus.

Over the course of the next half hour, the three of them combed the walls for any sign of another way to leave the room. During that time, Lady Kate's detection spell ran its course, causing the blue glows throughout the room to vanish. When at last the three secret door seekers came together at the opposite side of the room, Charka was forced to admit that Reneeke's idea about moving the statue's arms would have to be attempted.

"I don't like it," he said, once he and his Springers had returned to where the other two waited. "Too many dire things could happen."

There was silence for a moment before Reneeke asked, "Do you want me to do it?"

Charka glanced to Lady Kate. "Any suggestions?"

She shook her head. Then to Reneeke she said, "Good luck."

"Thank you."

Leaving the others, he made his way to the statue of the naked, golden man. First, he moved to the arm on the left, the one with the black stone. Very cautiously, he placed his hands against the underside of the statue's forearm, and pushed. The arm moved a fraction of an inch, then came to a stop. He tried using more strength, but the arm simply would not budge any farther.

The thought that perhaps the other side had to be moved first prompted him to leave the left arm and crossed over to the right. This time, he grabbed the forearm and pulled down. Again, just like the left arm, it moved only a miniscule distance before coming to a halt. Reneeke even tried lifting his feet from the ground, causing his entire weight to hang from the arm, yet even that failed to accomplish anything. He finally let go.

"I can't get them to move," he hollered to the others.

"Maybe your theory was incorrect," replied Charka.

Reneeke was certain that it wasn't. Then an idea occurred to him. "Jaik, come here and give me a hand."

Moving to his friend's side, Jaikus asked, "What do you need?"

"It could be that the arms must move simultaneously. You push up on the left while I pull down on the right."

Not looking very thrilled at being in such close proximity to the cursed item resting upon the statue's palm, Jaikus moved to do as requested.

Reneeke grasped the arm once again. Once Jaikus was ready, he said, "Now."

He pulled down, Jaikus pushed up, and the arms moved.

"It's working," he said and strained all the harder. Jaikus did the same. Together, they managed to move the arms twenty degrees before they would move no further. As Reneeke let go of the arm, he heard a grinding noise coming from behind him. A section of the wall was slowly sinking into the floor. They had found the way out.

—11—

At Charka's urging, Jaikus lent Seward a shoulder as they made ready to leave. Reneeke, with rope still secured about the middle, took lantern in hand and directed its light into the opening as he approached. Therin he discovered a tunnel extending outward at a slightly upward slant. Narrower by half than the previous passageways encountered, the tunnel continued past the reach of the lantern.

"Looks like an escape route," commented Charka as he came to stand beside his Springer.

Reneeke nodded. "And unlikely to be trapped, wouldn't you think?"

"Yes, I would. But then I wouldn't trust my life to that assumption either. Be careful."

Flashing him a half-grin, Reneeke stepped through the opening and began making his way through the tunnel.

Charka followed, all the while keeping a firm grip upon the rope, just in case Reneeke ran afoul of another trap. Behind him came Lady Kate, with Jaikus aiding the still much weakened Seward.

The tunnel continued its upward slant for a good hundred feet before coming to a dead end. Attached to the stone wall at the end was a sliding bar whose end was firmly ensconced within a receptacle cavity in the wall on the right.

Getting the go-ahead from Charka, Reneeke slid the bar free of the cavity, and pushed on the stone wall. It slid open several inches before coming to a stop. Sunlight filtered in through the newly formed opening.

"It *is* an escape route," he concluded. For a moment, he stood with face upraised, reveling in the sun's warmth.

With Charka lending his strength, he and his Springer managed to push the wall far enough to allow for their passage. They discovered that the secret exit had been built as part of a wall, less than thirty feet from where they originally began their exploration earlier in the day.

"We made it!" exclaimed Jaikus jubilantly.

Charka glanced to the sun. "Still have several hours left."

"You can't be serious," objected Lady Kate. "Seward is in no condition to continue rooting around through ancient buildings."

Turning a questioning look toward his man, Charka asked, "How about it?"

Legs trembling, dots flashing before his eyes from the exertion of having traversed the tunnel on their way out, panting and feeling as if he was on the verge of passing out at any minute, Seward replied, "Sure. Let's go."

All it took was a glance and Charka could clearly tell by Seward's pale countenance and the sweat dotting his brow that he was at his end. The welfare of his man outweighed the possibility of recovering further treasure. There was always next time. "You're right, Kate. Let us return to camp."

With the prospect of triggering traps now no longer a concern, Reneeke untied himself from the rope. Then after returning it back to Charka, went to lend his aid in supporting Seward.

"At least this trip wasn't a total loss," stated Charka as they left the site of the recently explored ruins. "We did recover a few items that will bring a coin or two."

"Thanks to Reneeke," added Lady Kate.

The Springer shrugged, or at least as well as he could with Seward's arm draped across his shoulders. "It was nothing."

"*Nothing?* I would hardly call gems, rings, and new sword for yourself, nothing."

"I suppose. But those aren't the treasures I'm glad to have brought out with us."

"Oh?" she asked. "You have something else?"

"You know you are supposed to inform Charka of any treasure you find?" Seward's voice was raspy from exhaustion.

Reneeke smiled. "I am referring to my life, and Jaikus'. Going in, it seemed one or both of us were doomed to not return."

"You can thank Seward for that," Charka explained. "If not for his current condition, we would even now still be delving into the unknown."

They found that their camp had remained undisturbed. Everything was exactly as they had left it.

"Master Hymal hasn't returned?" observed Jaikus.

Lady Kate shook her head. "We won't see him until just before dawn. That is when he normally returns."

She directed the two Springers to bring Seward near the fire-ring and lay him down.

"I tell you, my strength is coming back," Seward complained.

During the last half hour of their return, Seward had been blustering about how he no longer needed to be coddled, that he could walk on his own. It hadn't been until they allowed him to make the attempt, and the ensuing crash to the ground, that he had finally ceased his squawking. Now however, his objections at having to rest were resurfacing.

Lady Kate knelt beside him. Then just as she had before, she placed her hand on his chest. "If you can get up, I'll leave you alone."

Time had rejuvenated his strength to the point where he managed to gain a sitting position against her efforts to keep him down. "Perhaps you are no longer in such a poor condition after all."

Pale from the exertion, Seward was breathing a bit harder than he should have. As sweat once again began to form on his forehead, he said with some forced bravado, "See."

She gave him a smile. "Just don't go wandering off and collapse."

He knocked her hand from where it still rested on his chest. "I'm not a baby that needs to be looked after." Pulling his flask from out of his pack, he took a long drink.

Lady Kate glanced over to Charka. "I think he'll live."

"He better," their leader replied. "I don't fancy having to haul his carcass back through the Swamp."

Draining the last of the water, Seward flashed him an annoyed look. "You won't have to."

"Good." Charka had just settled down and begun breaking out some rations when the shadows of his two Springers fell upon him. Looking up, he glanced to Jaikus who was slightly more forward than Reneeke. "Yes?"

"We, uh," Jaikus said before pausing a moment to clear his throat. "We were wondering if you wouldn't mind if me and Reneeke did a little more exploring."

"Haven't you lads had enough for one day?"

"We thought to have a look through that building I investigated this morning."

Acquiring a stern look, Charka's glance passed from one Springer to the other, then he chuckled. "I suppose you can't get into too much trouble, seeing as how we have already gone through there a couple of times. It should be safe."

Jaikus' eyes lit up. "Thank you, sir."

Charka nodded. "Be back by sundown."

"We will," he assured their leader. Then indicating for Reneeke to follow, Jaikus said, "Come on, Rene."

As they rushed off to explore on their own, Lady Kate moved to sit next to Charka. "Think they will find anything?"

"No. But I well understand the need compelling them." He watched the pair disappear before starting in on a package of trail rations.

Before they entered through what Jaikus now understood to be a window, Reneeke insisted they secure themselves together with one of their ropes. When it looked as if Jaikus was about to object, Reneeke reminded him that the rope had already saved his life once. "Despite Charka's assurance that this building is secure, I would feel better if we used the rope."

Jaikus gave in and tied the rope around his middle.

Since the lantern had remained back at camp, they each lit one of their torches supplied by Bella. Then with Jaikus taking the lead, they entered the building and quickly passed through the room with the mural depicting a keep under siege. After that, he made a beeline for the darkened area that earlier he had figured to be a way down. He wasn't disappointed. A spiral series of steps led to the unknown depths below.

"Isn't this great?" he asked as he quickly began taking the steps down. The sheer ancientness of the place made him giddy with excitement.

Reneeke nodded. "Yeah." In the back of his mind, he knew they wouldn't find anything as Charka and his crew had already covered this area. But there was still an element of thrill in the hunt.

They descended the steps to the next level, only to discover they continued still farther. "Let's see how far down we can go," suggested Jaikus.

Shrugging, Reneeke replied, "Sure."

After giving the room on this new level only a cursory examination, Jaikus continued down the steps to the third level. Again, the steps continued down where they ended at the fourth and Jaikus pressed on.

"We're quite a ways down now," stated Reneeke as he left the steps and entered the fourth level. Jaikus simply nodded as he took a quick look around.

The room was of average size with a single doorway looming in one wall. Naught but dust and a carcass left behind by a long ago scavenger was to be found. Jaikus moved to the doorway and passed through into a hallway lined with doorways spaced every twenty feet or so.

Pausing at the first, he moved his torch within the room and saw where dirt had cascaded through a window from the outside to form a large mound on one side. A brief glance at the rest of the room revealed nothing of interest.

Moving on, he encountered further rooms that must have been located along the outer perimeter of the building as each bore windows and held similar mounds of earth. After the tenth such room, they encountered another series of steps down. Jaikus glanced to Reneeke who nodded for him to continue.

They descended deeper beneath the surface; making their way down to the fifth level, then the sixth, until finally coming out into a room on the seventh.

"Can you believe it, Rene? We've come down almost a hundred feet."

"I wonder how much farther until we reach what would have been ground level in Sythal's time?"

"I don't know."

Level seven was little different than the ones preceding it. The only real difference was that the passageway leading from the room was slightly wider. Such a change could possibly indicate that they were getting close to the original "ground level."

Not far after leaving the room, they came upon a gaping hole where the floor should have been. The hole was roughly the same size as the trap that had attempted to drop Jaikus to his death. Moving to the edge, they peered down into the shadowy depths below.

"Think there could be treasure down there like last time?"

Reneeke shrugged. "Possibly."

Jaikus laid his torch so the burning end extended past the lip of the opening. "Lower me down."

Reneeke set his torch down as well, then grasped the rope. Once Jaikus had swung his lower half from the passageway and into the opening, Reneeke started lowering him down.

This trap's shaft wasn't nearly as deep as the other, merely fifteen feet. Aside from the two dozen, foot and a half barbed spikes set in the floor of the shaft to impale the unwary, there was naught to find but a single, human skull skewered by one of the spikes.

Disappointed, Jaikus hollered up to Reneeke, "Nothing here. Lift me back up." As he neared the top, he heard Reneeke say, "Can't expect to find treasure all the time."

"No. But it would be nice to bring *something* away."

"If you expect to do that, we first need to find an area Charka has yet to explore." Reaching down, he took Jaikus' hand and hauled him the rest of the way out.

"How do you propose we do that?"

Reneeke shrugged. "Haven't a clue."

Leaping across the opening, they continued down to the next doorway. There, they discovered another windowed room full of dirt. Only this time, the window was not completely clogged with earth. In the lower left corner, a small hole had been bored out by what may have been some small, burrowing animal, and not that long ago either. For beneath the hole, loose dirt cascaded its way to the floor. Jaikus entered the room to give the hole a more thorough inspection.

He was no stranger to gophers, moles, and other burrowing animals, they were enemy number one when you lived on a farm. Though he couldn't tell exactly which one had made the hole, he was certain that the hole couldn't have been more than a day old.

Moving the torch so its light could pierce the hole's dark interior in full measure, he peered down its length. Three feet in, something glittered in the torchlight. Excitement!

"There's something in there!" Jaikus cried.

"What?" Stepping closer, Reneeke tried to see what had caused Jaikus to get all excited. When his friend moved aside to allow him to peer into the small tunnel, he saw where the glittering object was still buried within the earth filling the window. That only a very small portion was visible. However, that small portion glittered like gold.

Jaikus stuck the end of his torch in the pile of earth beneath the window. "Give me a hand," he said as he grabbed a rock and began scrapping dirt from out of the window.

Picking up a flat rock suitable for excavation, Reneeke set to with gusto. "I bet Charka never knew this was here."

"No way," agreed Jaikus. Excited with the untold possibilities of what it could be, he scrapped with fevered enthusiasm.

Dirt flew and the pile beneath the window grew larger. The hole widened until they were finally able to excavate the dirt surrounding the glittering object. It was revealed to be a hand, a human hand.

As more dirt was removed, the hand turned into an arm. The arm in turn was attached to an upper torso. Removing still more dirt revealed a head attached to the torso.

"It's a statue," announced Reneeke. Covered in dirt, his dust-tinged face streaked with rivulets of sweat, he grinned. "I don't think we'll be able to carry it out, Jaik."

"What do you mean?"

"A statue of that size, made entirely of gold, would weigh far too much for us to move, let alone haul it up eight flights of steps."

"Oh, come on. It can't be that heavy!" Encouraging his friend to move aside with a well placed nudge, Jaikus crawled into the recently excavated cavity and grasped the hand. He shook it, causing clods of dirt to be dislodged. "See?" he said. "I can move it." Then, giving it one last shake, he started backing out of the cavity when the hand moved.

In stunned silence, Jaikus watched as the portion of the statue they had thus far uncovered shook, then toppled backward. He could hear a solid thud as the statue came to land somewhere below.

"Rene!" Jaikus shouted.

"What did you do?"

"I...I don't know. Hand me one of the torches."

When Reneeke passed him the burning brand, Jaikus climbed further into the hole with torch held before him. "Oh man, Reneeke." Voice filled with awe, he glanced back over his shoulder. "You have *got* to see this." Scooting forward, he disappeared into the hole.

A circle of over a dozen statues, each looking to be constructed of solid gold, leaned toward a central point at a roughly forty-five degree slant. Their upper ends had come to rest against the bole of what appeared to once have been a massive tree. Its upper reaches couldn't be seen as an earthen dome had formed over the backs of the statues, leaving an open area beneath.

Half a dozen other, smaller statues were either standing, or lying, within the dome's interior. Three others were partially encased within the earthen wall of the dome, just like the first one had been before Jaikus dislodged it, causing it to topple over.

Sliding down the embankment to the area below, Reneeke said, "This is incredible." The reflected light from the golden silhouettes gave the area a surreal glow.

"How much do you suppose these would be worth?"

"More than a man could ever hope to spend," replied Reneeke. "Though I doubt if any of these could be brought to the surface." Stepping toward a small statue of a fawn, he tried lifting it. Strain though he might, all he managed to accomplish was to rock it slightly on its base. "Far too heavy."

"Too bad."

Jaikus went to the bole of the tree and was surprised to find it rock-like. "This is stone!"

"It is?" Leaving the fawn statue, Reneeke joined his friend at the tree. Running his hand along its surface, he nodded. "It sure enough is."

"A tree statue?" questioned Jaikus.

Shrugging, Reneeke replied, "Why not?"

Turning his gaze toward the statues forming the ribcage of the dome, he shuddered at the thought that they were watching them. Why he felt that way he didn't know.

"We must be at ground level," surmised Reneeke. "This may have been a garden, or maybe a plaza at one time."

"I wish there was more here than just statues," Jaikus complained. "A ring, or better yet, a sword like yours would be great."

"True. Though we couldn't keep it."

"Why not?"

"Anything we find belongs to the group," explained Reneeke. Jaikus made a rude noise. Reneeke fixed his gaze upon his friend. "That is what we agreed to, and that is what we will *do*."

Jaikus frowned, but finally nodded beneath Reneeke's withering gaze. "I suppose."

They spent some time going over the statues and testing the earthen wall of the dome, though not too intrusively. The last thing they wanted was for the dome to lose cohesion and crash down upon their heads. When they failed to turn up anything, they made their way back through the window.

"Sythal must have been a great place to live in its day," observed Reneeke. Following Jaikus from the room, he allowed him to take the lead.

"You may be right." Not really thinking about what his friend was saying, Jaikus instead had visions of hidden areas secreted in the building's basement. "Wonder if we can find another stairway leading down?" he mused. A short time later, they did.

It was after coming across what had once been the entrance hall. Most of the large room was choked with earth, having come through the massive opening that at one time must have held a pair of double doors. They followed one of the several passageways still opened to them from the hall and came to a fair sized room to which three other, smaller rooms were attached. It was in the middle room of the three that they discovered the stairwell; a flight of narrow, stone steps descending in a tight spiral.

Before they went down, Reneeke took a moment to study the floor area surrounding the stairwell entrance. When he saw the holes where hinges had once been attached, he nodded to himself. "I thought so."

"You thought what?" questioned Jaikus.

"Oh, that there was a trapdoor here. Whether it was hidden at one time or not is hard to tell." He flashed Jaikus a grin. "I like it when I'm right."

"Aren't you always?"

Reneeke laughed. "You know me better than that."

Jaikus joined in with laughter of his own. "Even still, you *are* right more often than I am."

"You simply need to take the time to see what's before you. Why, just take a look…"

"Not again, *please*," he interjected, cutting his friend off. Reneeke had for years tried to explain how and why he did things, explanations that did little to improve the way Jaikus saw the world. He simply figured Reneeke was smarter than he about such things and left it at that.

Jaikus took the lead as they headed down to what he hoped to be the dungeon, or basement. *What treasures could be waiting in the dark for a pair of intrepid adventurers to uncover? Jewels? Gold? Magic rings?* How he had always wished to have a magic ring all his own.

Spiraling around three times, they finally came out at a passageway extending straight ahead. As they made their way from the stairwell,

Jaikus' torch illuminated something they hadn't seen before in all of Sythal: a door.

True, there wasn't much left of it. Constructed entirely out of metal as it was, the door sat skewed in a doorway with a covering of rust reminiscent of an animal's fur coat. Jaikus drew his knife and tapped upon the door with the tip. The door disintegrated with the first blow to collapse in a cloud of rust.

Taken by surprise, Jaikus jumped backward as the cloud of rust spread throughout the passageway. "I guess that's why we haven't come across any other doors," he surmised.

"Yeah," agreed Reneeke.

Once the rust cloud settled, Jaikus moved to the doorway and extended his torch through to the room beyond. As he made to enter, Reneeke grabbed him by the shoulder and pulled him back. "We need to be extra careful from here on out."

"Why?"

"I don't think Charka and the others ever made it down here," he explained. When confusion appeared on his friend's face, he explained. "The door, Jaik. If they had come this way, they would have been the ones to have caused its collapse, not you. I seriously doubt if Charka would have forwent taking a look at this room because he didn't want to ruin a door."

"You mean, there could be treasure down here?" he asked excitedly.

Reneeke nodded. "Treasure, *and traps*. Keep in mind, Jaik, that we don't have any healing scrolls or potions should things go badly for us. And it's a long way back to the surface."

Jaikus took a moment to digest that. When he was done, he said, "Let's go until we find something. Then we'll head back to the surface."

"Okay. It's probably getting late anyway. Just be careful."

"You worry too much."

Reneeke's eyebrows creased in a frown as he asked, "After what we've been through today…?"

Turning back to the doorway, Jaikus stepped over the remains of the door and into the room. He could feel tension on the rope as Reneeke kept a firm hold on it in the event Jaikus ran into trouble.

Evenly spaced recesses dotted the wall across from the doorway as well as the walls to the right and left. Each wall held four, two rows of two, one atop the other. In the dim torchlight, they could make out that each recess contained something. Eager to discover what awaited them, Jaikus crossed over to the *quad* in the wall opposite the doorway.

Three held mounds of red powder, the remains of metal having long succumbed to rust. The fourth held a crude black stone. As it was almost an exact duplicate of the stone Lady Kate's spell had indicated was cursed back in the underground room, Jaikus decided to play it safe and pass it by. After all, there were still eight more recesses to check.

Next he headed over to the right side and found only disappointment. Each of those four recesses held nothing but mounds of powder. One mound still retained the shape of the object it had once been: a small, curve-bladed knife. Jaikus blew on the knife's shape causing a small cloud of rust to fill the recess.

On his way over to the left side of the room, he glanced to where Reneeke waited in the doorway. "Nothing," he announced. "Not one thing has survived intact except one of those black, lumpy stones like what that golden naked-man statue had held in the palm of his hand."

"The cursed stone?"

Jaikus nodded. "I thought it best not to touch it."

"Good thinking. We'll have to let Charka know it's down here so maybe he could recover it on his next trip."

The remaining four recesses held but four more piles of rest as well. Jaikus was not happy. He had figured to have come away with at least something after all this.

"Are you ready to head back up to the surface?" inquired Reneeke.

"Not yet, no," he replied as he made his way from the room and re-entered the passageway. "Let's see what's at the end, first." Taking the lead once more, Jaikus proceeded down the passageway.

The next room yielded nothing of interest, and the one after that was just as void of treasure. Hoping the third to hold something of interest, he hurried along, a little too fast as it turned out. For just before reaching the doorway, the floor fell away beneath him.

Screaming, his arms and legs flailed wildly before the rope snapped taut. The suddenness of the halt brought his outcry to an end with an, *"Oof."* As he crashed against the side of the shaft, the torch slipped from his grip.

"Are you okay?" came Reneeke's voice from above.

It took a second or two before he could get his wind back. "A bit sore around the middle from the rope, but I would rather have that, than hitting the bottom." Glancing downward, he saw where the torch struck the bottom some forty feet below. This was a deep one!

"Do you want me to pull you up?"

Jaikus searched the floor at the bottom before answering. He could see the barbed spikes protruding upward to snare the unlucky that ran afoul of the trap. In the flickering torchlight, it looked as if there might be something down there, but it was hard to tell. The shadows kept shifting about as the torch's flame flickered wildly.

Maybe it was his turn to be observant, or perhaps it was simply the years spent with Reneeke that caused a thought to cross his mind. "Rene?

Should a torch be burning quietly, or wildly when it sits at the bottom of a hole?"

"It should burn fairly steady. Why?"

"The torch slipped from my hand and is now lying down there. The flame is whipping around pretty good."

"The only thing that would cause such an occurrence is a breeze, and you don't get those at the bottom of a hole," Reneeke explained.

"Unless there is some sort of access at the bottom, like a tunnel?"

There was quiet for a moment before Reneeke, replied, "I take it you want me to lower you down?"

"Is there enough rope? It's still forty feet to the bottom."

Another silence, then, "I think so. It will be close."

"Then lower me down."

—12—

At the bottom he found a narrow opening, barely wide enough for him to pass. The breeze was coming from there.

His torch lay among dust, dirt, and naught else. Unlike the pit Reneeke had earlier investigated, during which he had found his sword, this pit was lacking in victims. Either it had yet to claim any, or they had been removed.

After retrieving his torch, he crossed the spike-covered floor to peer into the opening. A narrow passageway extended barely eight feet before turning sharply to the right.

Turning his attention to the rope tied about his waist, he gauged there to be roughly three feet of slack. "Can you lower down any more rope?" he hollered. "I need at least another ten feet."

"Sorry, Jaik. I'm at the end as it is."

Jaikus was beginning to contemplate removing the rope when Reneeke said, "Don't you have a rope too? You could tie the two together. That should give you all the play you need."

Good ole, Reneeke. He could always count on him to come up with a solution. "Yes, I do."

"Once you tie them together, I'll pull up the slack then let it out as needed."

"Good idea."

Quickly removing the rope from around his waist, he pulled his rope from out of his pack and secured an end to Reneeke's. "It's done. Pull it up." While the rope began to be drawn to the passageway above, Jaikus secured the other end around his waist. He didn't have long to wait before Reneeke had taken up all the slack.

Two quick tugs on the rope signaled that Reneeke was ready.

"Don't let go!" He waited long enough to hear Reneeke's *"I won't"* before entering the passageway. From above, Reneeke played out the rope just enough to keep it semi-taut.

Jaikus felt truly alone for the first time as he entered that passageway. Even though Reneeke stood above with rope in hand to pull him out should the situation warrant, he felt isolated.

Perhaps it was the confined feeling the narrow passageway produced, or maybe the fact that he was in a dark, unknown place with no other human in sight that played upon his nerves. But whatever it was, he felt decidedly uncomfortable.

Upon reaching where the passageway crooked to the right, he saw something white lying along the floor just around the bend. It was a leg bone, one of two attached to a complete, human skeleton.

Both legs showed multiple breakages, as did the right arm. The left was stretched above the head, almost as if this person had crawled along and died in the process. Jaikus figured the long dead human to be one who had succumbed to the trap. Having survived the fall, the person had tried to make it out, only to die in the attempt.

Lying next to the skeleton was a sword whose metal had only begun to be ravaged by rust. Stepping upon it with his foot, Jaikus discovered the blade still retained its strength. He found that curious, as every other blade in this long forgotten city had been reduced to rust. This person, like himself, had to have come along at a later time. Interesting.

Aside from the sword, there were metal snaps from what used to be clothing, the material being no longer present. Also, intermixed with the pelvic bones were three small gems, a score of coins varying from copper to gold, and a silver ring. Jaikus gasped when he saw the ring and immediately picked it up.

"I wonder what you do?" he asked as he held it close. There was a single strip of a red metal running along the outer side which was the ring's sole marking. He slipped the ring, gems, and coins into his pouch and thought about continuing down the passage to see what else there may be, when, for a fleeting moment, he caught sight of movement in the shadows ahead.

He froze. His sense of isolation increased tenfold. Sweat broke out on his forehead as he stood still and tried to pierce the darkness for another glimpse of what had moved. Could it have been his imagination? Deciding not to tempt fate any further, he began backing up.

"Yes," he said quietly to himself, "I think it may be time to return to the surface."

Backing away, he held his torch aloft as he kept constant vigil upon the darkness. There was no scent other than that of the earth being borne upon the breeze coming from farther down the passageway. So it couldn't be an animal. Then he came up with the thought: *whatever it was, it couldn't be alive!*

Visions of ghouls, specters, and other nefarious spirits generated an increase in his backward momentum. Imagination running wild, he turned and raced around the corner back toward the shaft.

"Rene!" he shouted. *"Get me out of here!"*

He tossed the torch in amongst the floor spikes, and then gripped the rope with both hands as Reneeke began hauling him out.

Terror filled him as he slowly began to rise. Images of ghastly hands reaching for his dangling feet prompted him to shout, *"Hurry!"* From above he heard Reneeke holler back, "I'm going as fast as I can, Jaik," as he continued his steady, upward ascent.

It was with great relief when he reached the top and Reneeke gripped him by his pack to haul him the rest of the way out.

"What happened?" his friend asked, concern and worry etched upon his brow.

"I...I thought I saw something."

*"Some*thing?"

Jaikus nodded. "In the darkness. Something moved!"

"Are you sure?"

"Yes. Rene, I wouldn't make up something like this."

"All right, calm down." Moving to the side of the shaft, he looked down to the torch burning far below. "I don't see anything moving now."

Coming to stand next to his friend, Jaikus gazed down to see for himself.

Seconds ticked by and nothing appeared. Jaikus was beginning to think it had been nothing more than an overactive imagination when they saw the torch move. It jerked back and forth, paused a moment, then slid across the floor to disappear into the narrow opening.

"...and me and Rene got out of there as fast as we could," concluded Jaikus.

After returning to camp, they had spent the last hour regaling the others as to their adventure and what they had found. This last episode produced a guffaw from Seward.

"Probably a mole-rat," he explained. "We've seen them a time or two while exploring the lower recesses of Sythal."

"Would a mole-rat grab hold of a burning torch?" asked Jaikus. "None that I've ever heard of."

"Hmmm, possibly," replied Charka. "Though I agree with you that it is unlikely. But it is even more unlikely that you came across a member of the undead world. If you had, it wouldn't have been content to merely allow you to catch a glimpse of it. It would have come and introduced itself in unpleasant ways."

"You got that right," agreed Seward. "The undead hate the living and will seek to destroy those that still retain life whenever possible."

Charka nodded. "Now, let's see those coins and gems."

Jaikus emptied the items onto the ground between them. All that was, but the ring. Not even Reneeke knew about it, and he intended to keep it that way. Reneeke would make him hand it over.

"Not bad," said Lady Kate, "for your first solo adventure." Glancing to Charka, she asked, "Don't you think we can allow them to keep this?"

A frown creased their leader's brow. "I suppose so. It isn't worth much anyway."

Jaikus' eyes lit up. "Really?"

"Yes, lad. It's yours."

"All right!" Scooping up the coins and gems, he slipped them in his pouch, an act which caused Charka's frown to deepen.

Jaikus caught the change in expression and glanced to the others who wore similar expressions of disapproval. "What?"

"Look, boy," Seward began, "you didn't find those all by your lonesome. Shouldn't you share them with your friend?" His nod toward Reneeke left no doubt as to what he and the others were thinking.

"What? Of course I am going to share with Reneeke. I wouldn't think of doing otherwise."

"Jaik wouldn't hold out on me," stated Reneeke. "He and I share everything, right Jaik? No secrets between us."

"Uh, yeah. Right." His hand unconsciously went into his pocket where he was keeping the silver ring. He almost pulled it out and announced that he had it. Almost. He simply could not take the chance of Charka demanding that he hand it over. So with feelings of guilt, he divvied up the coins and gems, giving the lion's share to Reneeke.

After a brief session of going over in greater detail their time spent with the golden statues, and Charka making sure he understood enough about how they reached that area so he could find it on a subsequent venture, they turned in. Everyone was tired, especially Seward who had already nodded off.

Jaikus volunteered for the first watch, with Reneeke taking the second, and Charka finishing out the watch schedule at the end. Lady Kate and Seward would be allowed to get a full measure of rest in anticipation for the return journey in the morning.

While everyone settled into their bedrolls and drifted off to sleep, Jaikus pulled out his ring and almost slipped it onto his finger. Memories of the curse that befell Seward stopped him before completing the maneuver. He intended to find out what properties it held, for good or bad, before putting it on.

All in all, this had been a good Adventure, much better than even his wildest dreams could have come up with. And they had survived! Grinning, he slipped the ring back in his pocket and began pacing the perimeter. When it was time for Reneeke's turn, he woke his friend and turned in.

The first rays of morning crept across the land until finally falling upon five, sleeping forms. A sixth sat before the campfire watching a pot of stew as it grew warm for breakfast. Charka added a few more trail rations and half a flask of water so there would be enough for all once the others awoke.

Nearby, Master Hymal lay beneath a blanket, three full packs lying on the ground beside him. He had wandered into camp not long after Charka had taken over the watch and promptly went to sleep without a word.

From past trips to Sythal, Charka knew a little of what the bags contained, but not in any great detail. There were some things Hymal avoided speaking of, and the reagents he harvested was one.

His two Springers, after a rocky beginning, had turned out to be a boon. Having been responsible for the majority of treasure they would be returning with, he couldn't see himself denying even the smaller one a chance to join the Guild. Of course, just because he put them forward for membership, it didn't follow that their acceptance was assured. There were other considerations to be taken into account. Still, he would do what he could.

Not long after the stew began bubbling and was ready to eat, the rest of the sleepers began to awaken. True to form, Hymal was the last to shake sleep's grasp.

"Ready for the return trip, Master Hymal?"

The apothecary nodded. "Yes. I was most fortunate in the reagents I found." Which is what he always said, never expounding on what he meant.

The two Springers joined them for stew. During which, Charka filled Hymal in on the highlights of the adventure, spending an extra long time detailing Seward's brush with the cursed gems. "I have half a mind to bring a cleric along next time to see if we can't lift the curse."

Shrugging, the apothecary replied, "Up to you. Just so long as you deliver me here and bring me back in one piece."

"Can we come?" asked Jaikus.

"Sorry, lad. I won't have need of you."

Jaikus was seriously disappointed. Despite his time as a Springer, he had rather enjoyed adventuring with *Charka's Troupe*.

"I'm sure we can find something equally exciting to do," added Reneeke. "Perhaps an adventure with less risk to life, limb…" then with a glance to Seward, added, "and health."

"There are plenty out there, that's for sure," agreed their leader.

Once the meal was over and the pots cleaned for travel, they began their return through Sythal's ruins. When they drew close to the fringe area, Charka had them pause and secure themselves with rope.

Jaikus hated this part. Passing through Sythal's fringe was disorienting and frustrating. And the return trip proved to be just as bad as going in had been. He kept count, and by the time Charka announced that they had cleared the fringe area, Jaikus had been brought up short by the rope a total of nine times when the protective properties of the fringe caused him to wander off on a tangent. Reneeke claimed a solid baker's dozen.

Three nights in the Swamp, and they would be back at Reakla. Jaikus couldn't wait to return and have Charka fulfill his vow to see they became members of the Guild. But first, they had to make it out of the Swamp. And if the inbound trip had been any indication, they should have very little trouble.

Their first day back through the Swamp was stressful as trolls seemed to be in greater abundance than their inbound trip. Each time one was spotted, they remained still and quiet until the beast had wandered off. Jaikus endured stares promising retribution during each encounter, but he had learned his lesson and no longer sought to incur an attack.

The second day was less stressful as troll encounters fell off dramatically. There were but two sightings, one they were forced to fight as their scent had been detected. But since it was but a single beast, they readily dispatched it.

It was during the late afternoon of the third day, about an hour or so before they would have planned to make camp, when things got interesting.

Jaikus and Reneeke were bringing up the rear. Reneeke led the mules while Jaikus regaled him with yet another rehashing of their adventure in the bowels of Sythal.

"I tell you, Reneeke, we need to find a way back there somehow." Ever since leaving the ancient city, Jaikus has been hot to return. "There's no telling what we could find there if we but had the time."

"First of all, Jaik, you would have to discover a way to even find the place. I for one couldn't even begin to retrace our steps. Secondly, a way must be found to bypass the misdirecting wards that seek to lead us astray. You figure out how to do those two things, and I'll return with you."

Jaikus rolled his eyes. "I'm not saying we are going to return there next week, or even this year. But *someday* we will, Rene. Someday."

Reneeke couldn't help but crack a smile at his friend's enthusiasm.

The others were some distance ahead. As the *Troupe* was beginning to leave behind the worst of the bogs, muck, and mire of the Swamp, things had grown lax. Jaikus and Reneeke had gradually fallen behind so they could talk without fear of being overheard by the others.

Currently, they were making their way along a fairly wide expanse of dry, level ground that ran alongside a small, stagnant pond. The mirror-glass smoothness of the water reflected the thinning forest of moss-covered trees. It was really quite a peaceful locale. At least it was, until a roar heralded the descent of a young mossback from out of a tree to land upon Master Hymal's horse.

Razor-sharp teeth and curved, dagger-like claws raked into the horse's flanks. Master Hymal was thrown free as his horse reared and bucked in an attempt to dislodge the beast. But, before anyone could react, the mossback had completely eviscerated the poor horse.

"No!" cried the apothecary as the severely injured horse managed to win its freedom and bolted away with unbelievable speed. With entrails trailing along behind, Hymal's horse didn't get far before collapsing, but it did progress far enough for it to no longer be the focus of the mossback's attention. With the horse having fled the attack, the mossback turned its attention upon the next closest victim: Master Hymal.

"Stay with the mules," shouted Reneeke as soon as the horse bolted. He handed the mules' reins to Jaikus. Then drawing his sword, he rushed forward to join the melee.

"Rene, no!" cried Jaikus, but it was too late. His friend was already on his way.

Lady Kate's fire bolts impacted along the creature's side in an attempt to draw its attention from the apothecary, but had little effect. The mossback's hide was much too tough and it simply ignored the attack. Snarling, it continued its forward charge.

"To me!" cried a much revitalized Seward. The last two days of travel had done much to return his strength to normal. Wielding sword and shield, he interposed his body between the apothecary and the charging beast. Seward struck the beast a resounding blow along the side of the head, but all his efforts did was elicit a swipe by one of its massive claws. Striking dead center on his shield, the blow knocked him back a step.

Master Hymal was in full flight; the mossback hot on his tail.

Before Reneeke could reach the battle, Charka pulled forth an oil bladder from his pack. *"Kate!"* he shouted, then threw, aiming so the bladder would land in front of the mossback.

His aim was true and the bladder fell between the mossback and its prey. Just prior to it striking the ground, Lady Kate cast a fireball which detonated with the bladder, igniting the oil mere feet before the mossback's snout.

The sudden conflagration caused the beast to halt its forward charge, rear back, and then race off to the side.

Reneeke was now closing fast on the creature. He saw how it turned from the flames with fear maddened eyes. "You didn't like that, did you?" he mumbled to himself.

"Get back, boy," Seward shouted as he and Reneeke came abreast of each other.

The mossback had maneuvered around the burning area and was still closing on the apothecary.

"I can help."

"You'll just get yourself killed."

Ignoring him, Reneeke sprinted ahead to leave Seward struggling to keep up.

"Charka!" screamed Hymal. *"Do something!"* Fleeing for his life, he darted around dead and dying trees. From not very far behind him, he could hear the mossback crashing through the underbrush in pursuit.

Lady Kate cast her *Webs of Binding* around the rear legs of the mossback, causing the creature to slow, but not stopping it. Its powerful hindquarters were strong enough to work against the potency of the webbing, enabling the creature to continue the attack.

"Hyah!" shouted Reneeke in an attempt to draw the creature's attention from the apothecary. Seeing it slowed by the webbing, he raised his sword and quickly closed the distance.

"Reneeke!" Charka shouted as he rounded the other side of the conflagration. "Fall back!"

Ignoring his cries, the farm boy from Running Brook hollered at the top of his lungs. Having come within striking distance, he leapt forward to land a fell blow with his sword. Using both hands, he brought it down on an area a little up from where the tail merged with the back.

The creature screamed in pain as the blade parted its hide. To Reneeke's disbelief, the blade sank in deeply, far deeper than he would have thought possible. Flesh and bone parted until the mossback's hind legs collapsed when the blade severed the lower end of the spinal column. His sword was yanked from his grasp when the powerful forelegs twisted its body about so its head was now facing Reneeke.

It seemed for a moment as if the passage of time was suspended; Reneeke stood weaponless facing off against the mossback whose forelegs were readying to lurch forward. Then, time resumed with Seward's appearance at Reneeke's side.

"Get out of the way!" he cried, shoving Reneeke to the side with the front of his shield. In that moment, when his shield was busy knocking aside Reneeke, the mossback sprung.

Leaping forward with incredible speed, it slammed into Seward. The force of the impact knocked him back a foot, and together, he and the beast crashed to the ground. Claws raked across Seward's armor. The creature's first blow created furrows in the leather, the second peeled it off.

Seward tried to interpose his shield between his body and deadly claws, but they were too close for that to work. Then there was pain.

"Die!"

Coming up behind the creature, Charka leapt into the air with sword gripped in both hands. Bringing down the weapon with both hands, he impaled the creature through the opening Reneeke's strike had created. Angling the blade so it would progress toward the chest cavity, he was rewarded by a piercing squeal. A shudder ran through the creature and its forward body began convulsing.

Reneeke quickly moved to grab Seward's hand and pull him from beneath the creature while it was distracted. The sight of his man almost made him retch. Blood was everywhere. When he pulled, Seward screamed in pain. Unwilling to stop as the creature's thrashing posed a greater risk than what he may be doing to him, Reneeke pulled all the harder and slid him free.

"Gods," he exclaimed when he saw how the front portion of his armor had been ripped asunder. Flayed skin was intermixed with the shredded leather, and he could even see the white of bone underneath.

"Kate!" In the heat of the moment, he neglected to add the honorific. He dragged Seward until the injured man was completely free of any danger posed by the death-throes of the mossback.

She appeared beside him. "Remove his armor. *Quickly!*"

While Reneeke worked to get the gory mess off the man, she upended her pack. Potion flasks, scrolls, and a sundry of other items spilled upon the ground. "Is he still alive?" she asked. A loud groan of pain answered her question.

She grabbed one scroll, and as soon as Reneeke removed the remains of Seward's armor, she laid it across his chest and spoke the word of activation. Even before the scroll finished flaring and vanished, she had a second scroll in position. Once its power was activated too, she poured half a healing potion onto the wound, and the other into the unconscious man's mouth.

By this time, the thrashing of the mossback had subsided. Charka, Master Hymal, and Jaikus had gathered around where she worked to keep Seward from expiring.

"Will he live?" asked Jaikus.

"I don't know," she replied. Then glancing to Charka she said, "He needs a priest. There is so much damage, I...I don't know if he'll be able to recover."

Charka gauged what remained of the sunlight. "Still two hours until dark, and I figure another six to Reakla. Can we keep him alive that long?"

She nodded. "I think so."

He turned to his two Springers. "Put him on a mule and let's go."

"Bind his chest, first," said Lady Kate. "Or the ride will more than likely kill him."

"Yes, ma'am," replied Reneeke.

Master Hymal came and laid a hand on Charka's shoulder. "I hope your man lives."

"So do I." Seward looked none too good. Now unconscious, the pallor of his face was very pasty.

Reneeke had just set Jaikus to tearing one of their bedrolls into strips to be used in binding Seward's chest when a curse from Master Hymal drew everyone's attention.

Standing near the spot where his horse had collapsed after being disemboweled, the apothecary was swearing a blue streak. He turned toward Charka, face filled with rage. "My reagents! *They're gone!*"

Not only were his reagents gone, but the entire horse to which they had been attached was gone as well. A bloody trail was evident. Starting from where the horse had collapsed, it then traveled all the way to the water's edge. From there, it worked its way around the shoreline until disappearing into the trees farther down. Something had dragged it away while they were distracted by the rampaging mossback.

Turning to Charka, Master Hymal said, "I demand you retrieve them."

"My man needs a priest or he's going to die," he replied. "We dare not spend the time to hunt for something that may never be found."

"We have a contract!"

"*Yes*, to escort you safely to and from Sythal. We do ***not*** have one to chase after what looks to be an adult mossback, on the *off chance* it *hasn't* dragged its dinner, carcass and all, to the bottom of some pond." Scanning the area from where the horse had been dragged, he nodded. "From the tracks, I'd say it's a rather *large* mossback. It would have to be considering it was able to drag away your horse."

Reneeke listened to the exchange while binding Seward's chest. Once he and Jaikus had the man up and secured to the back of a mule, he left Seward in the care of Lady Kate, then walked over to where the two men were standing toe to toe.

"Seward's ready," he announced.

Charka glanced to him and nodded. "My thanks, lad."

"Are you going after my reagents?" asked Hymal.

"No."

"Then I consider this a breach of contract."

"Take it up with the Guild," replied Charka. "I have a life to save." Then turning his back on the apothecary, he stalked away.

"What does it mean when there is a breach of contract?" Reneeke asked Master Hymal.

"It means that he failed to live up to his side of our agreement."

"But if your reagents were recovered, then there wouldn't be a problem, right?"

The apothecary glanced to the young man before him. "True."

"Rene, what are you thinking?" asked Jaikus, though he already knew the answer. Before he could stop his friend, Reneeke said, "Jaik and I will recover them for you."

Charka paused in mid-stride and spun about. "Are you out of your mind? The two of you, against a fully grown mossback?"

Master Hymal ignored him. "Do you mean it?"

Reneeke nodded. "If it is possible, we shall recover your reagents." Jaikus didn't look thrilled at the prospect of going off into the Swamp on their own.

Stalking back, Charka rounded on Reneeke and demanded, "How do you expect to make it back? Can you even find your way to Reakla?"

Pointing off through the Swamp, Reneeke asked, "It's that way, right?"

"Correct," answered Master Hymal.

Charka scowled. "Boy, you've lost your senses."

"I do not plan on engaging the mossback," he explained. "Merely track it and recover Master Hymal's packs from the carcass."

Lady Kate came forward leading the two mules. Seward was slumped across the neck of one. "If we wish Seward to live, we best leave now."

"Right you are." Then to Master Hymal, Charka asked, "Do you plan to accompany us back to Reakla, or would you rather remain with our two, completely inexperienced and most likely soon-to-be-dead, Springers?"

To Reneeke, Master Hymal asked, "*Can* you recover my reagents?"

"Unless the carcass has been taken somewhere we can't follow, then yes."

"Like at the bottom of a bog or something," added Jaikus, just on the off chance they failed to retrieve the aforementioned packs.

"There are three packs that contain reagents," said the apothecary. "Return with them and I'll give you lads a bonus."

"Bonus?" queried Jaikus. The prospect of trailing a mossback lost a great deal of its terror at the mention of a bonus.

"Indeed." Then he turned to Charka. "I would be of little help to these lads. I shall return with you."

"As you wish." Then to his Springers he said, "You two be careful. It's better to come back empty handed, than not come back at all."

"Don't worry about us. We won't take any unnecessary chances," Reneeke assured him.

Lady Kate opened her pack and handed him two flasks. "These are our last two healing potions. Take them."

Reneeke hesitated. "Won't Seward need them?"

She shook her head. "We still have three scrolls. That will be sufficient to see him to Reakla."

Jaikus quickly snatched the flasks from her hand and slipped them into his pack. "Thank you."

"If you make it back, stop by the Guild," Charka said. "I'll leave word where we can be located."

"Yes, sir."

"And good luck, boys. You two have more brass than any Springer I ever had."

"Thank you," replied Jaikus with a smile.

And with that, Charka took the reins of the second mule and turned to begin the trek back to Reakla.

Lady Kate gave them both a quick embrace. "May the gods be with you."

"And with you, Lady."

She smiled and nodded as she hurried to catch up with Charka and the apothecary. Setting a quick pace, they soon vanished into the trees.

—13—

Standing next to the blood soaked-ground where the horse had collapsed, they saw how the creature had begun dragging the carcass toward the water, but then had altered course and skirted the water's edge.

"I wonder why it didn't drag it into the water?" queried Jaikus.

To illustrate, Reneeke grabbed a stick from off the ground. Then, stabbing an end into one of the many pieces of horseflesh that had been ripped from Master Hymal's steed, flung it into the water. The roiling of the water as the flesh-hungry little fishes tore into it was explanation enough.

"It didn't want to share."

The bank of the stagnant pond was soft, and the mossback's tread had been heavy. Tracking it wasn't going to be an issue. Reneeke shouldered his pack and made sure it rested comfortably.

"Are you sure this is a good idea?" asked Jaikus. "Charka didn't seem to think we have much of a chance."

Pack now situated comfortably, he replied, "He didn't think we had much of a chance as Springers either. Yet here we are."

Slinging his own pack into position, Jaikus said, "This is different, Rene. You saw what that other mossback did to Seward, and that was even *after* you had rendered its back half useless." After a quick, nervous glance toward the trees wherein the mossback they were about to hunt for had gone, he added, "Charka said the one that took off with Master Hymal's reagents was much larger, too."

Reneeke flashed a serious look toward his friend. "Jaik, if we do this and survive, there's no way anyone would bar our admittance into the Guild." Reneeke could see his friend was having some serious reservations about following after the mossback. "I promise that we will not fight anything. We'll simply find out where it took the carcass, wait for it to leave, then retrieve Master Hymal's reagents." Slapping Jaikus on the back, he added, "Piece of cake!"

"I hope so."

"This is what adventuring is all about, right? Risking life and limb for glory?" But then he grew serious. "Unless of course, you have changed your mind about pursuing a life of adventuring? Returning to the farm would be no disgrace."

Jaikus knew that his friend would be more than happy to do just that. Farm life, though, was something Jaikus simply abhorred. "No, I still wish to join the Guild."

Putting hand to hilt, his face twisted into a wry grin. "Alright then. On to adventure?"

"On to adventure."

Reneeke took the lead as they followed the trail left behind by the thieving mossback. Tracking was simple as there were not only the mossback's tracks, but a wide swath of blood-streaked ground courtesy of the eviscerated equine with which the mossback had absconded.

Upon reaching where the trail left the water's edge and moved into the surrounding trees, Reneeke came to a halt. "We need to be extra careful from here on. Coming up on an animal with a fresh kill can often cause it to attack if it thinks its meal is in any way threatened."

"Not to mention the possibility that the scent of fresh blood could draw other creatures in to investigate," added Jaikus.

"Right. So like my father always said when we were on the hunt: *'Keep your eyes open and mouth shut.'*"

Jaikus merely nodded.

The trees they began to pass through were by no means closely packed together, yet it still took them some time before the mossback and its dinner came into view. Upon a knoll rising from a point slightly off-center within another pond, the mossback was in the process of greedily tearing into the horse's flesh. Half of the equine carcass still lay within the water. Reneeke was quick to note the lack of any tell-tale roiling which would indicate the presence of the voracious little fish. He deduced that this must in fact be the lair of the mossback. For with the pond being free of the parasitic little flesh eaters, it could take its ill-gotten bounty through the water to the knoll where it could eat in peace. Also, from atop the knoll, it would have a commanding view of anything enroute that might make an attempt to abscond with its supply of horseflesh.

Halting some distance from the water, the pair crouched down behind the roots of a toppled tree where they could observe the mossback without fear of being seen. "Look there," Reneeke said, pointing to the packs and saddle which were miraculously still attached to the horse.

Jaikus nodded. "But how are we to get them, Rene? That mossback will hear us in the water long before we reach it."

"Could be it will wander off once it's eaten its fill."

Annoyed by the insects buzzing about, not to mention the slight fact that night was rapidly approaching, Jaikus said, "Light's going to be gone soon." Already, the shadows were beginning to deepen. They had an hour before the last traces of daylight would be gone altogether. Maybe not even that long.

Reneeke didn't answer right away. He kept his eyes directed toward the feeding mossback. "You may be right," he finally replied. "But we dare do nothing until it's eaten its fill."

"But, night is almost upon us."

Shrugging, Reneeke said, "So? Night is going to catch us in the Swamp no matter what we do, anyway."

"Then, what *are* we to do?"

He gazed at his friend for a moment before realizing no answer was forthcoming.

Sometime after the sun had set, and before night had a chance to completely take over, the mossback moved off. Sliding from the knoll and into the water, it left the remains of the horse at the water's edge as it disappeared beneath the surface.

Reneeke could sense Jaikus was about to speak, so held up his hand for silence. Eyes scanned the surface of the water. The deepening shadows created a concealing patchwork that shrouded the pond almost to the point where details were lost. Almost.

Accustomed to the ways of animals, especially those inhabiting the mountains near Running Brook, Reneeke knew the mossback probably had a favored resting place that would most likely be both sheltered and secluded. Patience was the key.

A minute ticked by as the shadows continued their descent into full night. Then he saw it, a tell-tale ripple spreading across the pond's surface. It was easy to determine from the ripple's movement where the mossback had settled. Far to their left was a thick patch of moss drooping down from overhanging branches. It was thick enough to hide whatever might be on the other side. It was within that mass of sheltering moss that the creature had gone, he'd bet his life on it.

Pointing toward the moss, he whispered, "It went over there."

Predators, son, are mean and nasty when hungry. But if you wait until their bellies are full, they are prone to be slow and lethargic.

His father's words flitted across his mind as he considered their next course of action. What did he know of mossbacks?

Rene, always know what it is you're hunting. Know what its habits are, what it likes, and what it hates. With his father's words guiding him, he began to recall snippets of previous conversations.

...a mossback's habits were to kill and eat, preferably near water...

...young ones liked to drop out of trees...
...fire....
What did Charka say about mossbacks and fire? "*They don't care much for fire and tend to avoid it whenever possible.*" He remembered very well how the previous mossback had reacted to Lady Kate's fireball.

Turning to Jaikus, he grinned.

"What?"

"I have an idea."

"Is it a good one?"

Reneeke chuckled as he shrugged. "If we survive, yes. If not, no." In the fading light, he could see his friend's frown. With a sweeping gesture to indicate the area about them, Reneeke said, "Help me gather some of this dead brush and I'll explain."

Ten minutes later, they stood at the water's edge. Jaikus wasn't any more enthusiastic for this undertaking than when it first had been explained to him. "We're not going to make it. You know that, Rene." They both were able swimmers. It wasn't the fear of the water that had him concerned. Rather, it was the creature lurking beneath the overhanging moss that terrified him to the verge of calling this off and going home.

In his hands he held four branches. The ends of each had had their combustibility augmented with interwoven bundles containing as much of the dead and dried-out material that could be found.

The plan was simple. They would ignite one branch's bundle of combustible material, then slip into the water and cross to the knoll where they would then get the bags containing Master Hymal's reagents. It was hoped that having just gorged, coupled with the mossback's natural aversion to fire, the creature wouldn't sally forth to investigate what was going on in its pond. Should the first branch burn itself out, the next would be lit, and so forth, until they had returned back across the water and reached the shore.

Reneeke ignored Jaikus' prophecy of doom. Taking one of the four, make-shift super-torches from Jaikus, Reneeke used flint to strike sparks until the material caught. In no time, the fire spread throughout the bundle.

Standing up, he glanced to Jaikus. "Ready?" Chuckling when Jaikus shook his head, he stepped toward the water. "Come on." As Jaikus followed, he gestured to the remaining three branches his friend held. "Keep those dry."

Nodding, Jaikus entered the pond. He gasped at the icy water's first touch. "It's cold, Rene."

"So? Can't be any worse than the mid-week baths your mother gave you." He was, of course, referring to the fact that Jaikus' mother was a firm believer in a regular regimen of *cold* baths. Once a week, his mother

would make him haul buckets of water from the nearby creek for his
bathwater. The coldness was supposed to *'purge'* the evil out of him, as
everyone *knew* that evil spirits came from a place of fire. Therefore, a
good dousing in cold should scare them off. Jaikus' family was a bit
stricter than most when it came to such things.

"Don't remind me." Gritting his teeth, he stayed as close to Reneeke
as he could while making their way toward the knoll.

They kept constant vigil toward the moss-shroud wherein the
mossback lay hidden. Jaikus felt very exposed and vulnerable, feelings
that only increased the more submerged his body became. When the water
reached his chest, he was forced to hold the branches high above his head
to keep them from becoming wet.

"It's still there," commented Reneeke in the quietest of whispers. In
the light from the burning brand held aloft, he watched the hanging moss
and adjacent water for tell-tale signs that the mossback had taken an
interest in what they were doing. Thus far, that area of the pond remained
still and quiet, but he figured such a state would not last for long. They
were even now crossing the halfway point and drawing near to the knoll.

Chin now raised high due to the water's depth, Jaikus worked his way
along the bottom of the stagnant pond. The foulness of the water
occasionally found its way into his mouth, nearly causing him to gag.
What stopped the reflex was his fear that the mossback would take a
greater notice of their presence in its territory.

"Jaik," whispered Reneeke.

So quiet was his voice, that Jaikus almost didn't hear him.

"Hand me another branch." The flames of the one he held had begun
to die. Shadows started regaining lost ground, including that of the
mossback's hideaway.

Already precariously balanced on what he hoped was the branch of a
submerged log, Jaikus tried passing one of the branches to Reneeke. The
slight movement toward his friend caused a foot to slip off the branch, and
under he went.

He didn't panic, as both he and Reneeke were fair swimmers, having
during their youth frolicked in the ponds and lakes near Running Brook.
Reflexes quickly took over, and after locating the bottom, used his foot to
propel himself back toward the surface. Just before breaking through, he
felt Reneeke take hold of the branch he had been in the middle of handing
over, providing some much needed leverage with which to regain the
surface and stay afloat.

"Shhh!" urged Reneeke when Jaikus broke through and began
sputtering.

Pond scum coated his hair, eyes, mouth, and every other nook and
cranny from the neck up. Nasty was a mild description for the way he felt.

Once his balance had been restored, he began treading water since the bottom was no longer within reach.

"Are you okay?" Reneeke took the branch from Jaikus and set it against the almost burned out one. Instantly, the tinder of the second flared to life.

"Yeah," replied Jaikus. Now with only two branches in his left hand, he moved closer to Reneeke in order to lay a hand on his friend's shoulder to aid in his effort to keep afloat. Supported as he was with his new-found grip, Jaikus was able to wipe the scum from his face on a relatively dry patch of Reneeke's shirt.

"Uh-oh."

"What?" Looking up, Jaikus' panic returned anew as he glanced back and forth across the water for signs of danger.

Reneeke directed Jaikus' attention to the mossback's hideaway with a nod of his head. There was a gap in a section of the overhanging moss touching the water that hadn't been there before. In a voice as silent as he could make it, Reneeke said, "The mossback…it's out." He felt Jaikus' grip tighten on his shoulder.

"Let's get out of here," urged Jaikus.

Not moving, Reneeke held the torch up as he scanned the surface of the water. When he saw no signs of the mossback, or the tell-tale ripples indicating its passage, he shook his head. "We're close, Jaik." A short silence, then, "Hang on."

He began moving toward the knoll. Jaik held onto his shoulder and kept his eyes peeled for the mossback as Reneeke worked to bring them through the water.

They could see very clearly the remains of the horse where it lay half in, half out of the water. Of the three saddlebags Master Hymal had mentioned, two were clearly visible. The third could very well be hidden beneath the carcass.

A slow minute passed. Reneeke moved as quickly as he dared. Footing was treacherous, but at no point had the water grown so deep that it prevented him from reaching the bottom. Then his foot sank into a depression, causing his head to momentarily dip beneath the surface.

Terror shot through Jaikus as his friend suddenly went under, frightened that the mossback had attacked.

An instant later, Reneeke passed beyond the depression and his head once again broke the surface.

"You scared the life out of me," exclaimed Jaikus in a hushed whisper.

"I'm okay," he replied. "Hole."

From there on, the depth of the water gradually diminished. Jaikus was soon able to let go of Reneeke's shoulder and walk on his own. When the water was once again at mid-chest level, Reneeke brought them to a halt.

Mere yards away from their objective, he held up his hand, then pointed off to the right of the knoll. A small wave was making its way across the surface. It wasn't making directly for their position, but then, it wasn't moving away from them either. The wave's trajectory would bring it to within three feet of where they now stood.

"I think we have finally got its attention," Reneeke announced. Glancing to Jaikus, he could see the fear in his eyes. "Be ready with the last two branches."

Nodding, Jaikus tightened his grip upon them.

"Stay close."

Jaikus didn't need Reneeke's warning to practically tread on his heels; fear of being ripped apart was doing an ample job all on its own.

Two pairs of eyes tracked the wave's movement. Now that they knew they were discovered, they quickened their pace toward the carcass of Master Hymal's horse.

Reneeke turned to face the bow of the wave, all the while continuing to progress closer to the knoll. He put both burning branches in his left hand, then held out his right. "Give them to me." Once he held all four branches; two burning brightly in one hand, the other two awaiting their turn to be lit in the other, he said, "Get the packs."

As Jaikus hurriedly splashed across the last few yards to the carcass, he heard Reneeke add, *"And hurry!"* There was a definite edge to Reneeke's voice. Afraid to waste even the brief time glancing over his shoulder would take, he raced forward.

Drawing near the carcass, he saw the two blood-soaked packs, bulging with Master Hymal's reagents. In an instant, his knife was in hand as he fell to his knees in the bloody froth. Grabbing a strap, he put blade to leather and easily severed its hold.

Whoosh!

Light blazed forth as Reneeke ignited the last two branches.

"Back!"

Jaikus pulled the first pack free then glanced over his shoulder. There, not more than fifteen feet away, stood Reneeke with twin blazes now raging from both hands. In the water before him, the mossback recoiled from the sudden conflagration of the remaining branches.

"Hyah! Back!"

Sidestepping to match the creature's movements, Reneeke moved to interpose himself between it and Jaikus. Waving the branches to and fro, he shouted again as the mossback tried to outflank him. Leaping forward, he scored a direct hit on the creature's face with an intensely burning brand.

Roaring, it twisted about and vanished beneath the surface.

"Where did it go?" shouted Jaikus.

Reneeke kept eyes on the water as he said, "You let me worry about that. *Get those packs!*"

Pack two took another second to free, and now that he was close, could readily see where the third was pinned between the ground and the ribcage.

From the corner of his eye, he could see Reneeke moving closer as he scanned the surface for signs of the mossback's return. But he couldn't worry about that now. He had to get the third pack free.

The ravaging of the mossback had left ample opportunities for him to acquire a good grip on the horse's remains. By grasping two protruding ribs, he pulled with all his might. Fortunately, the mossback had consumed most of the meat, and thus had reduced the weight sufficiently to enable Jaikus to drag the carcass from atop the pack. Once it was free, he quickly cut the strap and gathered it up along with the other two.

"I got them!" he shouted just as a shadow leapt toward him from further up the knoll. The mossback had doubled back.

"Rene!"

Panic lent strength to his leap as he sought to escape the creature's attack. Easily clearing four feet of the knoll's surface, he landed awkwardly upon a pile of rocks and immediately crashed to the ground.

"Hyah!" shouted Reneeke as fiery brands rushed forward to Jaikus' aid. *"To me, creature!"*

Arcs of fire danced in the air and the mossback paused at their approach.

Jaikus scrambled back to his feet.

"Get to the water, Jaik." Holding the fiery brands as a mighty swordsman would his trusty blade, Reneeke jerked his head toward the water. "Get going."

"What about you?"

"I'll be right behind you." Then he saw the rear legs of the mossback bunch, readying for a leap. *"Hyah!"* he shouted as he stepped forward, wielding the brands before him. The mossback snarled, but remained where it was. His bravado had squelched the creature's impulse to attack.

When he heard the sound of Jaikus entering the water, Reneeke began backing up to follow. Never taking his eyes from the mossback, he stepped from the knoll and into the water. Brands of fire still held before him, he watched the mossback as it moved to place itself next to the carcass of the dead horse. Snarling a couple more times, it seemed, for the moment, quite content to allow them to leave. Reneeke was more than happy to oblige.

Step by step he entered the water. Farther behind him, he could hear Jaikus swimming with all speed toward the far shore. But such an act he could not afford to emulate, for to take his eyes from the mossback would be the worst sort of folly.

Knee-deep, he waved the brands back and forth. Their fuel now all but spent, the fire was beginning to subside. He hoped that with the threat to its food moving off, the mossback would no longer wish to pursue. After all, it had just eaten its fill, and that was normally the time when predators were the most passive. Though the way it continued snarling and pacing back and forth along the edge of the knoll, passive this creature definitely was not.

As soon as he reached the point where the water was to his upper chest, he tossed two of the brands aside. Having been the first ones lit, they were now little more than charred remains. With one hand free, he was able to increase his departure by using it to swim while still retaining the two burning brands in his other.

Stroke, stroke, glance back to the knoll. When he saw the mossback still near the carcass, he would continue on. It took six repetitions of that cycle before reaching shallower water where he could dispense with the swimming and return walking along the bottom.

"We did it!" cried Jaikus. Grinning broadly, he held up the three packs.

Reneeke returned his grin. "Yes we did, Jaik." Moving through the last of the water, he once again glanced back to the knoll. But with the withdrawal of the torches, the area had returned to darkness. Of the mossback, there was no sign.

He held the burning brands before him and saw how they were all but spent. "We better get out of here."

Jaikus nodded vigorously. After handing Reneeke one of Master Hymal's packs, and taking a burning brand in return, he turned toward the trees.

A god-awful roar split the night as a troll's nightmarish visage entered the radius of the brand's waning light. In the blink of an eye, the memory of something Charka once said flashed across his mind...

Where fire keeps mossbacks away, there are other creatures that it will attract.

Roaring once again, the troll attacked.

—14—

The sheer unexpectedness of the appearance, and subsequent attack, of the troll froze Jaikus into immobility. However, such paralysis was short lived. Darting back, he escaped certain death as razor sharp claws raked the space he had occupied only a split-second before. And the creature kept coming.

He tried to draw his sword as he fled backward, but the terror produced by staring into the merciless eyes of the troll kept him from succeeding. Even though his hand was on the hilt, he couldn't seem to draw it forth.

Then Reneeke was there.

Coming alongside his friend, sword drawn and shouting *"Hyah!"* to draw the creature's attention, he allowed Jaikus time to back away unfettered. But in so doing, had now become the focus of the troll's attack.

Jaikus finally managed to free his sword as the creature's claws shot forward in an attempt to ravage Reneeke's flesh. But his friend had been too quick. Dodging backward, Reneeke simultaneously brought the blade down. To his surprise, the blow struck the thick, tough hide of the troll's forearm and cut clear through to the bone. Yowling in pain and rage, the toll yanked its arm back, almost taking Reneeke's sword with it in the process.

Spine now somewhat firmly back in place, and feeling that perhaps his undergarments might need a thorough cleansing when all was said and done, Jaikus charged forward. He hit the troll with a resounding blow to the side as it moved to attack Reneeke yet again. But for all the strength he put into it, the blade barely left a mark.

Jaikus' lack of success was not lost upon Reneeke. "Get out of here, Jaik!" he shouted, as claws again shot forward bringing terrible, ripping pain. Unable to react swiftly enough, he was left with a shredded jerkin and furrows oozing blood from mid-breast to collarbone.

Though woefully outclassed, he wasn't about to give up without a fight. Thrusting toward the creature's face, he managed to score a hit dead

center to the troll's left eye. Four inches of blade sank into the optical
cavity before the troll's head jerked backward. A fraction of a second
later, it let loose a scream so primal in its intensity, that it caused both lads
to take a quick step backward.

Unwilling to disgrace the god of luck by refusing to take advantage of
such a fortuitous blow, Reneeke turned, grabbed Jaikus by the shoulder,
and shouted *"Run!"* as he propelled him away from the pain ravaged
beast.

In the hand of Reneeke, their single remaining, burning brand lit the
way. The one Jaikus had carried lay somewhere upon the ground near
where the troll first appeared. From behind, the troll's outcry quickly
turned from one of pain, to that of sheer, unadulterated, rage. It wasn't
long before they heard it crashing through the undergrowth in pursuit.

"Rene…"

"Just keep running, Jaik."

Keeping to the densest parts of the Swamp, they were gradually able
to put distance between them and the troll. Its great bulk was hindered by
the thick growth of trees and brush through which they ran.

Even in the shadowed landscape through which they ran, Reneeke had
a fairly good 'bump of direction.' He directed their progress toward where
he was certain Charka had said Reakla lay, only diverging when the lay of
the land required. When they came to an area the moonlight revealed to be
one of open water or deep, sucking muck, he would circumvent such
obstacles before returning to the proper heading.

"It's not gaining," said Jaikus.

Reneeke nodded, then paused as they came to the edge of yet another
scum covered pond. Behind them, the sound of the troll's pursuit could
still be heard. "Get a pair of torches."

"But, it'll see us!" exclaimed Jaikus. It was one thing to have a
solitary brand that barely gave out much light. But to have two torches
burning at full capacity, it'll be a beacon announcing to every nearby
creature that dinner has arrived.

That's when Reneeke turned and revealed the deep scratches the
troll's attack had opened across his chest. As Jaikus gasped at the sight,
Reneeke said, "I don' think a little extra light is going to matter, Jaik. I'm
sure he can track us by smell alone. At least with torches, we can find our
way around these quagmires much more readily."

"Right." Quickly removing his pack, Jaikus produced two torches that
he then lit from the all but spent brand. Flaring to life, the torches brought
their immediate area into full view.

"Perfect." Then tossing the nearly exhausted brand to the ground,
Reneeke took charge of one of the torches and searched for the optimal

route around the pond before them. By the time Jaikus had his pack back in place, he had found the route. "This way."

The short pause at the side of the pond had allowed the troll to gain ground. A cry from behind alerted them to the creature's closer proximity.

Once around the pond, Reneeke led them forward along a span of dry ground between an all but dried up quagmire on their left, and a small, pond to the right. The sound of the troll's pursuit kept them moving faster through this unfamiliar territory than Reneeke was comfortable with. But still, better the unknown ahead, than the flesh-ripping, life-ending 'known' behind.

The strip of land soon turned into a full fledged expanse of dry, solid ground populated by a dense grove of trees having long since given up the ghost. Shadows danced ominously within the dead forest.

"We didn't come this way," said Jaikus. Glancing into the trees, then back toward the darkness concealing the approaching troll, he couldn't decide which one frightened him most.

"No, that's true, Jaik. But it looks like we're going this way now."

As he passed through the outer fringe of the treeline, Jaikus asked, "How's the chest?"

"Stings something awful."

"We could use one of those healing potions Lady Kate gave us."

Reneeke shook his head. "Save it for when we really need it. I can deal with the pain."

Jaikus could hear the sound of pain in his friend's voice. He worried that the wounds would become angry, as such wounds often did, if they weren't taken care of soon. "Any idea how far we are from Reakla?"

"Not exactly. Hours, I would think. And that's if we aren't forced to double back."

"Let's hope not." Doubling back would surely cause them to encounter their persistent adversary. He couldn't understand why the troll was still pursuing them. Didn't they ever give up?

The trees were an off-brown color, almost as if their pigment had gradually been leeched away. Not a leaf was left on any of the branches above, nor were any present upon the ground below. Farther up on the trunks, at a point where the torchlight faded away, the color looked to be bleached out altogether, not being much more than a pale white.

Nocturnal sounds that had accompanied them throughout their flight from the mossback's knoll, gradually began fading away. The deeper within the forest of dead trees they progressed, the quieter the world around them became. Except, that was, for the intermittent roar of the troll, and the sound of its passage.

"I don't like this place," Jaikus said. Shadows produced by the torches created dark, ominous shadows amidst the trunks around them, fodder enough to fuel Jaikus' overactive imagination. Ten minutes hadn't passed before he began seeing fell beasts lurking to either side, beasts that only existed in his mind.

A demonic serpent turned out to be a fallen trunk. An ogre bearing a double-headed battle axe was revealed as nothing more than a misshapen tree. *Get a grip on yourself, Jaik,* he told himself. But such assurances had little effect in taming the wild thoughts that transformed shadows into fearful apparitions. He kept as close to Reneeke as he could.

Reneeke kept a furious pace. Alternating running with periods of walking, they were able to maintain their lead on the troll. When he unexpectedly came to an abrupt stop, Jaikus failed to notice in time and ran into his back.

As he rebounded off his friend, Jaikus gave a quick, "Sorry," before seeing why it was that Reneeke had stopped. Not six feet from where they stood, a rivulet cut its way across their path. Wide enough to prevent either of them from attempting to leap across, it effectively barred their way.

Then from out of the darkness behind them, came the sound of the troll's roar, which only served to amplify the direness of their situation. It wasn't close, but definitely closer than it had been.

Moving to the rivulet's edge, Reneeke gestured along the bank to the right. "See if there's a way across down that way," he said. "I'll check the other. Hurry."

Jaikus looked toward the ominous shadows, imagination once again working overtime. "Down...*there*? By myself?" he asked nervously, but Reneeke was already moving off and failed to reply.

As if he wasn't terrified enough, their ever present pursuer gave out with another roar. Their momentary pause along the water's edge had allowed it to narrow the gap still further. If they didn't ford this rivulet, and soon, the troll would very shortly be upon them.

Jaikus stiffened his resolve, and set forth along the bank of the rivulet. *Thirty paces,* he told himself. If a way hasn't presented itself in that time, he would return. Counting his steps, he raced forward as quickly as he could.

At no point along the thirty-pace dash did the rivulet narrow to such an extent as would allow them to leap across. If anything, it grew wider. At thirty paces, Jaikus paused and held his torch high as he gave the area one last look. No fording opportunities presented themselves. Turning about, Jaikus began racing to rejoin Reneeke.

As he ran, Jaikus spotted the light from Reneeke's torch through the trees and altered his course to intercept. "Find anything?" he asked as he came up behind his friend.

Reneeke glanced over his shoulder and said, "Maybe. You?"

Jaikus shook his head. "It only grew wider." Sounds from deeper within the trees drew his fearful gaze. "What are we going to do?" Glancing back to Reneeke, he saw his friend pointing toward a sandbar some fifteen feet from shore.

"If we can get there, we can easily cross the rest of the way." The span of water on the far side of the sandbar was less than five feet across.

"But I can't leap from here to there."

"You don't have to," replied Reneeke. He then drew Jaikus' attention to a tree rising not far from the water's edge. It was slightly askew and leaned in the general direction of the rivulet. "All we have to do is knock this tree over and walk across."

Having grown up on a farm, Jaikus understood all too well the impossibility of what Reneeke was suggesting. "Can't be done."

"We have no choice."

Just then, they heard the grunting of the troll followed by the snapping of a dead branch. They turned and looked in the direction of the sound. The beast couldn't be more than a hundred feet away. "Then we fight."

Jaikus blanched at the prospect of trading blows once again with the troll. Returning his attention to the tree, he asked, "So, how are we to get this down?"

Maybe it was his friend's quick reversal on his stand for knocking over the tree, or maybe it was due to the tension and fatigue wracking his body, but Reneeke couldn't help but grin. Drawing his sword, he said, "Lady Kate said there was an aura on this blade. It has already proven itself against troll-hide." Then he stepped toward the askew tree. "Let's see how well it does now."

"You might break the blade."

Reneeke shrugged. He handed Jaikus his torch then gripped the hilt with both hands. Raising the sword over his head, he said, "With or without it, we stand little chance against the troll." Then, using every ounce of strength at his disposal, he swung the sword in a mighty slice.

The finely honed edge struck the trunk and bark went flying as it cleaved its way a solid six inches within the tree.

"Yes!" exclaimed Jaikus.

Reneeke worked the blade out and hacked again. This time, a wedge of wood fell away leaving a pie-shaped cavity. With a nod of his head, Reneeke directed Jaikus' toward a low hanging branch on the rivulet side. "Give me a hand," he said as he raised the sword.

The tree emitted a slight cracking noise as Jaikus took hold of the branch. When Reneeke struck the tree for the third time, he pulled downward on the branch with all his might. Loud popping and cracking noises came from the hacked area and the tree tilted even more precariously toward the water.

"Almost there," said Reneeke a he drew his sword back for what he hoped would be the final blow required to fell the tree. But the blow never came. It was preempted by a loud crash heralding the arrival of the troll.

Seeing the two friends with their backs to the river, the creature snarled, then charged.

"Get that tree down!" Reneeke shouted as he turned to face the troll. With sword held before him, he started sidestepping away. *"Come and get me!"* The troll fixated on him, and followed.

Claws shot forward only to pass through empty space. Reneeke had anticipated the beast's attack and moved accordingly. In his younger years, he had faced down his share of distempered creatures; bulls and the like. This troll wasn't all that different. Sure it was bigger, stronger, and slightly more intelligent than animals found on a farm, but a beast, no matter how ferocious, was just a beast and would act accordingly.

After a second swipe that was just as ineffectual as the first, Reneeke glanced over toward where Jaikus was doing his utmost to bring that tree down. Grabbing the branch high up toward the trunk, Jaikus leaped up, tucked in his legs, and allowed his entire weight to drag on the branch.

There was a snap, and the branch broke.

Pain flared as his momentary, visual diversion cost him dearly. Talons ripped along the forearm wielding the sword. Simultaneously, the powerful hind legs of the troll launched the beast forward in a mighty leap.

Reneeke spun to the side to avoid the attack and struck out as the creature sailed past. The blade connected with the side of the troll's head, leaving a deep, blood-spurting, furrow. He dodged back as the troll twisted in midair, coming to land facing him. It sprang again.

Unable to dart to safety, he instead dropped to the ground and allowed the beast to pass harmlessly over him. Once it was past, he quickly regained his feet and ran for all he was worth. A second later, the troll came to land and raced in pursuit.

Rising from where the snapping of the branch had left him, Jaikus glanced over to see Reneeke racing off into the dark of the forest with the troll in hot pursuit. *"Get the tree!"* he heard his friend shout as Reneeke disappeared from sight. Returning his gaze back to the tree, he saw where Reneeke had all but cut his way through.

One more cut! One more and the tree would have fallen. Wracked with indecision as to the best course of action, he heard Reneeke's voice shout from out of the darkness, *"Hurry!"*

He considered using the rope in his pack to pull the tree down. And that would have been a viable solution had there been more shore between the tree and the water. But as it was, with the tree mere feet from the waterline, there wouldn't be sufficient leverage to make a difference.

Then, another thought occurred to him, one that he was loath to attempt. Although, when an inarticulate cry from Reneeke split the silence, he knew the attempt must be made despite the risks. Jaikus knew that should he climb up the trunk far enough, his weight, coupled with the degree of the tree's slant, would increase the pressure on the area hacked by Reneeke, and thus, bring it down. He dropped the two torches at the base of the slanted tree, steeled his resolve, then began to climb.

The climb was relatively easy as there were many limbs available for handholds during his ascent. When he reached five feet from the ground, he felt the tree start to bow beneath his weight. At ten, the trunk below gave off popping and cracking sounds.

Almost.

Moving another two feet along the trunk, he hopped. Driving his weight forcibly down upon the tree, he felt, as well as heard, the final crack as the tree finally gave way. Jaikus held onto the branches for dear life as the tree toppled. When it struck the rivulet, he was jarred loose and one hand inadvertently slipped into the water. At the same time, the upper reaches of the tree seemed to explode in a cloud of white when it came to land upon the sandbar.

Instantly, the water began to roil, and pain flared as tiny teeth sought to rip and tear away his flesh. Jerking his hand from the water, he discovered four of the little, meat-eating fish had their teeth firmly attached to three of his fingers. It was painful removing them as their jaws refused to relinquish their bits of flesh. Once the last had been removed, Jaikus turned back toward the forest and yelled, "Now, Reneeke! The tree is down!"

Jaikus began making his way back along the trunk toward the shore, and the two torches still burning upon the ground. When he reached the end and hopped down, Reneeke still hadn't appeared. Worried for his friend, he thought that perhaps Reneeke may have become turned around among the trees and couldn't find his way back. He reclaimed the torches and climbed back up onto the trunk of the fallen tree where he began waving them about.

"Reneeke!" he shouted. *"This way!"*

Torches moved furiously for half a minute before Reneeke broke free from the trees. Jaikus jumped in elation at seeing his friend, but was cut short as Reneeke drew close and he got a good look at him. Streaks of blood created a grisly patchwork along the left side of his face, and his clothes were shredded in three places, testament to having endured the troll's tender caresses.

Five paces behind him, came the troll.

"Get going, Jaik!" he yelled.

Jaikus turned about and was brought to a halt by the sight of glow-moths, hundreds of them, fluttering in and around the upper branches of the tree. *The white cloud created when the tree struck the sandbar. It had been the glow-moths!* The sandbar side of their tree-bridge was completely infested. And not only that, those closest to him were drawing nearer.

There wasn't sufficient time to cover himself in the protective mesh that had worked so superbly in the past. What with death nipping at Reneeke's heels, they had to press forward, and fast.

Jaikus held both torches in his left hand and began thrashing them about. He had just begun moving forward when small flares of flame erupted in midair as the business end of the torches set fire to flittering glow-moths.

Then all of a sudden, the tree beneath him shuddered as Reneeke leapt aboard and began following. It shuddered still further when the troll sought to follow, the branches proving to be a serious hindrance for it. Thrashing to and fro, the troll began snapping them away to clear a path.

"'Ware the water!" shouted Jaikus as more of the glow-moths became ready fodder for the flame. "It's full of those fishes. And in case you hadn't noticed, there's a glow-moth infestation up ahead."

"Less talk, more walk."

The route through the branches was anything but simple, wending his way around branches, even having to precariously lean out over the water in order to bypass an exceptionally obstinate one. And all the time, there were the moths.

His twin torches moved rapidly to halt the forward progression of the barbed critters. More than once, he had to singe the outer area of a limb in order to clear a space that was covered in glow-moths so it could be used as a handhold.

He was a mere ten feet from the sandbar when the first glow-moth struck. As he was waving his torch to clear the air before him, he felt a piercing jab of fire in his left forearm. Crying out in shock at the unexpected severity of the pain, he quickly brought his right hand over to pull the stinger out. The barb at the end was reticent to release its grip, but a quick jerk pulled it free along with a small bit of skin.

"One got me!" he hollered back to Reneeke.

"Keep going!" urged his friend. The troll was still very much in pursuit.

Jaikus tried to disregard the pain as he continued torching glow-moths and moving forward.

Reneeke had moved to just behind him and wished his friend would move faster. Glancing back, he saw how the troll worked to clear a path not five feet farther back. The creature was gaining faster than Jaikus was progressing. Working on removing a rather thick and gnarled branch that the two humans had maneuvered around with ease, the troll was for the moment, stalled. Retuning his attention to Jaikus and the dancing torchlight, he thought…*If it wasn't for the need to clear a path through the…*

"Hang on a minute, Jaik."

Jaikus came to a halt and felt Reneeke tug on his pack.

"I'm getting the mesh netting," he explained.

 Nodding, Jaikus continued weaving a fiery display in the air before him, torching moth after moth that then plummeted to the water below.

"Here." Reneeke said as he draped Jaikus' protective net over his friend's head. "Keep it close or the limbs are going to snag it." He paused a moment. Then as Jaikus was adjusting the mesh, said, "Hand me the torches."

"Thanks." Once the twin, burning brands were handed off to Reneeke, he was able to move the mesh into its proper, protective, position. That was when he saw twin streaks of fire sail over his head toward the sandbar.

"Are you mad?"

"They are drawn to the light, right?"

The two torches landed upon the surface of the sand some fifteen feet from the end of the tree. Almost immediately, glow-moths nearest the torches began moving toward the burning brands.

Jaikus nodded. "Yes."

"Okay, then. Now, *get moving!*"

With the mesh netting pulled tightly about his upper extremities, Jaikus started moving forward. It was much easier to traverse the limbs with hands free of the torches. The netting, however, snagged on the limbs, but such inconvenience was a small price to pay for increased speed.

Reneeke took his own netting from his pack and settled it into place. The time taken to thus protect themselves had allowed the troll to tear the limb from the tree and proceed forward. It was now almost within striking distance. Nimbly wending his way through the branches, Reneeke narrowly avoided the troll's lethal claws and began widening the distance once again. Behind, the troll roared in frustrated anger as its larger girth prevented it from following with similar agility. Claws ripping into the limbs, it continued at a much slower pace.

The glow-moths were dispersing. Fluttering about, they seemed to completely be oblivious to the two net-shrouded humans as they winged along in their roundabout way toward the torches lying on the sandbar. No longer having to worry about imminent attack, Jaikus was able to increase his rate of progression through the limbs and quickly reached the sandbar. Reneeke hopped from the tree a moment later.

The troll continued to be mired in the more thickly woven branches of what had once been the treetop. Its strength and tenacity filled the air with sounds of snapping wood and sundered limbs.

Glow-moths filled the air about them. The greatest congregation was concentrated in the area illuminated by the torches' glow.

"Leave them," Reneeke said when Jaikus moved toward the burning brands. "Let's get out of here while we can."

Jaikus nodded.

Reneeke took the lead as they crossed the narrow strip of the sandbar toward the far side. There, he took a running jump and easily cleared the narrow off-shoot of the rivulet. Jaikus followed with similar ease.

They paused but a moment to glance back at the troll. It had reached the end of the tree. Surrounding it was a cloud of glow-moths; and from the way its arms were flailing back and forth, the glow-moths were quite happy to makes its acquaintance.

In the dim shadows produced by the torchlight, they saw where a dozen or more had embedded their barbs within the creature. From its howls, it couldn't have been a pleasurable experience.

"Come on."

Breaking into a run, the two boys from Running Brook disappeared into the shadows, using what time the glow-moths may have provided to put as much distance between themselves, and the troll, as they could.

—15—

Once the light from the torches vanished in the darkness behind them, Jaikus called for a halt. "Hold up a second, Rene."

Panting hard, Reneeke asked, "Why?"

"You took a beating back there and I want to make sure you are all right."

Reneeke didn't reply. He merely found the trunk of an accommodating tree and leaned wearily against it. From the darkness he heard Jaikus rummaging around in his pack, then the familiar sound of striking flint. In a matter of moments, Jaikus had lit another of their torches.

"Now, let me take a look at you."

Moving the torch close, he examined the various wounds of Reneeke. Deep furrows lined his side, neck, face and chest. Hardly an inch of him had escaped unscathed.

He then peered into Reneeke's eyes. Not really knowing what to look for, he only knew that priests did it when examining the injured. "How do you feel?"

"Sore, exhausted."

"Ready to collapse?"

Reneeke shrugged.

"Here." Producing one of the two flasks containing healing elixir Lady Kate had given them, he held it forward. "Drink it all."

Again, Reneeke wasn't about to argue. Pulling the stopper, he placed the flask to his lips and upended it. He held it there until every last drop had crossed his tongue and slid down his throat. Immediately, warm sensations spread outward as the potion entered his bloodstream and carried it throughout his body. Strength returned, aches diminished, and his head cleared.

"Better?" asked Jaikus.

"Oh man, yes," he grinned. "I could get to like this."

Wounds closed as the elixir worked its magic. By the time the potion had run its course, all but the very worst had healed over completely, some to the point where it looked as if there had never even *been* an injury. The deeper ones were still red and tender to the touch, but much improved over the bloody furrows of a moment before. Jaikus concluded that magic potions were a wonderful thing, and vowed to always carry a supply on all subsequent adventures.

"It doesn't look as if there will be much scarring."

"That's a relief."

Very faintly, the troll's roar reached them from far away. "It must still be on the sandbar," commented Reneeke.

"Maybe it can't get off."

"I wouldn't count on that." Now reinvigorated by the healing properties of the potion, Reneeke pushed himself away from the tree. "Let's get going before it fords the water."

Jaik looked around the forest, confusion and uncertainty written across his face.

Reneeke pointed off toward a section of dark shadows. "Reakla's that way."

"Are you sure?"

"Fairly sure."

At that moment, the roar of the troll reached them again from a point almost directly opposite to that which Reneeke claimed Reakla laid. "Whether you are right or wrong, at least it will get us away from that." Jaikus took two of Master Hymal's packs to allow Reneeke less of a burden with but one. The odors coming from within filled the air with aromas neither had ever encountered before. The combination was less than appealing.

Jaikus took the lead, his torch pushing back the darkness as they hurried toward Reakla.

Less than ten minutes had passed before Jaikus' left arm spasmed in pain. *"Gods!"* It had been throbbing ever since the glow-moth sank its barb into it. But now, the pain had suddenly spiked in its severity. The spasming caused the torch to slip from his grip.

"Damn," he groaned, hugging his throbbing arm to his chest. "It hurts."

Reneeke came to a stop and turned to his friend. Jaikus stood hunched over his arm, face twisted in agony.

"The glow-moth?"

Jaikus nodded. "Same spot. It hurts bad, Rene." Perspiration began dotting his forehead.

Reneeke picked the torch up from off the ground and had Jaikus hold his arm out. As he pulled the sleeve back, Jaikus' arm began trembling.

"It's getting worse."

Red, inflamed and swollen, the site of the attack oozed a bloody discharge. A finger's length of dark purple extended from where the discharge emerged, then made its way up the forearm toward the elbow. Another swelling, about an inch in length and the width of a pea, marked the end of the dark-purple discoloration. It looked almost as if... Reneeke gasped when the swollen area moved.

"What?"

Reneeke ignored the question as he brought the torch closer. Something moved beneath the skin. "Uh, Jaik."

Turning his eyes upon the swollen area, Jaik felt a spike in pain that coincided with the movement of whatever was beneath his skin. *There was something alive in his flesh!* His voice took on a tinge of hysteria as he shouted, *"Get it out!"*

Knife appearing in his hand, Reneeke wrapped his arm around Jaikus' injured one to immobilize it, then pinched the area to either side of the internal intruder.

Jaikus cried out at the pain Reneeke was causing. When his friend looked questioningly at him, Jaikus gritted his teeth. "Just do it."

Reneeke nodded. Bringing the tip of his knife close, he made an incision. A pale, wormlike body writhed within the newly formed opening. Blood oozed forth as Reneeke dug the tip of the knife into the wound to draw forth the invader.

Jaikus moaned from the pain and clutched Reneeke's shirt. He buried his face in his friend's back as the knife dug deeper.

"Almost got it."

Fine, hair-like cilia covered the parasite's body, and wriggled under Reneeke's ministrations. The head had burrowed deeper within the forearm's muscle and thwarted every attempt at dislodging it. "Brace yourself," he told Jaikus, then dug deeper.

The pain was excruciating. Jaikus reflexively tried to withdraw his arm, but Reneeke had too firm a grip. Deeper the knife point went, and just when Jaik thought the pain would force him to heave all over Reneeke's back, it stopped.

"I got it."

Reneeke let go of the arm and pointed to a small, white, worm-like thing writhing on the ground. Jaikus shuddered.

"I think it might be a glow-moth larva of some kind." Reneeke then proceeded to grind the parasitic invader beneath the heel of his boot.

Jaikus' arm was a mess. Blood covered his forearm. The hole Reneeke had been forced to create in order to expel the parasite continuously oozed more. "There's another healing draught in my pack."

"Right." Reneeke quickly retrieved the flask and poured a small amount on the wound itself, just as he had observed Lady Kate do with

Seward, then had Jaikus drink a quarter of what was left. Almost immediately, the wound cleared of blood, and began to knit together.

"Now I can see why Charka insisted that the mesh was so important."

Reneeke nodded. "I still don't understand why the glow-moths avoid it. Perhaps it's made of something they don't like."

"Or it possesses a magical enchantment?"

"Maybe." Restoppering the flask, Reneeke replaced it within Jaikus' pack. "Either way, I think we should keep them handy in case we encounter more."

Both lads kept their mesh netting out, but had it rolled up and tucked beneath their arms. As Reneeke took the lead to resume their trek to Reakla, Jaikus fell in beside. He couldn't help but shudder anew at the thought of how the larva had been wriggling around beneath his skin. He couldn't wait to return to Reakla. How he could use a large mug of ale right about now.

Sunrise was imminent, and Charka paced impatiently before the Swamp Gate as he had for nearly the last hour. Nearby stood two Guild members who had volunteered to aid in the rescue of his two Springers. One was a bear of a man with twin axes strapped to his back, the other, an identical match except for the pair of swords in place of the axes. They were the twin brothers Khuodari, formidable fighters who had adventured with Charka a time or two. The promise of a night of debauchery upon their return had helped seal the deal.

Upon his *Troupe's* return to Reakla, Charka's first order of business had been getting Seward to a Temple. Once satisfied that his man would not only live, but make a full recovery through the ministrations of the priests, he left Lady Kate to keep an eye on him while he set about to gather a few cronies who wouldn't mind a quick jaunt into the Swamp to save a couple of lost pups. Now, he and the Khuodari brothers waited for the sun to strike the Gate, for the Gate would not open until that time.

There was nothing magical about such an occurrence, rather, the law kept it closed until daybreak. Only two instances would permit the Gate to be opened. One, of course, would be the appearance of a returning band of adventurers. The other necessitated procuring a letter from the Town Council which would allow it to be opened. But since the eastern sky had already begun to brighten, Charka knew better than to try and round up that lazy band of miscreants. By the time he succeeded in corralling enough councilors to make a majority, it would be dawn and their aid would no longer be required.

A glance to the ramparts above the Gate revealed Master Hymal pacing about in similar impatience. He'd been there since shortly after their return. Charka knew the reagents in the packs his Springer's had volunteered to recover constituted the bulk of his profits for the next few months. Without them, Master Hymal faced some lean times until the moon would once again rise in proper fullness to make another trip to Sythal worthwhile.

Charka caught site of the Watch Leader, the man whose primary responsibility was to oversee the area in and around the Gate, and to ensure the safety of the populace the wall protected. Coming toward the man, he said with no small amount of impatience, "Surely you can open the Gate now. The sun is almost up."

Watch Leader Reggie understood all too well Charka's impatience. Having, in the last hour, suffered no less than three separate bartering attempts and one threat of mayhem, his patience had worn thin. "I'm through talking, Charka. When the sun hits the Gate, we'll open it. *Not one second before!"*

"But my Springers might be dying out there!"

Reggie was unmoved. "Adventurers are always *'dying out there'*. It goes with the territory. Besides, the law is the law."

Charka felt like smashing in his face, but knew such an action would not get the Gate opened any sooner.

"Hey!" cried a lookout atop the wall. "I see something!"

Charka hollered, "My Springers?"

"Can't tell for sure. But there is definitely movement in the deeper shadows along the fringe."

A second later, Master Hymal yelled, "It's them!"

"Open that demon-damned Gate!" Charka shouted.

Visual contact of approaching adventurers constituted one of the few instances whereby the Gate could be opened before the rising of the sun. "Open it up!" shouted Reggie. One of his men rushed to the gatehouse. Shortly thereafter, the sound of the massive, internal locking mechanism filled the courtyard as the man threw the lever releasing them.

"Looks like one is hurt," Hymal shouted down to Charka. "The big one is leaning on the smaller."

"Reneeke?"

"I think so."

Just as the final *"clank"* signaled the Gate to be unsecured, a guard from atop the wall shouted, *"Troll!"*

In the early dawn, a time of day when night began rolling back in deference to the morn, two lads made their way through the Swamp. One had suffered grievous injury and leaned heavily upon the other.

The effects of the potion had worn off an hour ago, reminding Reneeke that the worst of the injuries inflicted by the troll still had a ways to go before it could be said they were healed. He suffered no great amount of pain, merely a dull ache and weakness. The healing properties of the potion had used a great deal of his energy to do its work. Reneeke had already consumed the last of the second healing draught, its revitalizing effect no more than a pleasant memory.

Legs wobbly, head pounding, and body aching all over; it was all he could do to merely put one foot in front of the other. He desperately needed a hot meal, warm bed, and a lengthy stretch of uninterrupted sleep.

As the sky began to brighten with the dawn, the protective wall of Reakla appeared through the trees.

"Look, Rene," Jaikus said. "We're almost back."

Weary eyes turned toward the towering walls. Nothing had ever looked so good. "We did it, Jaik."

"Yes, we did."

Three packs filled with reagents were slung over their shoulders, Master Hymal should be pleased. Jaikus could think of little else than the reward promised by the apothecary. Reneeke, on the other hand, was simply satisfied by a job well done. That, and the fact they returned with their lives intact. Although considering the amount of discomfort inflicting him, he amended that sentiment with "almost intact".

Clearing the tree line, they started across the final expanse of open area toward the Gate. It remained closed, but hopefully that would change once the guards atop the wall became aware of their presence.

"Come on, Rene. Not much farther."

With Reakla's wall now an immediate goal, a small measure of strength returned to him. Although, not so much as to enable the putting aside of Jaikus' aid. He still required a supportive shoulder to remain upright.

The snapping of a branch prompted Jaikus to glance over his shoulder to the trees from which they had recently emerged. His eyes widened when he saw the troll. *"Gods!"* He increased their pace dramatically, but such fear-induced acceleration across uneven terrain only caused his weakened partner to take a misstep. Reneeke hit the ground with a groan, taking Jaikus with him.

Jaikus immediately sprang back to his feet. Grabbing Reneeke's arm, he strove to get him up. "Come on, Rene!"

Reneeke saw the troll coming and knew that though he might be able to regain his feet, he would never sustain an effective flight. Pulling his arm from Jaikus' grip, he said, "Get out of here, Jaik. I'll never make it." He tried drawing his sword, but the maneuver was beyond him. His strength was gone.

"No!"

"Go. There's no point in both of us dying."

Jaikus reached out once more to try and pull him to his feet, but Reneeke batted his hand away. *"Go!"*

"I'll not!"

How could he leave? To abandon not only the best friend he ever had, but his *only* friend? Reneeke had always been there for him. When Jaikus left to join the Guild, he agreed to come along. He didn't have to. Reneeke would have been much happier on the farm. But he did it, because Jaikus was his friend.

Drawing his sword, Jaikus placed himself between the oncoming troll and the single most important person in his life.

"Jaik."

Glancing back, he saw that Reneeke had managed to draw his sword halfway from the scabbard. "Here," he said, straining to move the hilt closer to Jaikus. "Yours won't do any good."

Jaikus didn't even hesitate. Transferring his sword to his left hand, he drew Reneeke's with his right. Wielding the two swords helped to drive back his fear to a more manageable level. It gave him a feeling that all was not lost. Then, the troll attacked.

"What's going on?"

As the Gate began to open, a familiar voice drew Charka's attention. It was Viruloxi, a Guild magic user of some power. "I got two Springers in trouble."

"A troll's after 'em," added the sword-bearing Khuodari brother.

"Need some help?"

Moving toward the opening Gate, Charka asked, "Cost?"

"Say, a third?"

"Done."

Racing through the opening, he broke into an all-out run. Flanked to either side by the Khuodari brothers, with Viruloxi following on their heels, he raced across the open grassland. Charka saw Jaikus bearing double blades as he faced off against the troll, willing to defend Reneeke with his life.

"Your Springer's got grit," said the sword-wielding brother on his right.

"I guess he does," Charka replied, with just a touch of surprise tingeing his voice.

From his other side, the axe-wielding Khuodari brother said, "May we be in time."

There was something odd about the troll. Jaikus couldn't quite put his finger on it, but it didn't roar like before. Its mouth opened as if the troll wanted to, but naught more than a gurgling sound issued forth.

"Back!" he shouted in mimic of Reneeke in his friend's earlier battle with the mossback. Much to his surprise, his voice came out strong and sure. A remarkable feat considering he was a quivering mass of nerves inside.

Charka's words came back to him in the fleeting moments before the troll's attack

....***Keep your wrist in line with your elbow and the blade. Think of the area from your shoulder to the tip of your blade as one.***

The sword moved into proper position.

I'm trying!

A dead man tries, an Adventurer does. Or don't you want to be an Adventurer? What if your buddy's life depended on you being able to take out your opponent? Is he going to want you to try and help him? Or would he want you to help him?

Jaikus was through with trying. *I am an Adventurer!* Firming his resolve, he braced for the attack.

The troll launched itself forward.

Bringing up Reneeke's sword, he struck with all his might. Before the blade could connect, the troll struck it aside with a mighty swipe.

Snap!

His wrist had twisted slightly out of position, and just as Charka had prophesized, the blow snapped the bone. Reneeke's sword, the one weapon with which Jaikus could have dealt damage to the troll, slipped from his non-responsive fingers.

An explosion of pain erupted from his broken wrist followed a second later by even worse as talons ripped into him.

He tried bringing his other sword into play as the troll plowed another set of bloody furrows across his upper body, but it merely bounced off the beast's hide. His legs gave way, dropping him to the ground as deadly talons again penetrated his flesh.

Time seemed to slow as he gazed at talons stained with blood, *his blood*, that were being drawn back to rip into him again. Unable to look away, he braced himself for what he knew would be his end.

Thunk!

An axe appeared as if by magic to embed itself in the beast's skull. A split-second later, the crackle of electricity preceded a blinding explosion of brilliant light. The troll's blow never fell.

Eyes recovering from the flash, Jaikus saw the charred and blackened section of the troll's chest. Through vision growing ever more obscured, Jaikus watched the troll yank the axe from its head and stepped forward to continue the attack, only to be hit by another bolt. The lightning strike knocked it from its feet and sent it reeling backward.

The last thing Jaikus saw before his vision failed completely, were *Webs of Binding* appearing to encase the troll from the neck down.

"See to the troll!"

Somewhere on the edge of consciousness, he heard Charka's voice.

"Jaik! Come on, lad!"

His mouth was forced open and a sweet liquid passed between his lips.

"We're too far from town. He's not going to..."

The last thing he knew before slipping away into oblivion, was being raised from the ground by many hands.

—16—

Quiet conversation drew him from a realm rampant with valiant deeds and daring-do, to one of achy-weariness. He tried lifting his arm to minister relief upon a rather itchy span covering most of his chest, but found even such a meager effort beyond his current capabilities. He did manage to raise his hand an inch above the woolen blanket before weakness drew it back.

If he couldn't scratch, he'd just as soon sleep. Unfortunately, the voices continued unabated and kept him from descending past the final stage into the welcoming arms of slumber.

Jaikus cracked an eye open to find Reneeke conversing at the foot of his bed with a man in priestly robes. "Rene?" Voice cracking and hardly more audible than the squeak of a mouse he failed to draw his friend's attention. He mustered more effort. "Rene."

Two heads swiveled toward him. Reneeke broke into a wide grin and hurried to his side.

"Jaik, praise the gods."

The priest joined him at Jaikus' bedside. "I thought he might awaken today."

"Thank you, Father Balicci."

"You are welcome, my son." Stepping forward, he passed a hand over Jaikus' chest, then paused it momentarily above his head. "He still requires much sleep. Keep your visit brief."

"Yes, Father."

The priest gave Jaikus a grin. "I shall leave you in the hands of your friend."

As the priest departed, Reneeke sat on the edge of the bed. "Man, we didn't think you were going to survive."

"We?"

Reneeke nodded. "Charka, Lady Kate, and Father Balicci. Even Seward stopped by once he recovered, to see how you were doing."

"Seward?" he asked in disbelief.

Reneeke chuckled. "I know. Couldn't believe it myself when he appeared."

Three other cots shared the room with his. Two were empty, each having a single, neatly folded blanket perfectly situated at the end. The fourth looked to have been slept in as its blanket was rumpled with half dangling over the side to the floor.

"Where am I?"

"Fjerl's Temple in Reakla," replied Reneeke. Fjerl, God of Earth, was one of the more popular and prolific faiths in the realm. The people knew that if they were ever in need, succor could be found within its walls, *and* at a reasonable price. The very poor rarely had to pay for the simpler healings. For care of a more serious nature, healings such as being brought back from the dead or the removal of a curse, payment of one kind or another had to be given.

Most temples accepted industry as well as gold. If a person could not meet the required sum, the temple offered them the chance to perform a needed service. Often, such services required nothing more than helping to keep the grounds clean or minor maintenance. The Priests of Fjerl turned no one away. Perhaps that explained Fjerl's position as the patron god of Adventurers.

"I'm not dead, then?"

"It was close, Jaik. If it hadn't been for Charka appearing with the Khuodari brothers and a magic user when he did, neither one of us would be here."

"Kh...Khuodari brothers?"

"They're friends of Charka, you'll get to meet them later. Nice fellows to have on your side in a tight situation."

A lad attired as a novice of Fjerl arrived bearing a cup of cool water. Their conversation took a brief hiatus while the lad aided Jaikus in rising so he could drink. Once the cup had been emptied, the novice laid him back down. Then the lad glanced to Reneeke.

"Father Balicci said your friend needs to rest."

Reneeke nodded. "I understand. I shall leave momentarily."

The lad nodded, then gave each a brief bow before departing.

Jaikus gazed upon his friend. "How are you?"

"I'm fine." Indicating with a quick nod toward the rumpled cot next to Jaik's, he added, "Two days of rest have done me a world of good."

"Two days?"

"Yep, two days." His expression grew solemn. "You were hurt pretty bad, Jaik. Real bad."

"I feel like it." Every part of him ached in one manner or another. His chest was heavily bandaged, as was his head and arms. "I thought priests could do a better job than this."

Reneeke grinned again. "They can, if they must. But Father Balicci explained, '*a few aches and pains are good for the soul*'."

"I'd rather do without them if it's all the same."

Seeing the novice standing not far away giving him a disapproving glare, Reneeke rose from the cot. "I better let you sleep before that novice comes over here again."

Yawning, Jaikus nodded and closed his eyes. "I could use more sleep anyway."

"I shall return later. I'm glad you are all right, Jaik." But Jaikus had already fallen asleep.

After another day of convalescing, Father Balicci announced Jaikus fit to leave. Though from Jaikus' point of view, he was anything but ready. It took Reneeke's help for him to get up off the cot, and every step produced pain. About the only place that didn't hurt was his left nostril…no…wait…that hurt too.

"Come on, Jaik." Reneeke said as they left the cot behind. "Charka wants to buy us an ale over at the Guild."

"The Guild?" He had forgotten all about that. "Are…are we…in?"

"Not yet. Apparently they are still considering it."

"Oh." Disappointment filled his voice.

"But hey, we get to go in since we will be Charka's guests."

Inside the Guild. He could settle for that, at least for now.

They made their way through the temple and out to the street.

"Oh, and we have some coins, too."

"Your share of the trip to Sythal?"

"That, and Master Hymal's bonus for recovering his reagents. He was very grateful."

The news piqued Jaikus' interest. "*How* grateful."

"A hundred golds, each."

Jaikus almost passed out right then and there. *A hundred golds*! That was more money than his family could ever hope to earn in a decade, maybe two. "A hundred?"

"Yep. And there's more."

"More?"

"Remember that glow-moth larvae I removed from your arm?"

He shuddered. "How could I forget?" The band of newly grown skin over the area Reneeke had dug the larvae from was one of the more vocal of the voices in his chorus of aches.

"Well, as it turned out, the troll that almost killed you was infested with them. The Guild has a standing order for larvae of the glow-moth, and since we were instrumental in leading it to capture, received a percentage of the take."

"We're rich!"

"Uh, not exactly."

Casting a sidelong glance at Reneeke, Jaikus frowned. "What do you mean?"

"Well, there was the amount we owed to Charka for your, uh, indiscretion. The Khuodari brothers received a share since they helped bring the troll down. Also, that magic user I mentioned received a full third. I don't know why, you'll have to talk to Charka about that.

"Then, we had to pay the healers, time spent under their care, and...uh..." pausing a moment, he searched for the final item. "Oh, right, let's not forget the supplies we got from Bella."

"How much do we have?" Jaikus' hopes of being rich were quickly being dashed upon the rocks of fiscal reality.

"Together, we have ten golds, seven silver, and eleven copper."

Sounding less than excited, he asked. "That's it?"

Reneeke laughed. "That's it? Back on the farm, such an amount would be considered a fortune, and you ask '*That's it?*'."

Up ahead, the walls of the Guild came into view. Out front stood the one-armed man who during their last encounter had kept them out.

"Think he'll let us in?"

"Don't worry, Jaik. Like I said, we're Charka's guests."

Jaikus wasn't convinced. But when they came to the door, Jeral, a.k.a. Booba, merely nodded and opened it for them.

Exhilarated beyond words, Jaikus leaned heavily upon Reneeke as they passed from the world of everyday life, to that of sagas and epics. His knees grew wobbly as they entered the foyer, itself a small room. To one side sat a counter, beyond which a rather scruffy looking man dug beneath his fingernails with the point of a knife. In the area behind the man stood shelves and hooks bearing all manner of items from simple cloaks, to saddles, and before they passed from the foyer into the main meeting hall of the Guild, Jaikus thought he had observed three heads of a less than human nature.

Despite its size, the hall bore more of a tavern atmosphere than of a revered meeting place that had been the launching point for many a famous tale. Laughter, the clanking of flagons, a shout here and there all added to the cacophony.

Tables filled the hall, each packed with men and women dressed in armor, robes, and everything in between. Even a few non-human races were represented, races that Jaikus had heard about only in epics. Servants in the uniform of the Guild worked their way amongst the tables, delivering flagons of ale and trays of food.

No less than six, arched avenues gave egress to the rest of the Guild. Two sets of steps, one to either side of the hall, ascended to the floor above. Far to the right, at the head of the hall, sat a dais, stage really, whereupon bards and other performers would entertain.

What really drew his attention was the double-headed battle axe prominently displayed above the dais. *Reakla's axe!* Over a thousand years ago and yet…there it was.

"Greetings, friends."

Coming out of nowhere like it did, the salutation caused Jaikus to jump.

"It's just Chork."

"Chork?" Glancing around, he saw no one, only a bronze statue of a fully armored fighter situated just within the great hall. He received his second shock when the statue's eyes blinked.

"That's me," said the statue.

"What…?"

"Long story," explained Reneeke. "I'll tell you later."

"Welcome to the Adventurer's Guild, young Jaikus. Reneeke and I have shared many a tale of your exciting exploits."

"It talks?" Jaikus glanced to Reneeke, but his friend was busy scanning the faces of those seated at the many tables spaced throughout the hall.

"Talk? Of course I talk." Its eyes flitted to and fro, and the lips moved when it spoke, but that appeared to be the extent of Chork's mobility. "In fact, I would have you know that I speak over a dozen languages including that of the now extinct race of Tyllians, though for the most part they had very little in the way to say, as they did little but drift along with the ocean currents. Did you know that they have, or I suppose we should say *'had'*, seventeen separate and distinct ways in which to say hello?"

"Uh, no. I didn't."

"Well, now. Let me illuminate you."

As he began an ear-piercing series of shrieks, Reneeke spotted Charka at a table over against the far wall. "Sorry, Chork. Charka is expecting us."

Immediately, the shrieking ceased. "No problem at all, young Reneeke. I'm sure your friend and I can resume our conversation at a later date."

"I suppose so…"

"Wonderful. I will count the minutes until I again have the pleasure of your company."

Hurrying Jaikus toward where their friends sat, Reneeke said. "He'll talk and talk and talk if you don't walk away."

About to question his friend further, he was forestalled when Charka noticed their approach and waved them over.

"Good to see you up and about, lad."

"Thank you. I'm glad to be here."

Few tables offered more than one vacant place. Even Charka's held only the two empty seats that Jaikus and Reneeke soon occupied. Three others aside from Charka and his crew shared the table. Two were the Khuodari brothers, and the third was a wiry little fellow known as Slip. From the slightness of his build, and the lack of armor and magic user's robe, Jaikus deduced that he must be one of the Guild's thieves.

Slip eyed the two newcomers. "Heard about your fight."

Kerl, the axe-wielding Khuodari brother, slapped the table. "Stood up to a troll, he did!"

"Impressive." The wiry little guy nodded approvingly.

Lady Kate laid a hand on Jaikus' arm. "How are you doing?"

He flashed her a grin. "I'm alive."

"Ha!" Terl, the sword-wielding Khuodari twin, slapped the table then gave out with a loud and raucous laugh. "Then you met the first law of adventuring."

"What is that?"

"You came back alive." He and his brother Kerl repeatedly slapped the table as they broke into laughter.

Jaikus glanced to Reneeke, wondering if he might have understood the joke, but his friend looked just as confused. Returning his gaze to Charka, Jaikus said, "Thank you for inviting us. I've always wanted to see what it was like inside."

Raising his mug of 'kult in salute, Charka silently grinned before downing half of it.

Movement upon the platform at the head of the hall caught Reneeke's attention. Three men had mounted the four steps leading to it and were even now making their way to center stage.

They didn't look like any performers Reneeke had ever seen. Two were heavily armored while the third, though he wore a simple suit of leather armor, had the bearing of command.

Charka took note of Reneeke's interest in the stage. "Looks like old Ellantho plans on giving another speech."

Both Khuodari brothers groaned. "That's why I don't like spending my time here. It's more fun over at *The Dented Helm*."

Taking on a sour expression, Seward said, "You got that right."

Charka eyed the trio with annoyance. "Show some respect. He *is* the Guildmaster, and if he likes to make speeches, then we should at least do him the courtesy of listening. You just might learn something."

Seward rolled his eyes before turning them on Reneeke. "His last speech was on the best way to take down a specter."

"Wouldn't that be worth knowing?" asked Reneeke.

"From the other side of the grave? According to him, the best way is to become one yourself."

"That's..." began Jaikus, then paused. He didn't want to run the risk of offending anyone by speaking ill of the highest ranking Guild member.

"...stupid?" finished Kerl.

Jaikus glanced at those around him, then nodded.

"Don't worry, lad. Few around here will think ill of you for knocking Ellantho's words of wisdom."

Over on the stage, the Guildmaster raised his hands. Conversations died, heads turned toward him, and the hall quieted.

Jaikus glanced to Charka only to have his one-time leader place a finger before his lips, indicating quiet.

"Greetings, my fellow adventurers." Ellantho's arms lowered as his gaze roved across the assembled faces.

"We have business here tonight..."

"No speech?" interrupted a shout.

The Guildmaster shook his head. "No, not toni..." Thunderous applause drowned out the rest of his words. He flashed an annoyed look to those in the crowd, subduing their outburst and restoring a sense of propriety. Once the noise level diminished to a respectable level, he continued.

"As I said, we have business here tonight and I shall keep my comments brief."

Another round of applause and table thumping.

"Honor and bravery have ever been the hallmarks of our beloved Guild. Only those who exemplify these attributes can ever hope of joining our exalted ranks."

Slip glanced to Charka. "Sounds like a Vote's about to happen."

Charka shrugged. "Perhaps."

Transferring his gaze from Ellantho to Slip, Reneeke asked, "A Vote?"

"Whenever someone wishes to join the Guild, they put it to a Vote. At that time, those who object are allowed to come forth and state their case. Once everyone has had their say, we vote."

"Most times," added Kerl, "there are no objections and this is merely a formality."

Terl chuckled. "Remember when Kog tried to join? No less than forty-five members stood in objection, almost caused a riot."

"Did he get in?" queried Jaikus.

Kerl shook his head. "Not then. Later, though, he proved himself by slaying the Glenriver Raptor. Brought the beast's head back and chucked it at the Guildmaster. Such temerity demanded that he be allowed to join. None blocked his entry after such a display of courage."

"Wonder who's up for the Vote," mused Slip.

Very interested in the inner workings of the Guild, Jaikus returned his attention back to the Guildmaster. His eyes flicked to and fro in an attempt to discover who may be the one to join.

Reneeke, on the other hand, turned a knowing look toward Charka. The *Troupe* leader failed to meet his eye.

A growing murmur throughout the hall made Guildmaster Ellantho difficult to hear. Jaikus tried to listen, but the growing buzz of speculation proved too obstructive. He continued scanning the assemblage, he couldn't for the life of him see anyone that appeared more anxious than the rest.

Finally, the murmuring grew too loud and the Guildmaster once again signaled for quiet. Jaikus turned his attention from the crowd, back to the Guildmaster and found Ellantho staring in his direction. "Now, I believe Charka, leader of *Charka's Troupe*, a longtime and respected member of the Guild, would like to say a few words."

Every eye in the hall turned toward their table as Charka stood.

Jaikus listened in shocked surprise as Charka began to speak.

"You all know me. I've been around long enough to remember some of you as Springers." That elicited a murmuring chuckle. "A couple probably should still *be* Springers." More laughter and several guffaws followed. "During my last venture into the Swamp, I had the privilege to get to know a couple lads who may have had more desire than brains when it came to adventuring, but let me tell you, they acquitted themselves with great courage. And like you, courage is the attribute I admire most in any individual.

"Mistakes were made; for what Springer knows a troll from a hole in the ground. But they righted the wrongs, went forward into the unknown, and never backed down. When faced with death, they stood their ground. When faced with entombment, they found the way out. These lads may come from modest stock, but they have the spirit of adventurers.

"When my man, Seward, was grievously hurt and had to be rushed back to Reakla, they went alone into the Swamp to retrieve items stolen by a fully grown mossback." More intakes of breath. "Not only did they return to tell the tale, but they recovered that which I believed irretrievable."

Eyes that had gazed upon Charka, now turned toward Jaikus and Reneeke. Between their youthful appearance and Jaikus' nearly mummified appearance, all understood of whom Charka spoke.

"Over the last two days, you've heard the tale of their last heroic deed, facing the wrath of a maddened troll infested by glow-moth larvae." Many in the audience nodded while others who hadn't heard the tale, spouted expletives. "I am not the only one who can attest to the bravery these two lads exhibited. The Khuodari brothers, Viruloxi, Master Hymal the apothecary, and over half a dozen guards who watched the events as they unfolded from atop the wall, witnessed their heroic deed."

Terl and Kerl nodded in affirmation.

"If ever two individuals deserved to be accorded the honor of joining the Guild, assuredly, it must be them."

Jaikus was completely taken aback.

Charka glanced toward his former Springers. "Stand up, lads."

Aches and pains melted away as Jaikus rose from his chair. Reneeke offered him a hand, but he shrugged it off with a shake of his head. Making it to his feet, he stared at the men and women looking his way. Many bore grins, others gave nods. Not one held a negative expression.

From the stage, Ellantho raised his voice and asked, "What say you? Do we welcome these brave lads into the Guild?"

Silence hung in the Guild hall for what seemed an interminable time. For a brief instant, fear and doubt sought to squelch the exhilaration of the moment. But it was thunderously thrust aside as a hundred voices shouted, *"Yes!"*

Here ends the first book of:

The Adventurer's Guild.

Be sure to watch for further installments in the continuing adventures of Jaikus and Reneeke.

Check out the epically adventurous worlds of fantasy author

Brian S. Pratt

The Morcyth Saga

James, a high school senior, went looking for a job. But instead, he begins what turns out to be an adventure of a lifetime. Whisked unexpectedly to a world where magic works, he must learn to master its power, all the while searching for the meaning of why he was brought there and what he must do.

The Broken Key Trilogy

Four comrades set out to recover the segments of a key which they believe will unlock the King's Horde, rumored to hold great wealth. Written in the style of an RPG game, with spells, scrolls, potions, Guilds, and dungeon exploration fraught with traps and other dangers.

Dungeon Crawler Adventures

*For those who enjoy dungeon exploration
without all the buildup or wrapup.*

Fans of his previous works, especially *The Broken Key*, will discover *Underground* to be full of excitement and surprises. First in a series of books written for the pure fun of adventuring, *Underground* takes the reader along as four strangers overcome obstacles such as ingenious traps, perilous encounters, and mysteries to boggle the mind.

Ring of the Or'tux

In many stories you hear how *"The Chosen One"* appeared to save the day. Every wonder what would happen if the one doing the choosing bungled the job?

In *Ring of the Or'tux*, that's exactly what happens. Hunter was on his way to a Three Stooges' marathon when in mid-step, he went from the lobby of a movie theater to a charred tangle of stone and timber that once had been a place of worship. From there it only gets worse for the hapless *Chosen One*. First, an attempt to flee those he initially encounters (who by the way are the ones he was sent there to save), lands him into the merciless clutches of an invading army (those whom he was supposed to defeat).

www.ingramcontent.com/pod-product-compliance
Lightning Source LLC
Chambersburg PA
CBHW021103130626
46554CB00002B/500